Thou Shalt Submit

Crimson Rose

This book is dedicated to my sanity – a once dear friend with whom I could no longer see eye to eye. You will not be missed.

Contents

Chapter	Page
1	1
2	10
3	17
4	25
5	31
6	41
7	49
8	57
9	67
10	74
11	80
12	87
13	94
14	101
15	110
16	117
17	123
18	131
19	140
20	145
21	153
22	160
23	166
24	171
25	179
26	186
27	192
28	200

29	208
30	214
31	223
32	231
33	238
34	245
35	255
36	264
37	272
38	279
39	285
40	292
41	299
42	305
43	311
44	321
45	331
46	341
47	348
48	354
49	361
50	369
51	376
52	387

Acknowledgement

I would first like to thank all of my readers as without you I would not be where I am today.

I would also like to give a very special thank you to Joyce Meyer for taking time away from her busy schedule to edit my works.

And to Nicole Dixon, Anthony Robson, and Max Reynolds for being the best beta readers an author could ask for.

And finally I would like to thank my family and friends for understanding the many long nights I've spent secluded in my small office with a computer and a case of coke as I wrote the night away.

1

Natalie Holt was walking through the park on her way home – a trip the nineteen year old had made four days a week for the last year from her classes at Maple Grove College where she majored in biology. Sure, she could have driven, but she enjoyed the walk, the serenity of nature and the birds chirping their joyful song. It was her time to relax and let her mind go after a long day of having her nose stuck in books and she took advantage of it whenever possible.

It was a beautiful day and Natalie was leaning against an ancient oak admiring the clear blue skies and breathing in the aromas of wildflowers she never bothered learning the names of, when she was suddenly broken out of her reverie by something large ramming into her side, knocking her off her feet and to the grassy ground below. "Watch where you're…" her words of rebuke cut short when she looked up to see a tall, possibly handsome (it was hard to tell with the many cuts and bruises covering his face) man staring down at her through frightened eyes. "Oh my god! Are you alright?" she asked, climbing to her feet.

"Take this!" the man wheezed as he shoved a manila envelope against Natalie's chest, his face growing more paranoid by the second – eyes darting left and right as if in search of whomever delivered the beating upon him. "Tell no one you've got it!"

"W-What is it? I don't want to get mixed up in your troubles, Mister," Natalie said holding the envelope out for him to take back. "Who are you?" she asked, her eyes fixed on his bloody face.

"Please, you have to keep it! It's no longer safe with me," he said refusing to take it back. Taking a pain-filled breath, he ran off as quickly as his battered body would carry him.

"Wait! What in the heck am I supposed to do with it?" Natalie yelled after the man, her voice trembling with fear of its own as she suddenly began looking around for whomever was going to jump out of the bushes and attack her for the package. Having no idea what was going on, or why she was listening to a stranger in the park, she tucked the envelope into her backpack alongside her books and went home as quickly as she could – alternating between running, jogging and walking while constantly looking over her shoulder.

Meanwhile, back in the park, the mysterious man leaned against an elm and smiled as he wiped the makeup and fake blood from his face – making a mental note to thank his good friend Connie for the excellent job in making him look like he had just gone ten rounds with Ali.

Running into the house, Natalie nearly knocked her mother to the floor. "Oh god! I'm sorry mom!"

"Ahem," her mother cleared her throat. "You in a hurry?"

"Huh?"

"Are you alright, sweetie?" her father asked. "You look worried."

"Hmm? Oh, I'm fine," Natalie lied. "I was just thinking of the weird man that ran into me at the park.

"A strange man?" Her mother asked.

"I don't know who he was, but I think he was in trouble. His face was all bloody like he was on the losing end of a bad fight. He…" Natalie started. She was going to say he shoved an envelope at her, an envelope now in her backpack, but then remembered his words. "He apologized for running into me and then ran off. So, you guys going out on a date?"

"Yeah," her mother smiled radiantly "we're going to dinner and a movie with Luke and Gina. We'll be out late so don't wait up," her smile turned to an almost seductive grin.

"Um, alrighty then. Do I even want to know why you're grinning like that?"

"Probably not," Her dad answered. "Come on honey, we don't want to be late to the party."

Her dad out the door, Natalie's mom leaned in close and whispered in her ear. "Your father and I will be out most of the night. I left a gift on your bed." Winking, she walked out of the house leaving her daughter standing there looking more confused than ever.

With her parents thankfully out of the house, Natalie ran up to her bedroom and locked the door behind her. Tossing her backpack on the bed, she barely missed the colorfully wrapped gift

3

her mother left for her. Temporarily forgetting the envelope, she picked up the package and was surprised at the weight of it. Tearing off the wrapping, she opened the cardboard box and picked up a folded piece of paper.

With the paper out of the way, she stared down in wide-eyed embarrassment at three dildos. "Jesus Christ mom!" she gasped, picking up the largest of the three – a monstrous black dick with suction cup base measuring more than a foot long and nearly three inches thick. The other two toys were a purple dildo, again with suction cup base, but this on a more modest seven inches long and about an inch and a half thick; and a nine inch long, two inch thick blue one with a cord and bulb pump handing out of the base.

Putting the huge black dildo back in the box and sitting it on the bed, Natalie unfolded the paper and read it.

I know this is a hell of a gift for a mother to give her daughter, but I'm worried about you, sweetie. You're nineteen years old and have never had a boyfriend, or girlfriend for that matter and it just isn't natural. I know you can be shy, but come on, Natalie, you're a beautiful young woman who should be out experimenting, not sitting home alone every night with her nose in a book.

Use the toys and learn how great sex can feel and then go out and get yourself laid! Your father and I will be out most of the night so feel free to go hog wild.

Love, Mom

"I'm a virgin and I intend to stay that way until I get married," Natalie sighed, dropping the note back into the box and then moving the box to the furthest reaches of her closet. Mildly embarrassed, she stripped out of her shirt and pants and plopped down on the bed while cursing the still broken air conditioning. Retrieving the envelope from her backpack, she looked the orange colored package over – guessing it to be about an inch or so thick and filled edge to edge with something hard, yet somewhat flexible.

There were no names, addressed or postage stamps and the only thing holding it closed were the small metal tabs on the back. *Well, seeing as how it's not really sealed shut no one will know that I opened it.* She reasoned as she scoot back on the bed and leaned against the headboard.

Fingers trembling, she lifted the tabs and opened the flap. Looking inside, she saw what appeared to be a photo album. Holding the envelope by the sides, she turned it upside down and gently shook it, being careful not to ruin the envelope or the photo album as it slid out and landed on the bed. Turning it over, the first thing she saw on the black cover was a picture of a stunningly beautiful brunette woman with the caption: **Fiona Delmarco's Album of Perversions** written below.

"What in the fuck?" Natalie said as she opened the album. The first page was head and body shots of the lovely Fiona Delmarco with what looked like some sort of dossier on her including name, age, address, place of work, and all the vital statistics. Flipping the page, the photos became more revealing. In place of shirt and jeans, or dresses, Fiona was now wearing lingerie. In one picture her large breasts were revealed showing she had pierced nipples.

For some reason intrigued and unable to stop herself, Natalie flipped to the next page and Fiona's clothes were gone. But on the next page things really got interesting. It was titled ***Thou Shalt Eat Seed*** and showed Fiona kneeling on the floor surrounded by at least a dozen men with their hard cocks pointed at her. Page after page it showed her sucking and jerking off all those men. Her face was blasted with semen, her mouth filled with it.

"OH MY GOD!" Natalie gasped at about the halfway point – a page showing Fiona with a cock in each hand and two shoved in her gaping mouth. "I've never seen anything so disgusting in my life!" Closing the album, she tossed it on the bed as the trembling in her hands spread to the rest of her body and she looked down at the lacy purple thing she was wearing – a lacy purple thong that was now damn with pussy juices.

Shocked, Natalie reached into her panties and did something she had never done before. Rubbing along her moist slit, she withdrew her fingers and held them up about a foot in front of her face – her eyes focusing on the pussy juices covering them. "No way! There's no fucking way that turned me on!" But like it or not, the seed of curiosity had been planted. Unable to resist the urge, she picked the album back up and flipped through a few more pages as the feeling of butterflies swarming in her belly grew by the second.

"My god!" she half moaned. "How can she let them shoot all over her face like that?" Turning the page, her hand grew a mind of its own and slowly slithered into her panties where her fingers gently massaged her clit as she looked at the degrading images of Fiona Demarco covered in the semen of at least a dozen men. The rubbing intensified the further into the album she went and just as she felt her entire body tingling, on the verge of her first orgasm, a slip of paper fell out of the back of the album and landed on the soft swell of her sweat-covered belly.

In the event this album is lost or misplaced please return to 372 Belmonte St SW. Men's room, middle stall. HUGE reward offered for safe return.

"Belmonte street…Belmonte street," Natalie said thinking out loud, her fingers still rubbing her clit. "That's on the way to the school. I'll just stop by and drop this off and collect the reward on my way to class and no one will be the wiser." Suddenly hitting the right buttons, she jumped out of bed and ran into the closet where she grabbed the first dildo her fingers wrapped themselves around. It wasn't until she was placing it on the wall – the only flat surface the suction cup base would stick to, that she realized it was the huge black one.

Nearly chewing a hole through her bottom lip, her clit throbbing with excitement and apprehension, Natalie took several deep breaths and backed up onto the toy until the bulbous head was spreading her open. *OH MY FUCKING GOD! This is it!* She thought taking another deep breath. *I'm really going to do it. I'm going to lose my virginity!* Biting her lip again, she closed her eyes and rocked her hips back as hard as she could and for a brief moment nothing happened. Or at least her startled mind did not register anything.

And then it did. "Aahhgghhh! Oh my motherfucking god!" she yelped as the massive silicone cock plowed through her hymen like a hot knife through butter until the head was pressed against her cervix. Her knees growing suddenly weak, she leaned down and braced her hands on the floor – looking back between her legs to see at least two more inches of dildo remaining. "W-Why did…oh god! I had to grab the largest toy, didn't I?" she panted as she slowly began working herself back and forth along the rigid shaft in the hopes the pain would soon turn to pleasure. Unfortunately, she had no such luck and after about three dozen thrusts she dropped off of it and onto the floor – her fingers going to her pussy where three slid in without trouble.

"Oh my god!" It was not until she added her pinky that it became really tight and started to hurt and when she pulled them out she could see traces of blood – a mood-killer for sure. Popping the huge dildo off of the wall, she took it to the bathroom and dropped it into the tub. And after setting the water she turned on the shower and got in.

2

Natalie woke to the sound of light knocking on her bedroom door and she rolled out of bed feeling rather well rested. The ache in her loins a thing of the past. Unlocking the door, she opened it enough to see that it was her mother. Remaining behind the door since she was only in her bra and panties, she let her mother in before closing it.

"What's up, mom?"

"I just thought I'd drop by before you headed out to class to see if you opened your gift."

"I did. What in the hell were you thinking buying me dildos? You know I was saving myself until marriage."

"Was? Does that mean you put them to use?"

"Are we seriously going to have this discussion?"

"Yes. So, did you?"

"I don't know what in the hell I was thinking. I was looking at some pictures and I got really excited and…and…"

"And what? Don't leave me hanging sweetie. Which one did you use?"

"That giganormous black one. I just grabbed one out of the box, put it on the wall and did it."

"Holy shit! Are you alright? You were supposed to start with the smaller one and work your way up. Not the other way around."

"It hurt like hell last night, but I feel fine now. I can't believe how much it stretched me open."

"Honey, that thing in nearly three inches thick. I'm surprised you managed to fit it in you right off the bat."

"Well, it didn't go in easily that's for sure. I kind of slammed myself back on it. Anyways, can we never talk about this again?"

"Did you at least enjoy it?"

"Not really. It hurt entirely too much to be enjoyable."

"Well, the good news is you'll be able to handle pretty much any dick from now on. Now do us all a favor and go get yourself a boyfriend and stop being a damn recluse."

"I'm not just going to go out and let the first man I see fuck me, mom! And even if I did get a boyfriend I still wouldn't let him have sex with me on the first date."

"I'm not asking you to, sweetie. All I'm saying is you need to go out and meet more people. Socialize, have fun and experiment while you're still young enough to enjoy it. Your father and I have to leave early so I'm afraid you'll have to fend for yourself."

"I think I can manage breakfast on my own," Natalie rolled her eyes. "And thanks for the gift."

"Anytime, sweetie."

∞ ∞ ∞

With her parents gone, Natalie did something she rarely ever did. Dressed in something sexy – figuring the tight skirt showing off her toned thighs and round ass, paired with a nearly sheer white blouse her pink bra could be seen through would through people off enough they would not recognize her and she could get the delivery over with as quickly as possible. Putting her normal, baggy clothes in her backpack, she left the house and drove to Belmonte – looking at addresses until she found 372.

Fucking perfect! She thought as she looked at the windowless brick building with a sign hanging over the door reading: XTC Toys.

Pulling into the parking lot and parking as far in the back as possible, she got out of her car and ran into the adult toy store with the envelope in hand, the promise of a huge reward the only thing keeping her feet moving in the right direction. Entering the building, she looked to her left where a man sat behind a counter looking at her with a creepy grin. Quickly turning to the right, she saw row upon row of magazines, DVDs and sex toys galore. And then there were the five other shoppers perusing the wares.

"Can I help you?" asked the man behind the counter. If his nametag was accurate his name was Steve.

"Um, I um," Natalie stuttered "I'll just take a look around."

"Suit yourself," Steve replied "if you need any help just let me know." He sat back in his chair, kicked his feet up on the counter and flipped through the pages of Beautiful Bondage Scenes magazine.

Natalie hoped that the other shoppers would go away so she could go into the men's room and drop off the package without everyone looking at her funny, but luck was not on her side. After twenty minutes of looking at rubber dicks, anal beads, gags and a myriad of other sex toys she decided to just go for it. Walking down the short hall towards the restrooms, looking behind her to make sure no one was watching, she turned to the left and entered the men's room.

The bathroom was dark. She felt around for a light switch but found none. "Damn it," she said through gritted teeth "I can't see a damn thing." She fished her cell phone out of her purse and with the limited light found the middle stall. No sooner had she entered the stall then the lights came on. Freaking out, she sat on the toilet and pulled her feet up so no one could see her. *Of all the rotten luck,* she thought.

"You see that hot piece of ass?" one man said. "She looked as nervous as a deer caught in headlights."

"Yeah," another man laughed "probably her first time in an adult shop."

"Wouldn't mind having those full lips of hers wrapped around my dick though," a third man said. "I bet she gives great head."

"It's all I could do not to pull that skirt up over that sexy ass and fuck her right there in the shop," the first man kept the humiliating conversation going.

"Oh," Natalie gasped quietly. *Those perverts are talking about me out there.* She slapped her hand over her mouth.

"What do you guys think about an old fashioned glory hole?" the second man said nodding at the stall Natalie currently occupied.

Glory hole, Natalie thought. *What in the hell is a glory hole?*

A dick slid through a hole in the left stall door and Natalie looked at in in shocked fascination. This was the first real live dick she had ever seen and she immediately began comparing it to the dildo she fucked herself on the night before as another dick popped through a hole in the right stall wall which was followed by a third through the door. A forth joined the one on the left. A fifth, this one black and longer than the rest, joined the one to the right.

"Come on sexy," one of the men said "suck my cock. We know you're in there. Wrap those beautiful lips around my shaft. "

"You can jerk me off while you suck him," another said.

"You guys are fucking crazy," Natalie shouted. "Let me out of here right now. You guys are nothing but fucking perverts."

"Perverts?" one of them replied. "You're the one in the men's room. Who's the pervert now, missy?"

"My dick isn't going to suck itself, honey," the black man said. "You're not afraid of a little cock are you? I'm sure a sweet thing like you has seen plenty of big dicks."

"I've never seen a dick of any size," she said back instantly regretting it.

"Ah ha, you've got to be kidding me," laughed a man to the right. "You're telling us you've never seen a cock ever?"

"So what," Natalie said defensively. "What difference does it make that I've never seen a cock before? Let me out of this damn stall right now."

"Well, now you have five cocks ready and willing, sweetheart," the black man replied. "Why not give us a go. Maybe you'll learn a thing or two about how to please a man."

"What do you mean?" Natalie said confused.

"Come on honey," said the man at the door "hop off that toilet you're trying to hide on and play with our cocks. Jerk us off, suck us, fuck us, just do something. I know you're curious otherwise why would you be in the glory hole stall?"

"I was just dropping off a package," Natalie answered. "Now let me out of here before I call the cops on you."

"Go right ahead. By the time they get here we'll be long gone. Besides, Steve has you on camera entering the men's room of your own accord."

"Why are you doing this to me? I'm not a whore!"

"Maybe not, but you are a hot piece of ass and we're a bunch of men that got horny looking at you. So, seeing as how all these stiff dicks is your fault, why don't you do something about it?"

3

Natalie could not deny the effect she was apparently having on the five hard cocks stuck through the walls and door and despite her apprehension and inexperience with all things sexual, she was getting more than a little curious as the dicks were having an effect on her. Images of Fiona Delmarco kneeling on the floor sucking and jerking all those men suddenly popped into her mind and she felt her pussy moisten.

Still sitting on the toilet she reached a hand out and touched the cock in front of her. She rubbed her fingers over it, felt it twitch at her soft caress. Emboldened, she reached to her right and started stroking another. *This isn't so bad,* she thought.

"Mmmm, that's it," said the man with his dick stuck through the four inch hole in the door. "Stroke my cock."

"The slut is stroking me as well," said the man to the right.

"I think this bitch has been playing with us this whole time," said the black man.

"If not, she sure is playing with us now!" Another added.

Without really thinking about it, Natalie scooted off of the toilet and fell to her knees in front of the door and stared intently at the cock her hand was slowly jerking off. It looked much like those she saw in the pictures with Fiona – long and hard, yet soft to the touch. She could feel every raised vein as her hand pressed slowly back and forth. Overcome with a mix of emotions, she stuck her tongue out and gave the head a lick.

"That's it, lick my cock. Come on babe, you know you want to put it in your mouth.

Images of what she saw in the picture album flooded Natalie's mind. Her lips parted and wrapped around the dick sticking through the door in front of her. Having no idea what she was doing, she bobbed her head back and forth, taking as much as she could without gagging on it as she continued to jerk off two more. When the first blast of semen landed on her face, she felt her heart flutter and the excitement grow in her loins. And then her mouth was filled and she instinctively gulped it gown – surprised at the taste, but finding it somewhat delicious.

Alternating between jerking and sucking the five men until they came in her mouth and all over her face, all that remained was the large black cock that reminded her of the big black dildo her mother had bought her and which she lost her virginity on last night. Taking it into her mouth while cupping his full balls, she let it stretch her throat as she gagged on it.

"Aahhh yeah, that's it you dirty fucking cunt!" the black man grunted. "Take it down your throat! Eat my fucking jizz you nasty whore!"

Being talked to like a slut had an effect on the naïve Natalie that she could not yet make sense of. All she knew was that she thoroughly enjoyed it and did not put up much resistance when he began fucking his thick cock down her throat. Her knees starting to cramp, she rose into a bent over position, her skirt hiked up over her ass and panties pulled to the side as she furiously rubbed herself. Her ass was pressed firmly against the back wall and she suddenly felt something sliding along her pussy. And as she felt it sliding into her, she jumped forward, taking all ten inches of black cock down her throat in an attempt at getting away from it.

"You can't fuck me!" she proclaimed loudly.

"Ah come on, babe," the man said "I was so damn close. Back that ass up to the hole so I can get it all in this time."

"I'll suck you off, but I won't have sex with you. None of you are wearing condoms and I have no intentions of getting knocked up today."

"We're in a sex shop, babe," one of the men said. "Give me five minutes and I'll go buy a whole god damn box of condoms."

"I'm not having sex with five men!" she protested, though the thought made her even weaker in the knees. Silently, she thanked her mother for buying her the dildos, and her own craziness for using the largest of them to lose her virginity on. Looking around the stall at the dicks, she knew she would have no trouble taking any of them all the way.

"You're not getting out of that stall until you do," another said.

"You going to force me to have sex with you? I believe that's rape and I'll have the police on the phone in ten seconds if you don't open the door right god damned now so I can leave."

"Ah, come on. I was only kidding. You can at least suck us off like you promised. A line is forming so you've got your work cut out for you."

"A line? How many are out there?"

"Not many. Maybe fifteen or twenty"

"FIFTEEN OR TWENTY! I can't suck that many more dicks! My jaw is already starting to hurt."

"Then let us give your lips a break. Press that ass against a hole."

"I said no sex!" Bending over in the small stall, she took another dick into her mouth and felt her legs pressing against the opposite wall. In seconds, she felt a dick poised for entry, but not into her pussy. Before she had time to move, she felt her asshole splitting open as another black man popped her anal cherry. Though he was not quite as large as the first black man she sucked off, he was still well above average, and she jumped up and grabbed her aching ass. "MOTHER FUCKER! You put it in my ass! I've never taken it up the ass before you son of a bitch! And I said no sex!"

"No, you said you didn't want to get knocked up. Well, I can guarantee there's no way in hell you'll get knocked up taking it up the ass. So back that tight hole up and let me fuck it."

"Shit babe, now I really want to get my dick into you. I haven't popped a virgin ass in years." Pushing his dick back through the hole, he was pleasantly surprised when he felt Natalie back up onto it, easing the head into her ass and then stopping.

"Please go slow. And if it starts to hurt I'm leaving and I don't give a shit how many of you are out there waiting."

"Fair enough. But without lube it's going to hurt. Let me coat it in your pussy juices first."

"Fine." Pulling off of the man's cock, Natalie raised up a little and then pushed back – taking the entire length into her pussy. "Aahhhh! Oh my fucking god that feels good!" she moaned as she fucked herself on her first real cock. Pleasure taking over, she forgot all about her no sex policy and rocked her hips hard and fast. Bracing her hands against the wall, she took another cock into her mouth and slipped into another realm where orgasms roamed free – getting so lost in the moment that she failed to realize that the man had filled her with semen, was replaced by another man that had shot his load into her and a third man was now plowing into her. "Oh god! D-Did you c-cum in me?"

"Honey, I just started fucking you. But the first two men gave you a couple of creampies. But if you continue squeezing my dick like a vice, yeah, I'm going to give you a nice big load."

"I told you not to cum in me!"

"Hey, you're the one in there having orgasms like this is the last time you'll ever have one. If you didn't want us breeding your sexy ass then you probably should have stopped before the first man filled you. Now be a good little slut and take my load! There are ten more men waiting patiently for their turn."

He has a fucking point, Natalie thought to herself as she felt the semen running down her inner thighs. "Fine, you can cum in me, but you had better hole like hell I don't get pregnant."

"I'm kind of hoping you do," the man said redoubling his efforts.

"Hey, I've got the condoms and lube," she head one of the men say.

"We can use the lube on her ass, but the freaky cunt just gave us permission to creampie her," the man fucking Natalie replied. "I'm about to give her load number three!"

∞ ∞ ∞

Hours after entering the middle stall at 372 Belmonte, Natalie felt something thick and hard pressing into her now gaping asshole and then something else slide into her well-fucked pussy – trapping the semen within. "W-What did you just put in me?"

"We sealed you with a couple of plugs," Steve answered. "Don't worry, they're on the house for letting us gang bang your sexy ass."

"Um, thanks I guess. So, will you let me leave now?"

"Of course."

The stall door unlocked and then swung open as Natalie straightened up her skirt and pulled her hair back into a ponytail. Looking upon the faces of about nine men that had just used her, she flushed deep red and wanted to crawl under a rock and die. The men moved out of her way and she ran out of the shop, got into her car and drove away as quickly as possible. Smelling strongly of sex – her face, hair and clothes covered in semen, she opted to skip the rest of her classes and drove home instead.

I can't believe what I just did! She thought as she ran into the house before the neighbors could see her disheveled clothing and ruined makeup. *Twenty-six men! What in the holy hell fuck was I thinking? I swallowed their semen! They came inside of me! What in the hell am I going to do if I end up pregnant?* Stripping out of her clothes as she ran through the house, she went to the bathroom, climbed into the tub and gently tugged the large plugs from her pussy and ass.

"Jesus Christ!" she exclaimed as she looked at the two massive cone-shaped toys she now held in her hands. "How in the fuck did they fit these in me?"

After taking a shower so long it used up every last drop of hot water, Natalie took her new toys into the bedroom and added them to the box in her closet. Exhaustion set in out of nowhere and no sooner was her head on the pillow then she was out like a light.

∞ ∞ ∞

"How was your day, dear?" asked Regina Holt, Natalie's 39 year old mother as they sat around the dinner table.

"Oh you know, same old boring classes," Natalie lied.

"Would you like some cream sauce for your pasta?" Henry, her father, asked.

"More?" Natalie said absentminded.

"More? Replied Regina "What do you mean more? You don't have any at all."

"Huh? Oh, sorry dad. Sure I would love some cream sauce on my pasta," she said looking at the white sauce her father ladled out of the bowl and drizzled onto her pasta. "You make the best cream sauce I have ever tasted." *Second only to man sauce,* she thought hungrily licking her lips.

4

That night Natalie dreamt of sucking cock and drinking cum. She was back in the stall of the XTC men's room taking one cock after another down her throat and in her hands while trying to avoid the poking and prodding dicks trying desperately to steal her virginity until she remember it was already long gone and allowed them to take those holes as well. So intense were her dreams she woke up twice – her pussy dripping wet, and she was unable to get back to sleep until she rubbed her clit to orgasm.

The next day was Wednesday, the one day during the week that she was free of classes. Exhausted from lack of sleep, Natalie did not climb out of bed until noon. After a quick shower and another finger-induced orgasm, she headed to the kitchen to grab a bite to eat. Her mother was sitting at the table sipping coffee and flipping through the pages of a magazine.

"You're up late," Regina said. "A package came for you in the mail. It's over there on the counter."

"A package," Natalie said slightly confused "what kind of package? I don't remember ordering anything." After pouring a glass of orange juice, she walked over to the counter and picked the familiar looking manila envelope. It was addressed to her, but there was no return address and she got a sinking feeling in the pit of her stomach. Opening the sealed flap, she looked inside to see the all too familiar black cover of a photo album. "Oh fuck!" she gasped, seeing a headshot of herself on the front.

"Is everything okay?" her mother asked.

"I'm fine," Natalie lied. "It's just an important book for school I forgot all about." She closed the envelope and downed the juice before returning to her room, locking the door behind her. Sitting on the edge of the bed, she opened the envelope and withdrew the contents. After staring at it in wide-eyed terror for several agonizing minutes, her brain finally registered what she was seeing.

Below her picture – obviously taken before the glory hole gang bang began, was written: ***Natalie Holt: For she has eaten seed.*** Fingers trembling so much she was barely able to control them, she opened the album to the first page and saw another headshot along with personal information very few people should know.

> Name: Natalie Holt
> Age: 19
> Height: 5'7"
> Weight: 123 lbs.
> Hair: Brown
> Eyes: Brown
> Measurements: 36C-25-36

Following the personal information was a brief history of her life that appeared to be written by someone that knew her better than even her best friend followed by a summary of her visit to XTC Toys that to her surprise included all of the blowjobs and hand jobs, but none of the sex. Flipping the page, she saw herself entering the shop and walking around as is nervously shopping for sex toys.

The next two pages were of her inside the men's room stall with five different flaccid cocks poking through holes in the walls and door. That was followed by another twenty pages of her sucking and jerking off over two dozen men. But missing were the pictures of her bent over sucking one cock while taking another in either her pussy or asshole.

This can't be happening, she thought. *If these pictures get out my life will be ruined. Who in the hell would do this to me? What do I do now?* She started to cry in shame and humiliation was about to shove the album back into the envelope when she saw another piece of paper down in the corner of the back cover.

The Second Commandment: Thou Shalt Love Thy Neighbor

If you don't want these pictures released to your family, friends, and school, bring this paper to 1256 Fulton Rd by 3pm TODAY!

What in the hell have I gotten myself into? If I don't go my life will be ruined, but if I go there's no telling what they will have me doing.

Maybe it's another adult store and they want me to suck them off again. I can do that I guess. She thought, a now familiar tingling sensation in her clit as her nipples grew hard.

Unable to think of a way out, she hid the photo album in her closet and headed out, sneaking by her mother so she did not have to come up with another lie. She hated lying in general, but to her parents above all else. They had a relationship built on trust and she knew all too well that all it took was one loose brick for the entire house to come tumbling down. But, a small fib was much better than the truth in this situation and so she gave it very little consideration.

The address on Fulton road turned out to be a rather nice and large Victorian home set well off the street surrounded by a high brick wall and double, black-iron gates. Natalie drove up and looked at the intercom. No sooner was her window down and her hand reaching for the button then a voice spoke.

"Can I help you, Miss?" asked a woman at the other end.

"I have a 3 o'clock appointment," Natalie replied nervously.

"Name?"

"Natalie Holt."

"Alright Natalie, if you'll be so kind as to get out of the car and strip naked I'll go ahead and open the gate for you."

"Strip? But people driving by will see me and call the police!"

"Not likely. You're on private property and far enough off the road no one can see you. Now strip naked, or leave."

Looking around to make sure no one was watching, Natalie got out of her car and quickly stripped naked before getting back in. "I'm naked so please open the gate."

"No one told you to get back in the car. You will leave it running and get out. When the gate opens, you will drop down onto your hands and knees and crawl the rest of the way to the house. Is that understood?"

"Jesus Christ, I'm not a damn dog."

"If you're not going to do as you are told then you may leave. I don't have time to repeat myself over and over."

"Fine! Anything else you want me to do?"

"Oh, there's plenty, but it can wait until you're inside."

Huffing, Natalie stepped passed the iron gates and dropped onto her hands and knees on the hard, rough gravel and began crawling down the long winding driveway – cussing and screaming in pain the entire way as the small stones dug into her hands, feet, knees and shins. By the time she finally reached the porch, she was so pissed off she nearly got up and stormed back to her car, but then thought of her life spiraling down in flames when everyone saw what a complete and total whore she was.

Unsure if she was supposed to get up, or remain on all fours, Natalie stayed on her hands and knees as she knocked on the door. It opened a minute later and she looked up at a petite blonde wearing a sheer dress and nothing underneath. Her eyes lowering, she saw that the woman's nipples and clit hood were pierced.

"You must be out three o'clock," the woman smiled down at Natalie. "Please, come in."

"Can I get up now? My damn hands and legs are killing me."

"Of course."

Letting out an exaggerated sigh, Natalie got to her feet and looked down at her scratched palms, knees and shins as she entered the house.

5

The inside of the house was very spacious and decorated with modern art, plush furniture and plaster busts of more than fifty different women. Several women wearing nothing but lingerie walked around paying her little mind and Natalie got the sudden feeling she had just walked into a brothel. She stared from a tall blonde wearing a black and red basque with matching thong to a brunette wearing a sexy pink babydoll without panties of any kind, her pussy was shaved bald and a gold ring dangled from her clit hood – the second one she had seen today.

A strikingly beautiful raven-haired woman approached Natalie as she stood motionless in the doorway. She was wearing a two piece ribbon trimmed mesh cami garter with lace up sides and matching G-string that clung to her curvy frame like a second skin and she carried herself with an air of authority that told Natalie she was running the show.

"You must be Natalie," the woman said holding out a hand. "I'm Lady Raven and this is my home."

"Um, what exactly am I doing here?" Natalie asked. "What's going on?"

"You are here because you have completed the First Commandment and now desire to learn the Second."

"Beth," Lady Raven said to the blonde wearing the basque "please take our guest upstairs and get her into something more appropriate. When she is presentable take her to the play room."

"Yes, Lady Raven," Beth replied putting her arm around Natalie's waist and guided her up a wide set of stairs.

"What is this place?" Natalie asked. "What is this second commandment I'm supposed to be learning?"

"You'll see soon enough," Beth replied. "For now let's get you into something more comfortable."

"More comfortable? What in the hell can be more comfortable than my own skin?"

"Lingerie."

"That makes no freaking sense! Why would I be told to take my clothes off if you were just going to put something else on me?"

"Because as cute as your clothes were, they weren't lingerie. Not sure if you noticed or not, but that's all we are permitted to wear here."

"Is this some kind of brothel? Is the second commandment meant to turn me into a whore or something?"

"It is a brothel of sorts," Beth answered. "Now please follow me before I have to get Lady Raven. She'll punish you for disobedience if I have to call her for nothing."

"Punish…disobedience? What are you talking about?"

"If I have to ask you one more time to get your sexy ass in gear she'll come up here and swat you with a cane until you comply."

"OH!" Natalie gasped. And without further question she followed Beth down a long hallway to a set of double doors. Beth opened the right door and ushered her ward into what appeared to be a massive walk-in closet filled with every type of lingerie Natalie could think of and much, much more.

"You really are quite pretty, you know?"

"Um thanks, I think," Natalie blushed. "Can you tell me what's going on here? Why is everyone dressed in lingerie? What kind of brothel is this?"

"You'll find out soon enough. Come on, let's get you into something sexy."

Beth had Natalie try on several different outfits before settling on a sexy green and black split front babydoll with a matching g-string that accentuated her every curve. "God you're stunning. If I wasn't so afraid of Lady Raven punishing me I'd make love to you right here and now. Come on, the others will be waiting for you."

"The others?"

"You do love to ask a lot of questions don't you? Lady Raven will explain everything and then the fun will begin." Taking Natalie by the hand, Beth led her back out of the clothing room, through the massive house and to a large bedroom where Lady Raven and three other beautiful women lay in waiting on a king-sized bed. "I hope you're ready."

"Lady Raven sat up in bed and smiled. "Natalie Holt, you are here to complete the Second Commandment. Is that correct?"

"Yes, I guess so," Natalie replied nervously, still having no idea what she was accepting.

"You're an incredibly beautiful woman, Natalie and we're all going to enjoy your initiation."

"Initiation? What initiation? What's going on here? Why won't someone just tell me…" her sentence was cut short when Beth drew her close and groped her breasts while kissing her lightly on the neck. "Oh my god! W-What are you doing!? I'm not into women!"

"You will be before this day is done, sweetie," said Lady Raven, spreading her legs open and revealing her bare pussy. "Crawl over to me, Natalie. Crawl to me and lick my pussy."

"I'm not a fucking dyke," Natalie yelled. "I'm done playing these fucked up games. I'm out of here."

"Suit yourself, sweetheart. I'll make sure copies of the pictures make it to everyone you know."

"Did you take those pictures of me at the toy shop?"

"Nope. I am in charge of the Second Commandment, not the first. Now crawl over here and lick my pussy or everyone will know what you've done."

Natalie stopped in the doorway defeated. "That's fucking blackmail," she screamed. "Why are you doing this to me? What did I ever do to you?"

"You accepted the First Commandment, honey. And you've accepted the Second by showing up here today. Now, get on your knees and crawl to me. I want to feel your tongue on me pussy in the next thirty seconds or I'll send the pictures out regardless."

Natalie dropped to all fours and cringed as pain shot up her arms and legs from where she had crawled up the gravel driveway. Taking a moment to compose herself, she moved across the bedroom like a dog to where Lady Raven sat on the edge of the bed. She had never dreamed of doing it with another woman and had no idea where to begin, or what to do. Not that she had a problem with others doing it, but the idea never really turned her on. "I've never done this before," she said, her face turning red in embarrassment. "I don't know what to do."

"It'll come naturally to you," Raven replied. "Just give my pussy a few licks and you'll get the hang of it in no time."

Natalie did as she was ordered if only to save herself a lifetime of shame and ridicule from family and friends. First, she breathed in the almost intoxicating smell of honey, rose water and Lady Raven's natural scents. Then, she stuck out her tongue and gave Lady Raven's pussy a quick lick.

"Mmmm, that's it sweetie," Lady Raven cooed. "Don't forget to pay my clit some attention as well. And work that tongue as deep inside of me as you can."

Feeling a mix of excitement and revulsion, Natalie reluctantly pushed her tongue into Lady Raven's moist pussy and licked from bottom to top, flicking her tongue over her clit and nibbling her inner labia. And then she felt a sensation begin at her own clit, shoot up to her brain and then rocket right back down her spine causing her entire body to tingle. Looking back over her shoulder, she saw Beth kneeling behind her and the sensation was caused by the tongue so expertly licking her pussy and asshole.

"I thought you said she was supposed to be a virgin?" Beth said looking up Natalie's back towards Lady Raven.

"She is."

"Well, she's not. Based on how her holes are gaping I'd guess she's taken some pretty big dicks and a lot of them."

"That isn't right. I was told she would be a virgin. Did you lose your virginity, Natalie?"

"In a huge way. You can thank the first commandment for that. Well, actually I popped my own cherry with a fat dildo my mom bought me, but the two dozen or so men at the glory hole really opened up both holes. Before I left they stuffed me with two fat plugs."

"Jesus Christ! This is not good. This is not good at all. They were not supposed to fuck you at all!"

"No one told me that. What's the big fucking deal anyways? So what I had sex, isn't the whole point of this to turn me into some kind of sexual deviant like Fiona Demarco?"

"Well, yes, but there's a natural progression to these things, Natalie, and you skipped ahead in the worst way possible."

"I don't understand."

"No, you don't. Oh well. I'll let him worry about it. My job is to break your sexy ass open, but that's apparently already been done for me."

"Not quite, Lady Raven," said Beth. "I can barely get four fingers in so she's still got some work before her ass is ready."

"Um, what are you going to do to my ass?"

"What we're here to do. In the meantime, get back to licking my pussy and this time use your fingers. Drive them in and massage my clit with your thumb. The rest of you know what to do," Lady Raven said to the three women in bed with her.

The three women – a pale-skinned, freckle-faced redhead aptly named Ginger, a green-eyed, large breasted brunette named Heather and another brunette with pierced nipples named Connie crawled out of bed and followed Beth to a glass-front cabinet. Turning to see what was going on behind her, Natalie watched as they all stepped into strap-on harnesses and plugged a large dildo into the slot.

"Both of the slut's holes are stretched pretty well, so feel free to fuck them all," Beth said as she lubed her fake dick.

"Nix that," said Lady Raven. She is supposed to be a virgin leaving here so no one will put anything in her pussy except for a tongue. If I see even a single finger go in I'll personally flog the skin off of whomever does it. Am I understood?"

"Yes, Lady Raven," they said in unison.

"But I want them to fuck my pussy," Natalie said almost pleadingly. Whomever wants me as a virgin is about thirty dicks too late, so you either fuck all of my damn holes, or you fuck none of them." Taking a deep breath, she got up off of the floor and faced the door as if to leave.

"You don't understand," Lady Raven said. "We are not here to just fuck your ass. We are to stretch it open as wide as possible. Before you leave here tonight you must be able to take the largest of fists with relative ease. If you ask for them to fuck your pussy it'll get the same treatment and He will not be happy with any of us."

"I don't give two shits who's happy. This is my damn body you're playing games with and if I want you to fuck me then that's what you're going to do! So, what'll it be?"

"You'd risk your family and friends discovering your secret just to have sex with a house full of women?"

"Damn straight I would!" suddenly turning red in the face as she realized what she was saying, Natalie tried, and failed, to backpedal. "I mean no! I don't want to have sex with women, but if I have to then I want it to be on my terms and not those of some man I've never met. Who in the fuck is doing this to me anyways?"

"Sorry, that's privileged information," Lady Raven Answered. "Okay, you heard her ladies. If she wants us to fuck and stretch her pussy and ass open then that is exactly what we will do. He actually never told us what we should do if she asked for it so I'll take full responsibility for what happens tonight. As for you," she said directly to Natalie "get your sexy ass back over here and finish licking me to orgasm."

∞ ∞ ∞

The sex went on into the wee hours of the night and with every licked pussy and tweaked nipple, Natalie's views on lesbian sex changed for the better. After acquiring a taste for pussy juices and a knack for licking assholes, she came to the only logical conclusion that she could. Her pussy and asshole each stuffed with a four inch plug, she drove home knowing happy in the knowledge that she could count women on her growing list of sexual desires.

Dressed in a black and red latex split-front babydoll with matching panties, Natalie pulled into the driveway and took several looks around to make sure there were no lights on in the house, or those of her neighbors before getting out and rushing in as quickly and quietly as she could – biting her lower lip to stifle the moans encouraged by the two massive plugs rubbing together in her pussy and ass.

Having already showered before leaving 1256 Fulton, she plopped down in bed as she was and was fast asleep. Rolling onto her right side, her lips formed into a seductive grin as she dreamt of being playfully chased through the park by giant pussies and dicks.

6

All Natalie Holt could think about during classes was her encounter with the women at Raven's Hollow – the very gothic sounding name for the brothel ran by the raven-haired beauty, Lady Raven. She could feel the tongues licking her pussy, the dildos fucking her ass. She could taste the sweetness and smell the distinct aroma of each woman. And while the professor droned on about acids and bases, her thoughts drifted to the men's room at XTC Toys and she wondered how many more men she could suck and fuck before she got another package in the mail.

On her way home, Natalie took the long way through the park as she tended to do when the weather was cooperating as it was today with clear blue skies and sun shining bright even as it waned into evening. Nervously looking around for other hikers, she ducked off of the beaten path and into the trees – going several hundred feet before stopping and hiking up her skirt and pulling her panties down. Reaching into the bottom of her backpack, she withdrew a small box and opened it. After once more looking around to make sure the coast was clear, she quickly applied some lube to the massive four inch thick plug she took from the box and worked it into her overly stretched asshole.

Mmmm, god that feels so fucking good, she thought moaning softly. Pulling her panties up and her skirt down, she walked back to the trail and finished her hike home. But she did not go into the house. With the plug moving around in her ass, she was more turned on than ever so got into her car and drove across town to the adult toy store where it all began. Smiling at Steve, she opened the door and walked down the short hallway leading to the bathrooms and entered the men's.

Three men were standing at a urinal when Natalie entered and they all eyed her up and down as she pulled the door to the glory hole stall open and locked herself with. "When you're done pissing I'll suck and fuck those cocks for you," she said. It didn't take long for one of them to poke through the door and she dropped onto her knees and took it into her mouth. *Fuck the son of a bitch that thought he was going to get my virginity,* she though as the dick grew harder. Getting up, she turned around and backed up onto it – taking all seven inched in one quick thrust of her hips.

She heard the bathroom door open and another man enter. "Is she in here?" Steve asked.

"I am," Natalie answered. "Please tell me you've got more men out there ready to fill me with their fucking seed!"

"How many do you want?"

"As many as you can get! I want them fucking my pussy and mouth until I can't take it anymore."

"What about that sexy ass?"

"Sorry, I'm afraid it's plugged tight right now. And even if I did take the toy out no one could possibly enjoy such a stretched out hole."

"Speak for yourself," one of the men said. "Are you stretched enough to take a fist?"

"I am. The plug up my ass is four inches thick. I can easily take a fist in my pussy as well, but you wouldn't want to do that," she purred seductively."

"The hell we wouldn't! Open that door and come out here so we can gang bang you the right way!"

"Well, since you asked so nicely." Pulling off the man's dick, Natalie opened the door and stepped out. "Give me a minute to get out of my clothes and I'm all yours."

"What about your ass?"

"If Steve will give us a few bottles of lube on the house you can fist both holes as much as you like. But I have two conditions. First, you are to only shoot your loads in my pussy or down my throat. And two, I want you to call me every dirty name you can think of. The more humiliating and degrading the better. Think you can manage that?"

"I'll be right back with the lube," Steve grinned.

In the meantime, one of the men – a lanky, scraggly-haired guy named Chris, Pulled Natalie down on top of him. No sooner was his cock filling her pussy then another stepped up and pushed in alongside him. "Fucking hell! You took that pretty easily!"

"I told you I could easily take a fist. Now ram your dicks in me! And you, she said to the third man, get that cock in my mouth!"

Steve returned to the bathroom several minutes later with four more men and an armful of sex toys. "I've brought a few bottles of lube and some toys you can play with. Consider them yours when you're done being a whore. Unfortunately, I have a store to run right now, but I'll be back later to pound one out on you."

"Thanks Steve," Natalie smiled back over her shoulder. "I won't leave until you've had a chance to have your way with me. As for the rest of you, I'm your fucking whore for the next several hours so get to using me!"

One of the newcomers grabbed a pair of cloverleaf clamps from the pile on the counter and attached them to Natalie's nipples, making sure to give the chain a few tugs in order to pinch them tight. She let out a soft groan, but kept the dick in her mouth and down her throat. The man came, but did not pull out as she sucked him clean. And then something happened that she never saw coming. The man in her mouth grabbed her by the sides of the head and looked down at her with a wicked grin as he began pissing – the warm, bitter liquid sliding effortlessly down to her belly.

But it did not remain there for long. Jumping up off of the two men still double fucking her pussy, she ran to the toilet and threw up. "What the fuck, man? You pissed down my throat!"

"Yeah, I did. And you loved it didn't you? Now get your ass back over here so the rest of us can use you as our urinal!"

"Like hell!"

"I said to get your freaky ass over here right now, or so help my I'll take the cane to it! That's it, you piss drinking whore," he said when Natalie reluctantly returned to the action. "What are you?"

"I...I'm a p-piss drinking whore," Natalie stammered.

"And what do piss drinking whores want?"

"To drink all of your piss."

"That's right. So, what are you going to do for every man that walks through that door?"

"Drink his piss."

"And what's going to happen if you refuse?"

"You'll cane me."

"And you don't want that, do you?"

"No. I'll be a good and drink everyone's piss," Natalie said climbing back onto the man on the floor so he and the other man could finish fucking their loads into her pussy.

"Good. You're not going to up and leave on us now are you?"

"No. I want you to use me like the dirty whore that I am."

The bathroom door opened and another man stepped in. "Holy shit!" he exclaimed at the scene playing out before his very eyes. "He wasn't kidding when he said there was a woman getting fucked in here!"

"You here to join or use the bathroom?"

"First one, then the other!"

45

"If you've got to take a piss put it in her mouth and let the slut drink. That's what she's here for, right, Pisspot?"

"Yes. Though I'm just learning to drink it so I probably won't be able to keep it down long," Natalie replied as the butterflies swarmed her belly and her clit tingled as if receiving gentle jolts of electricity.

"Fine by me. I've never seen a woman drink piss before," the man said as he took out his limp cock and pushed it into Natalie's open mouth. Her lips closed around it and he had to fight back the urge to throat fuck her as he let the stream flow.

Natalie fought back the urge to throw up with the man's dick still in her mouth, but only barely – learning that if she just relaxed and let nature take its course the piss would slide down like warm, salty water. And when he was done, she took a few minutes to make sure she was not going to throw up and then smiled in triumph as another man stepped forward to give her another bellyful.

The two men fucking Natalie's pussy filled her with semen and then stepped aside to make room for another. The next one lubed her pussy and asshole and then worked his hands in, balling them into fists as he pushed then in and out harder, faster and deeper. "God damn! That's fucking hot! You really are a sloppy little slut aren't you? Look how easily she takes my fists! How can any man satisfy a stretched out, worthless cunt like you?" Yanking his hand out of her ass, he added more lube and then shoved four more fingers into her pussy.

"Aahhgghhh! W-What…uhn…uhn…what are y-you d-doing?"

"I'm going to stretch you open even more, you used up has been. I'm going to shove both of my hands into your cunt!"

"What? No! I can't take that much! Please, only use one hand in each hole."

"Sorry, bitch, one hand isn't enough for a worthless nympho like you is it? Go on, admit it. Tell us all how much you want both of my hands stretching you open!"

"No! I don't want that at all! My holes are gaping open enough! Take your other hand out or I'm ending…Aahhgghhh!" Natalie let out a blood-curdling yelp as the man's left hand joined his right in her pussy.

"You did it, whore! You've got both hands in that sloppy cunt of yours! Now tell me how much you hate it? Go on, lie to them. I can feel how you clamp down around my wrists to keep me from pulling out. I can feel your entire body shaking as the orgasm builds. Open your mouth and drink more piss and cum as I wreck your pussy."

Perverse thoughts overtaking any rational reasoning, Natalie opened her mouth and let out a verbose moan right before another man put his cock into her mouth, pissed, and then kept it in so that she could suck him off. Another added more piss and he was followed by a third. Her belly rumbled and she knew she was not going to keep it down for long. Jumping off of the two hands buried deep in her gaping pussy, she ran to the toilet just in time to purge the contents of her stomach.

"I think it's getting easier to," she half-smiled, going to the sink to wash her hands and rinse her mouth out. "I think I need a short break before we continue. When we resume, you can work on stretching my asshole open."

7

Let's see what the son of a bitch blackmailing me thinks about me now, Natalie thought as she parked her car in the driveway. Tightening her vaginal and anal muscles around the plugs in her pussy and ass, she suddenly remembered the clamps hanging from her nipples and reached up under her shirt to take them off – hiding them in her purse before getting out of the car and going into the house.

"You're home late," her mother said from the kitchen. "You got another package in the mail today. Is it another book for school?"

"Yeah," Natalie lied. "I'll probably be getting a few of them in the coming weeks," Natalie replied, certain it was going to be pictures of her encounter with Lady Raven.

"I thought you purchased all of your books at the beginning of the semester?"

"I did. These are workbooks so I can practice for my finals. I'll get it in a few minutes. I need to take a quick shower first."

"I'd say so," her mother said poking her head out into the living room. I can smell the sex all the way in here. Grinning ear to ear, she gave her daughter a wink. "I'm glad you took my advice and found yourself a boyfriend."

"Um, I wouldn't exactly say that, but, um, yeah, I've taken your advice and am enjoying myself."

"Glad to hear it. Now hurry up and get that shower before your father gets home."

"So, you're not mad?"

"Mad? Why on earth would I be mad? I'm the one that bought you the dildos and suggest you get a sex life aren't I? So, who's the lucky man? When will we get to meet him?"

"What makes you think it's a man?" Natalie grinned.

"Well, you may have been with a woman, but there's no mistaking the smell of sex radiating from you like a cloud. "I'm going to ask you a question and I want you to be completely honest with me, Nat. Just how many men and women have you been with?"

"Hmm…If my math is correct, forty men and thirty-nine women."

"JESUS CHRIST! You're kidding, right?"

"Nope. You were right. Sex is fucking amazing and I've been experimenting like a madwoman."

"I didn't mean for you to go out and become a whore for Christ's sake! And how in the hell could you have possible had so much sex in such a short time unless you've…OH MY GOD!"

"I can see you've answered your own question. Anyways, I better go get that shower before dad gets home.

Though in desperate need of a thorough scrubbing, what Natalie needed more was to get the two massive plugs out of her pussy and ass and to give them a much needed break. Grabbing some clean clothes from her bedroom, she went to the bathroom, stripped out of her clothes and turned the water on, tugging the plugs from her body as the water rose to temperature. The way her sphincter expanded and clenched around the toy as she popped it out nearly made her orgasm, and she shoved it back in. Out. In. Out. In. Taking hold of the one in her pussy, she tugged it out and shoved it back in as she pulled the plug from her ass – alternating back and forth until she had her orgasm.

Taking the toys out for the final time, Natalie sat them in the back edge of the tub and climbed in. As the hot water cascaded down her naked body, she stared at the massive plugs and was overcome with a sense of pride at how easily she could take something so big in her recently deflowered holes. And then she thought about her mother calling her a whore and she chewed her lower lip as a tingle of excitement caused her clit to throb.

The urge to pee coming out of nowhere, she thought to go right in the shower, but then drew the curtain back and grabbed the cup from the counter next to the sink – bringing it to her pussy just in time. Once filled, she brought it to her nose and cringed at the bitter-smelling liquid. She then moved the cup to her lips and drank until it was empty. Licking her lips, she finished her shower and washed the toys before getting dressed and taking everything, cup included, to her bedroom. Feeling empty without the toys keeping her stretched open, she sighed and went down to join her parents for dinner.

∞ ∞ ∞

"Are you ok Nat," her father Henry asked looking at his flushed and flustered daughter.

"Huh? Oh I'm fine dad. I was just thinking about school. Are you guys going out again tonight?"

"We're going to a party at Laura and Greg's," her mother replied.

"What kind of party? Can I come along?"

"Um, I don't think you'd be interested sweetie."

The look on her father's face spoke volumes and Natalie decided to roll with it. "Ah, come on, dad, you and mom never want to do anything with me. Let me come along."

"I thought you had a lot of homework," her mother shot Natalie a knowing look.

"I do, but I haven't been to a party in, well, forever. Unless it's some sort of weird sex party for swingers or something. Is that it? Are you and dad swingers?"

"WHAT!? Why on earth would you ask such a question?"

"Because you dress all sexy like and never let me go to these parties with you. They are, aren't they? You're swingers! Don't bother denying it. The look on your face is proof enough. So, how long have you been swingers?"

"We're not swingers!" He dad answered.

"Oh, stop it," her mother said shaking her head. "She's an adult now and I just so happen to know that she's more than capable of handling the truth. "Your father and I have been swingers for about ten years."

"Cool," Natalie said taking a bite of spaghetti. "How many couples do you have sex with?"

"We are not having this discussion at the dinner table!"

"Apparently we are," said her mother. "There's Laura and Greg and fifteen other couples."

"WOW! And you have sex with them all at the same time?"

"No, not all of them. Usually, it's only eight to ten couples."

"Still, that's eight men and eight women. Do you have sex with the women as well?" Natalie asked her mother. "Do you have sex with the men?" she turned to her father.

"Yes, and no," her mother answered both questions. "And yes, they all have sex with me at the same time, same as the other women."

"Cool. Well, have fun tonight while I'm stuck here doing homework."

After dinner, Natalie grabbed the large envelope from the counter and took it to her bedroom, leaving her parents to clean up the dishes and put the leftovers in the fridge. She was dying to open the photo album to see the kinky images within, but she knew what that would lead to and did not want her parents to hear her moaning in orgasm. Laying back on the bed, she thought about the openness at which her mother admitted to being a swinger and wondered if it had anything to do with her earlier confession.

When Natalie heard the car pulling out of the driveway, her clothes came off and she tore the envelope open to reveal the photo album she expected to see. In the center of the black cover was a picture of her kneeling between Lady Raven's legs while Beth stood behind fucking a thick dildo up her ass. Below the picture was written: ***Natalie Holt, Lesbian Lover***.

Instead of freaking out as she did with the first photo album she received, she flipped the cover open, and thumbed passed the dossier and clothed images to the page showing her stripping out of her clothes and crawling on all fours up the driveway of Raven's Hollow. Spreading her legs, she gently and slowly rubbed her clit. As she went through page after page, she saw that anything remotely alluding to her having vaginal sex had not been included and she let out an irritated sigh.

Turning to the back cover, she read the slip of paper tucked into the corner.

The Third Commandment: Thou Shalt Become a Woman

Unless you want these, and previous images released to your family and friends you will come to 903 Falcon's Run tonight at 9 o'clock. Wear something sexy for the special occasion.

"Thou shalt become a woman," Natalie repeated the words aloud. "If only they knew." Tossing the album aside, she went to the closet to grab the big black dildo when she heard a knock at the front door. Cursing whomever had the audacity to interrupt her play time, she threw on a robe and rand down. Opening the door, she saw Lady Raven standing there before letting herself in. "Um, come on in. What brings you by? How did you even know where I live?"

"I don't have time to explain. I know what's coming in a few hours and I know what you did at XTC Toys earlier today." Opening the small black bag slung over her right shoulder, she withdrew two photo albums identical to the two Natalie already possessed, and handed them to her. "Those contain the pictures that were cut out to give the illusion that you were still a virgin. But He will discover the truth soon enough."

"Who will learn the truth? Who is *He*?"

"You'll learn that soon enough as well. Assuming you are going to Falcon's Run, that is."

"Of course I'm going. So, how pissed is he going to be that I'm not a virgin?"

"Pretty pissed. You heard none of this from me, but He loves nothing better than to turn naïve virgins into sex-crazed whores and I'd say he succeeded with you in spades."

"How can he do this to women and not expect them to take the logical step and have sex? Why did he even pick me in the first place?"

"All I know is that He watches his targets for some time before approaching them. Now, you had better get dressed. And if you ever want a job at Raven's Hollow just give me the word and I'll make sure you get all of the pussy you can handle."

"Thanks. I don't know about a job, but I wouldn't mind dropping by so that you, Beth and the others can have your way with me."

"Stop by anytime, love," Lady Raven said. Giving Natalie a passionate kiss on the lips, she pulled the door open and left.

Natalie took the photo albums to her bedroom and hid them in the closet with the others to look at later.

8

No longer fearing the pictures getting out, Natalie could not wait to get to the house for her next encounter where an unknown and unnamed man was to make her a woman, presumable by taking her virginity – something she herself took before her roller coaster ride into kink began. Borrowing a little black dress from her mother's closet, as the once shy nineteen year old did not have sexy clothes of her own, she made herself up as stunning as possible and then headed out.

Arriving at a mansion that made Raven's Hollow look paltry in comparison, she got out of the car and knocked on the front door. It was opened by a middle-aged man that made no attempt to hide the fact that he was checking her out.

"May I help you, young lady?"

"I'm Natalie Holt. I have a nine o'clock appointment."

"Of course, Miss Holt," The master has been expecting you. "I've been instructed to escort you downstairs for this evening's events."

"What exactly are this evening's events?"

"I'm sorry ma'am I'm not at liberty to divulge that information. If you'd please follow me."

"Can you tell me who this master of yours is?"

"Afraid not. His identity must remain a secret until the event. It's just through there, ma'am."

"Please, call me Natalie. Will you be joining these events? Will I get to feel that hard cock of yours fucking me?" She grinned, looking at the growing bulge in the butler's pants.

"I can only be so lucky, ma'am. I'm afraid I'm going to have to blindfold you before we go down. I'll lead the way so you don't fall down the stairs."

"Um, thanks, I guess. What's your name?"

"My name is Adam, ma'am."

"And mine is Natalie. Use it, or I'm not letting you blindfold me."

"If you insist. I must blindfold you Natalie. Will you please allow me to do my job?"

"Very well. I want you down there with me during the events, Adam."

"I'm afraid I am not permitted. My duties are up here."

"I don't care what your duties are. I'm the guest of honor and I know exactly what's going to take place down there. If you won't join me, then I won't join them and your master can find himself another virgin to deflower. You may blindfold me now."

Adam's version of a blindfold was a latex hood with mouth and nose holes which he expertly placed over Natalie's head. Taking her by the arm, he opened the basement door and led her down one step at a time. She could hear murmuring and breathing followed by several minutes of clapping and cheer by both men and women as she was led across the room and up three steps. Hands groped her body and her dress was removed. A week ago she would have freaked the hell out, but tonight...tonight it only filled her with excitement.

"Kneel," the man that had just stripped her out of her clothing commanded. Natalie dropped to her trembling knees and wondered how many people would be screwing her brains out. "Tonight, ladies and gentlemen, we bear witness to this young lady becoming a woman. Tonight, Natalie Holt will be deflowered before your very eyes. Are you prepared?"

"More than you could possibly imagine," Natalie answered, barely stifling a giggle.

A finger gently traced along the backs of her shoulders, around to the front and lifted her chin. "You will suck my cock now," the man said, placing the head of his dick against Natalie's parted lips. She took him into her mouth and bobbed her head back and forth, breathing through her nose as it hardened and slid down her throat. Swirling her tongue around the head, she licked up the pre-cum. But just as the fun was getting started, he pulled out.

His cock hard, the man walked around Natalie and gently nudged her head to the floor while raising her ass. Looking down, he saw her asshole gaping open wide. His eyes lowering, the grin faded from his lips to be replaced with disappointment. Leaning down, he grabbed a handful of Natalie's hair and yanked her head back. "Why is your pussy gaping open as if you've been fucked a million times?" he whispered so that only she could hear. "You're supposed to be a virgin."

"I took my own virginity the night that envelope was thrust into my hands at the park," Natalie replied. "I fucked myself on a big black dildo and then the next day I let more than two dozen men fuck me at the glory hole. And then I had sex with thirty or so women at Raven's Hollow before they stretched my holes open with toys and fists. So go right ahead and deflower me, she laughed."

"Well, I suppose I can't win them all. Put your head on the floor so I can fuck my load into you." Looking out at the crowd, he did the only thing he could to save face. "Ladies and gentlemen, I've just been informed that our guest of honor not only took her own virginity, but has been taking cocks left and right ever since she was given the first album. After I fuck my load into her, she's all yours to do with as you please."

The men and women watching the show went wild with this turn of events and then Natalie rose up into a kneeling position to add her two cents. "After you fuck me, I want your butler Adam to take me. If he is not the next one I feel then no one will have me."

"You're in no position to make demands here," the man preparing to fuck Natalie replied. "Now get back into position."

"I don't think so. In fact, I think I want him to be my first." Reaching up, she unzipped the hood and pulled it off. Turning around, she saw the man that had handed her that fateful envelope in the park, though his face was decidedly less beaten and battered. "YOU! You were behind it the whole time?"

"Guilty as charged. My name is Glen Parker and I am ordering you to put your head down and ass up so I can fuck my load into you."

"I'm pretty sure I just said I wanted Adam to be the first to fuck me tonight. Come on up here Adam. I want your dick in my pussy in the next three minutes or I'm leaving." Looking out at the crowd, she saw everyone on the edges of their seats waiting to see what happened next.

"I will be the one to fuck you first and then everyone else may have you. Now, get into position or I'll cane your ass until you do."

"Go right ahead. You've manipulated me from the beginning and now I'm now longer playing by your rules. If your dick comes anywhere near me before Adam has fucked his seed into me I'll have the police here saying you threatened me with rape. Now, get the fuck off the stage and wait your turn. Come on, Adam, I want your cock in me right god damned now!"

Shrugging, Adam stripped out of his clothes with every step he took towards the stage. "Sorry boss, but there's no way in hell I can pass up the chance." Walking behind Natalie who was not in the position Glen commanded her to get in, he wasted no time in pushing into her gaping pussy. And while Glen turned red in the face with humiliation and anger, the rest of the audience went wild – cheering and clapping this hilarious turn of events.

"Uhn…uhn…t-that's it, slam your cock in me! Harder! HARDER DAMMIT! Slap my ass and call me dirty names! Tell me what a worthless fucktoy I am!"

"I can't do that," Adam said grabbing Natalie by the hips. "You're far from worthless, but yeah, you are a bit of a slut."

"A bit? I've had more sex in the last week than most women have in a lifetime! I've taken cocks in every hole, licked pussy and taken two fists at the same time in my pussy and again in my ass!" she confessed to everyone listening. "I've gone from innocent and naïve virgin to piss drinking whore and I loved every minute of it. Now slap my ass as you fuck your load into me! I may not be pregnant yet, so maybe, just maybe you'll be the lucky one to be the first to breed me like an animal!"

"You hear that Glen?" she continued as Adam fucked her. "I've taken so much semen in my pussy and womb that even if you did fuck me you most likely wouldn't be the one to knock me up! You," she pointed to a cute blonde sitting in the front row "come up here so I can lick your pussy! And then the rest of you. I want you all! Fuck me! Fist me! Use me as your personal urinal! I want to be used as the fuck toy I've become thanks to that man standing over there!" She grinned, motioning to the left side of the room where Glen leaned against a wall, arms crossed over his chest.

With every passing hour, Natalie added another dick sucked and fucked, another pussy licked and another bladder full of piss drank to her growing roster of sexual conquests. Her pussy was so full of semen that it was readily running down her thighs, but she did not care. Looking across the room, she grinned at Glen and for the briefest of moments felt sorry for him, but her concentration was broken by a large fist pumping in and out of her ass while another went into her pussy. Her vision of Glen blocked by another man offering her his cock, she saw him leave the basement out of the corner of her eye.

∞ ∞ ∞

It was late the next day when Natalie woke lying in a comfortable king-sized bed. Rolling over, she found herself staring at Glen and her eyes went wide. And then she remembered. The party ended well into the night and feeling sorry for the host, she searched the house until she found him in one of the mansions many bedrooms. There was a brief argument which she ended abruptly when she climbed into bed and took his cock into her mouth.

Glen rolled over and Natalie draped her arm over his side, feeling happier in that moment than she had ever been in her life. She felt sexy. Wanted. But most of all, in some bizarre and twisted way, she felt loved. Kissing his shoulder, she moved her hand down and gently squeezed his dick.

"Mmmm, you were magnificent last night," Glen moaned. "I'm so glad I ran into you at the park."

"According to a reliable source, you watch your targets for months before approaching them. Don't worry, I'm pleased you ran into me at the park as well. I'm a bit sore after last night, but it was well worth it. Sorry I was such a bitch towards you, but as far as I'm concerned you had it coming for what you did to me."

"What I did to you? As I recall, all I did was give you a package to keep safe. You're the one that opened them and you're the one that took it upon yourself to return it to the men's room of XTC Toys. And you're the one that went to Raven's Hollow."

"Only because I was being blackmailed. Had you never sent me those photo albums I never would have done any of it. And I can only assume the men at the shop that first time were there because of you. Now, I have to ask why. Why did you pick me for this kinky game of yours, Glen?"

"Have you looked at yourself in a mirror? You're an incredibly beautiful woman and I knew from the first time I watched you walking through the park that I had to have you. I needed to be the one to take your virginity."

"Why?"

"I guess you can call it my fetish. So, would you do it again?"

"Not today," Natalie giggled "but I think I would in the future. Right now I'm way too sore.

You have no idea how much sex I've had in the last week or so."

"No doubt," Glen said hugging her close. "You really were amazing last night even if I did have to wait until the end to have sex with you."

"So what does this make us now?" she asked biting her lower lip.

"What do you want it to make us?"

"I don't know. I've never had a boyfriend before. Prior to all of this, I was a complete virgin; too shy to really even talk to guys. How long have you been watching me anyways?"

"Long enough to know I had to risk giving you those first photos. I hoped it would peak your curiosity, but I never imagined you'd take it to such extremes so quickly."

"Who was the woman in the pictures? Did you do the same to her as you did to me? Was she a virgin too? Did you turn her into a slut like you did me?"

"I think you turned yourself into a slut, dear. I didn't make you do anything you didn't want to do. Deep down I think you were longing of sex and by happy coincidence I was the one to bring that hunger to bare. As for the woman in the pictures she was my first girlfriend. We met years ago in college."

"And did you make her a slut?"

"As a matter of fact it was all her idea. She was a sexual freak kind of like you are. In fact, there wasn't much she wouldn't do. She also loved to be watched like I think you do."

"Ok, I'll give you that. I do like to be watched. I also love the feeling of multiple cocks drilling my holes at the same time. I never thought sex could be that amazing, but I'm glad I took my mother's advice and did it."

"You're mother's advice?"

"As it so happened, the day you gave me that envelope, my mother gave me a gift of three dildos. While my parents went out for the night, I stayed home and looked through Fiona's pictures. The next thing I know, I'm grabbing one of the toys from the box and fucking myself on it. It was a big black monster nearly three inches thick and more than a foot long. The next day at XTC I wasn't going to let the men fuck me, but again, I was overcome with lust and the more they called me names, the more I had to have them. "So back to my original question… What does that make us?"

"I think it makes us slut and lucky guy," Glen smiled.

Natalie rolled over on top of him, his semi-hard cock pressed against her pussy. Grinding back and forth, feeling him growing harder by the second, she lifted up and his cock sprang to life. "Mmmm," she moaned, lowering herself on his dick, taking it fully into her. "I think I can get used to that, Lucky Man."

9

A week had passed since her night with Glen and she had still not received a photo album filled with pictures celebrating the special occasion. In fact, she had not even heard a word from Glen at all. After driving by his mansion several times, she came to the conclusion that he was either out of town, or simply did not want anything to do with a whore like her. On the verge of depression and feeling foolish for going along with the commandments in the first place, humiliation, shame and doubt set in and she began questioning everything she had done.

Feeling used in the biggest way possible, Natalie lay in bed deep in thought. *I sucked so many cocks,* she thought while lying in bed. *I drank cum and piss like water, savored it even. I jerked them off, ate pussy, and let them fuck and stretch my holes open like a common whore.* "What in the hell is wrong with me," she sighed. "Why did I do those things?"

"You did it because you're a whore," a voice in the back of her mind told her. *"You enjoyed all those cocks plugging your holes. You enjoyed everything they did to you, Natalie. Admit it… you're nothing more than a depraved slut and you loved everything they did to you!"*

Perhaps I am a whore, Natalie replied to the voice. *"But I only did it because I was being blackmailed. I never would have done it otherwise."*

"Blackmailed you say? Were you being blackmailed when you went back to the toy store and let all of those men use you for a second time? Were you being blackmailed when you went to Glen's mansion and took charge of the situation, demanding they use you like a fucktoy? Or did you love it and are only now pissed off because the man that turned you into a sex-crazed animal is nowhere to be found?"

"Fuck you!" Natalie yelled at the voice in her head, rolling over and doing her best to ignore all further communications.

∞ ∞ ∞

A large box arrived for Natalie the next day. Unfortunately, she was in class when it arrived and her mother accepted and signed for it. Carrying the box into the house, she sat it on the coffee table and stared down at it. "Nat sure is getting a lot of packages lately," Regina said to her husband. "This is the third one in the last couple of weeks."

"Did she tell you what she's been getting?" Henry asked in reply.

"She said it was stuff for school, but why would she be getting it this late in the semester? The term is almost over."

"Beats me," Henry replied flipping through the channels.

Picking the box up, Regina carried it into the kitchen and sat it on the table out of the way while she went about cleaning house, but her eyes kept going back to it as her mind wondered about its contents. Unable to take it any longer, she got a knife from the drawer and sliced through the clear tape. Pulling the flaps back, she looked upon the top photo album and her jaw nearly hit the floor when she saw a picture of her daughter on the front getting fucked by three men at the same time. Beneath the image was written: *Natalie Holt Becomes a Woman*.

Regina pulled the photo album from the box and found another. This one depicting her daughter on all fours licking another woman's pussy while another fucked her with a huge strap-on. "What in the hell is this?" she gasped. Tossing the second album on the table, she withdrew a third. "HENRY! Come in here right now!"

Thinking something was seriously wrong based on the tone of his wife's voice, Henry sprang out of the recliner and ran into the kitchen to see her sitting at the table flipping through a photo album. "What in the hell's going on? Why on earth are you screaming like a madwoman when you're sitting there all fine and dandy?"

"Look at this," she replied pushing the first album in his direction. Standing up, she emptied out the contents of the box. There were four photo albums and six DVD cases – each with an image of her daughter in a sexual position. The first DVD showed Natalie in a men's bathroom sucking cock after cock and swallowing one after another. It was titled: *Glory Hole Natalie*. The second DVD – titled: *Natalie Tries the Fairer Sex*, showed a picture of Natalie licking a raven-haired woman while another fucked her with a large dildo. The third DVD – titled: ***Natalie Becomes a Woman***, showed the nineteen year old stunner on her hands and knees getting fucked in front of a crowd. The last three DVD's were a trilogy titled: ***Natalie's First Gang Bang Volumes 1 – 3***.

"What in the hell," Henry said in surprise, slowly flipping through the pages of the first album. "What kind of pervert did we raise?"

"I have no idea, honey," Regina replied. "I thought she was kidding when she told me she had sex with so many people, but this…this is beyond shocking!"

"That's putting it…wait, I thought she was still a virgin? She's never even had a boyfriend. And how many people did she say she had sex with?"

"Um…a lot. But like I said, I thought she was kidding. I never even expected her to use the gifts I bought her, let alone do something like this!"

"Gifts? What gifts? You never told me you bought her anything."

"Don't be mad, but I was feeling sorry for her and bought her a few dildos. I was hoping she'd use them, figure out how great sex was and go get herself a boyfriend."

"Well, it looks like she found about a hundred of them!"

"I swear to god I never intended for any of this to happen! Our daughter is a god damned whore!"

"Don't say that," Henry said. "There's got to be a rational explanation for all of this."

"I think the names of these DVD's are telling enough. We have to do something about this. Nat has to explain herself or she can hit the road. I don't want a whore living under my roof."

"Calm down dear," Henry said. "Let's not get ahead of ourselves. After all, you gave her the toys and told her to go out and enjoy sex, and I'm pretty sure telling her that we're swingers didn't help matters. We'll sit her down and have a talk, but I'm not throwing my daughter out on the street with nowhere to go."

"From the look of these pictures she's got plenty of places to go." Regina slammed the album shut and tossed it into the box alongside the others.

Henry flipped to the last page of the album he was holding and pulled out a folded up piece of paper. "OH MY FUCKING GOD!" he gasped. "Did you see this?" With a shaky hand he handed the letter to his wife.

The Fourth Commandment: Thou Shalt Lay with Friends

Unless you want these and all previous photos, as well as the DVDs of your gang bangs released to your family, friends, and anyone else we wish to send them to, you will complete the Fourth Commandment within one week of receiving this package.

In case you don't understand what you must do, you are to lay with your friends; that is you are to have sex with them. We'll be watching and if you don't complete the Commandment everything will be released. To make the choice easy for you, we've picked the friends you are to have sex with. Jane Filmore, Maria Kimball, Susan Galloway, Roger Blakely, Mike Suffield, James Creedy, Tyler Beck, and Shane Gosselin.

Seems easy, right? WRONG! Not only do you have to have sex with those eight friends, you must do them all at the same time. That's right my curious little nympho, at least eight of your friends will not only learn your dirty little secret, they'll become part of it. HOW EXCITING!

P.S. I know you've been by the house a few times in the last week looking for me and I'm afraid I have some bad news for you, my slut. That's not my house and my name is not Glen Parker. Sorry dear but I'll be much harder to find than that.

"What in the hell do we do?" Regina said in tears. "Our baby is being blackmailed to do these perverted things!"

"What could she have done to deserve being blackmailed like this?" Henry wondered. "What in the hell did she do? Why wouldn't she tell us, or go to the police?"

Regina put the albums back in the box and folded the flaps to keep it shut. "We have to talk to her about this. You read that letter. It says she has to have sex with her friends. I take that to mean she has not done that and they do not know about this. We need to prevent this from happening before it gets too far out of control."

"I agree, but other than involving the police how are we going to stop it?"

"I think we should talk to Nat and figure out what in the hell's going on before her name gets smeared through the mud and leave going to the police as a last resort. You're right, I'm sorry I flew off the handle, but this is our daughter we're talking about and I really never expected something like this to happen to her. Perhaps you're right. I probably never should have told her we were swingers."

"This goes way beyond any of that. Let's just try to regain our composure and come up with a line of questions and answers before she gets home."

10

Natalie was walking through the park enjoying the weather and smell of fresh cut grass when she saw a familiar face headed in her direction. Smiling, she hastened her pace and was just about to say hi when Beth cut her off by kissing her hard on the lips – her hands reaching around to grab her ass and pull her in tight. "Why, hello to you too," she grinned when the embrace finally broke fifteen seconds later. "What brings you to the park this fine day?"

"You," Beth smiled. "Lady Raven told me I'd find you here. She also told me all about the, um, deflowering party," she added the last part with air quotes and a giggle. "Was it as amazing as she made it out to be?"

"Holy shit yes! I wish you could have been there, Beth. Not only did I find out who was blackmailing me to do all of this, but I put him in his fucking place."

"Lady Raven told me what you did, but I couldn't believe it. Man, I bet he was pissed."

"Yeah, but I made it up to him. It's a shame he up and left on me because I kind of liked him. Shit, Beth, I thought we wanted to be my boyfriend the way we talked in bed the day after. But I guess I was too much of a whore for him."

"Honey, let's get one thing straight right now. You are *not* a whore."

"Really? What else would you call someone that's done the things I have?"

"Open-minded and highly sexual? So, do you think you'll ever come back to Raven's Hollow? I hear Lady Raven has offered you a job and I really think you'd make a great addition to the team."

"Thanks, but even I have my limits and getting gang banged every night is more than I can take right now."

"You still wearing the plugs?"

"No. I haven't had them in me since the day after the party. I'm trying to get my holes to return to a more normal size."

"Is it working?"

"Yeah. They're no longer gaping open all the time and I've learned to do kegel exercises for better muscle control. I can squeeze them so tight now it's hard taking the big black dildo that started it all."

"Nice. You know, all of this talk about sex is getting me horny. How about we duck in the bushes over there and have some fun?"

"As much as I would love to do that, I need to get home. I have a shitload of studying to do for a couple of big tests tomorrow. You know, you could come home with me. I can shock my parents by introducing you as my girlfriend."

"Ha! Yeah, I'm sure they'd love that. Are they ultra-conservative or something?"

"Not exactly. Actually, they're swingers."

"Nice! So, is this just a ploy to shock your parents, or a not so subtle way of asking me out?"

"Maybe a little of both. God, I never even asked if you were married or dating anyone."

"It's okay. I'm single. And if you're being serious right now, I'd love to be your girlfriend."

Butterflied swarming her stomach, her heard beating like a drum, Natalie pulled Beth close and kissed her like she had never kissed anyone before and she did not care who saw it. "You know, you're the first person I've ever dated," she said with a nervous grin. "You sure you want a used up whore for a girlfriend?"

"First things first, you are not used up. You're a beautiful young woman with a lot of kinky sex under her belt and do you know what I love most about you?"

"My nipples?" Natalie giggled, remembering back to her first visit to Raven's Hollow and how much time and attention Beth gave her breasts and nipples.

"That too. What I really love is your willingness to try new things without bitching and moaning about it. I'm the same way and believe me, it's a lot harder than you think to find another like-minded woman."

"Very important question and I will respect whatever answer you give so please be honest with me."

"Always."

"Will we be having sex with other people, or only each other?"

"I'm fine with you having sex with others, if you're okay with me doing it as well. That being said, however, I'd like for us to do it together as much as possible."

"Agreed. And tell Lady Raven that I accept."

"Accept?"

"The job. I'll take it if it's still on the table. That way we can have as much sex as humanly possible, right? I mean, what could possibly be better than mixing work and pleasure with the woman I love?"

"I love you to. And don't be alarmed, but I'm seriously considering dragging you into those bushes and having my way with you."

"Come on, my place is only ten minutes away. We can do it there."

"After you. Oh, before I forget, I have something for you." Reaching into the huge purse slung over her shoulder, she pulled out an all too familiar manila envelope and handed it to her new girlfriend. "I was asked to deliver this to you before you got home."

"Pictures of the party, I presume? I was wondering when I'd be getting them."

"No idea. I was also told to tell you it's time sensitive and that you should open it as soon as you are home and alone."

"Then what are we standing around here for? Let's get back to my place and see what's inside, shall we?"

"You live with your parents, right? Do they know about all of this?"

"No. I told my mom I had sex with a bunch of men and women, but not about these albums and my being blackmailed."

"Don't think of it as blackmail. It's more like a hard nudge to expand your sexual horizons."

"So, do you know who this Glen guy really is? I've been by the mansion where the party was held several times and no one answers the door and he won't return my phone calls.

"No idea. I think Lady Raven is the only one at the Hollow that's ever met him as she's in charge of the second Commandment. All the rest of us do is help her fulfill it. Can I ask you a serious question?"

"Of course. You can ask me anything you like."

"Are you upset at what happened to you? I don't mean just at the Hollow, but all of it. Do you have any regrets over the things you've done?"

"I did. When Glen, or whomever he really is, stopped talking to me I felt betrayed, humiliated and degraded. I felt as low as a worm and about as filthy for falling for such a horrible trick. But then I kind of got into an argument with myself and after a lot of self-reflection realized the voice in my head was right. I loved every minute of everything I did. No one put a gun to my head and told me to enter that men's room. I could have just as easily thrown the photo album away and forgot the whole thing, but I didn't. I was curious and I acted upon it. Even when I entered the stall thinking I was going to get some huge reward and instead only got dicks, I still did not protest too much. And I certainly did not have to let more than two dozen men have their way with me. Fuck, for all I know I very well may be pregnant right now."

"Would that upset you?"

"Not in the slightest. I thought it would, but then when I remembered all the times I told the men to fill me with their seed, and how excited it made me feel, I think deep down I was really begging them to breed me."

"I have to admit that's really fucking hot!" Beth said, eyeing her new lover with unbridled lust. And just when she was about to lean in for another kiss, her phone rang. "Hello, Lady Raven," she answered. And after a brief conversation she hung up looking more than a little irritated. "I'm afraid we'll have to do this another time. I'm needed back at the Hollow. One of my regulars is due in any moment and she does not like to wait."

"It's okay. I really should try concentrating on my schoolwork tonight."

"Yes, you really should. Give those holes of yours a break and I'll talk to you later."

Natalie and Beth shared one last kiss before parting ways and Natalie knew there was no way in hell she was going to be able to think about anything else.

11

It was a good thing Beth was called into work because Natalie wasn't in the door five seconds when her mother started on her. "Sit down, Nat. Your father and I have something very important to talk to you about"

"I really can't right now, mom. I've got two big tests tomorrow and I need to study."

"I don't give a damn what you have tomorrow, young lady," her father said. "You'll sit your ass down right now and listen to what we have to say, or else!"

"Or else what?"

"We'll get to that later. Now please sit down," her mother answered.

"What's this all about?" Natalie asked as she took a seat on the couch. She had never seen her parent's this upset before and it profoundly disturbed her. She watched as her father walked into the kitchen and then returned a moment later carrying a cardboard box.

"This came for you today," he said sitting the box on the coffee table. "Your mother couldn't help but open it."

"What the hell, mom!" Natalie exclaimed, suddenly nervous about the contents and what her parents may have seen. "What gives you the right to open my mail?"

"I wanted to see what books you were getting so late in the semester," her mother said opening the box and pulling out one of the photo albums. "Care to explain this? Or this," she said adding a second album. "Or this, this and these? Can I assume the other books you got were more of these?" she asked, holding up the top photo album. "What in the hell have you gotten yourself into Natalie?"

Natalie's shoulders slumped in defeat and she knew better than to compound the situation with another lie. I had no choice. He said he was going to send the pictures to everyone I know if I didn't do as he said. No one was supposed to find out! What's the big deal anyways? You're the one that bought me dildos and encouraged me to go out and experiment with sex!"

"With a man or a woman!" her mother shot back. "I didn't tell you to go out and become a god damned whore!"

"Says the woman getting gang banged by at least eight couples several times a week! Neither of you have any fucking room to talk about being a whore!"

"She has a point," her father said. "But this isn't about you having sex with lord only knows how many men and women. This is about you being blackmailed, Nat. Who is this man? What is his name?"

"He said his name was Glen Parker, but I don't think it's real."

"What is this commandment shit?" Henry asked. "Do you have any idea what he wants you to do next?"

"I have no idea dad. I get the packages of the previous commandment I completed and he tells me what I am going to do next."

"Well, sweetheart," her father said angrily "for the fourth commandment you are to have sex with eight of your friends."

It took a long moment for this to fully sink into Natalie's distraught brain. "What? Wait, that can't be possible. He can't seriously think I could, or would do that!"

"I'm glad we're on the same page," her father said. "So, what do you intend to do about this? How long has it been going on? What has he made you do? Never mind, I've seen enough pictures to get the idea. And there are DVD's Nat. What are you going to do if he decides to sell the videos?"

"How do we know he hasn't already?" her mother asked.

"OH GOD," Natalie wailed. "He swore he wouldn't do that if I cooperated with him.

"And you believe a man capable of blackmailing you into being a slut?"

"I don't know. I didn't even know I was being filmed until now. I don't know what to do other than cooperate with him. I don't even know how or where to find him."

"You should have told us earlier. Why haven't you gone to the police with this?"

"And have all of our names dragged through the dirt? I couldn't do that to you and I sure as hell didn't want everyone I know finding out about any of this!"

"Too late for that now. So, what do you intend to do about the current commandment he's demanding of you?" her mother asked.

"I can't involve my friends in this," Natalie replied morosely "but if I don't he'll release everything not only to them, but to every one of my friends, family members, and to the college as well. My life will be ruined."

"How does this man know where all of your family and friends live?" her father asked. "Did you tell him that too?"

"Of course not, dad," Natalie said, shocked her father would even think that. "I'm sure he's done some digging. He at least knows where you and eight of my friends live. Probably isn't hard to figure out the rest."

"Do you like getting used like a slut?" her father asked.

"HENRY!" Regina shouted. "Don't ask her such things."

"It's ok, mom. I think you can tell from the pictures that I enjoyed what they did to me, dad. I admit it, I'm a slut."

"Don't say that, sweetie," her mother now joined in the sobbing.

"So you liked all those men fucking you, using you like a piece of meat? What if you they got you pregnant? Have you thought about that?"

"Actually, yes, I have thought about it and if I am then I'll have the baby and love it with all of my heart. I will not blame it for my stupid mistakes."

"Well, the way I see it, you've got exactly three choices. You can either have sex with eight of your friends and let the son of a bitch keep used you like the whore he's turned you into, you can pack up and more somewhere far away in the hopes that'll be enough to drive him off, or we go to the police and inform them of what's going on.

"We can't go to the police! That's the last thing we should do. Unless you want him to send everything out and ruin my life. And I doubt running away will solve my problems either. That leaves only one choice."

"You're just going to let that piece of shit walk all over you?" her mother asked. "I thought we raised you better than that!"

"What else can I do? If I do anything else all of our lives are ruined. My humiliation is a small price to pay to keep your names clean."

"Do you plan on spending the rest of your life being blackmailed into performing one sexual act after another?" her father asked. "This needs to end now!"

"And how do you plan on doing that, dad? I don't even know where Glen lives or even if that's his real name. I went to the mansion these DVD's took place and no one's there."

"I don't know," Henry said shaking his head in disgust "but we'll think of something."

Suddenly remembering the envelope Beth gave her in the park, Natalie opened her backpack and pulled it out. "I got this on my way home," she said tearing it open. "It was supposed to have come in that box. One the black cover were pictures of the eight friends named in the latest Commandments letter. Below was written: ***Kinky Friends of Natalie Holt***. With shaking fingers she opened it. Inside the cover was a slip of paper reading:

I forgot to include this with the box I sent so I asked Beth to deliver it for me. I hope it finds you well. If your friends are unwilling to comply feel free to show them the contents of this album.

"OH GOD!" Natalie gasped. "H-How is this possible?"

"What is it?" her mother asked.

"Pictures of Jane!" Flipping through the pages, Natalie stared in wide-eyes shock as they went from headshot and fully clothed to naked, masturbating with fingers and toys, showering and having sex with three men at the same time with the last picture showing a jet of pussy juices squirting two feet in the air. After Jane came photos of Maria depicted in much the same manner, but instead of three men, she was being screwed by six. And on it went for each of the friends depicted on the cover. The evidence was damning, but it told her one thing for sure. She had no choice but to follow through with the commandment. "They're all in here! All eight of them in very compromising situations."

"All of them?" her father asked. "And by compromising can we assume sexual?"

"Yes on both accounts. Wait, there's another note."

If the commandment is not completed in time, not only will all of your pictures and videos be sent out, but so will theirs. What I've sent is only a small sample of what I have on each of them so be a good little slut and do as you're told.

"Well, that settles it once and for all," Natalie sighed. "I have no choice but to comply with his wishes."

"Don't give us that bullshit!" her mother cried. "You want to do it don't you? I can see it in your eyes that you want to have a gang bang with them."

"Maybe I do. But that's beside the point. You heard what the note said. If I don't do this then their lives will be ruined as well."

"Then do what you must to protect your friends, but this has to end, Nat," her father sighed.

12

Natalie knew her friends well and she knew getting all of them to agree to what amounts to a gang bang with each other would be nearly impossible as some of those named had prior history, but she had a week to make it happen. Susan Galloway and Mike Suffield use to date until Jane Filmore got in the way and ruined the relationship for Susan. After a three month fling Jane broke it off with Mike and moved on to another man. Mike tried to get back with his ex, but she wanted nothing further to do with him. Convincing the three of them to do anything sexual together would prove the biggest hurdle she'd have to overcome if this was ever going to pan out.

In the wee hours of the night Natalie realized what she had to do. The only way to prove to them this it was not a hoax would be to tell them the truth. Climbing out of bed, she went to the closet and grabbed her box of photo albums and DVD's and sat it on the dresser with a very simple plan in mind.

∞ ∞ ∞

To Natalie's frustration it was four more days before she could get all eight friends together at the same time. That left her with only two days to complete the commandment before the pictures and videos of her and her friends were released to what Natalie figured would be a minimum of fifty people not counting the school and internet.

"What's this all about?" Maria asked, looking around the room.

"I have something to tell you all and it's not going to be easy," Natalie replied, her fingers tightening around the papers and photo album she held in her right hand. "The truth is, I've gotten myself into a huge mess and I need all of your help to get out of it."

"What in the hell did you do now?" asked Tyler. "And what does this have to do with us?"

Natalie handed each of her friends – a term that could change in the next minute or so, a piece of paper – a copy of the letter she received from her blackmailer. "When I give the word I want you to open the paper and read it. Before you do, let me stress that it is not a joke. I asked my parents to be here to verify that." Handing the last piece of paper to Shane, she took a deep breath and told them to open it.

They all read the paper in stunned silence and nineteen year old Susan Galloway was the first to respond. Standing up, she walked across the room and stood in front of Natalie – giving her friend a hard look in the eyes, her own light grey eyes seeming to pierce to the soul. She could sense the fear coming from Natalie and knew she was telling the truth. "If this is what it takes to get you out of trouble you can count me in."

"Thank you," Natalie replied barely able to hold back the tears.

"I've wanted to get in your pants since we first met," said Tyler. "I don't care for the others joining, but as long as I don't have to have sex with the other guys I'm in too."

"Are you people idiots or what?" Maria protested. "Can't you see what's going on here? How do we really know what she says is true?"

"It's all true," Natalie's mother replied. "Do you really think her father and I would be here to listen to this if it wasn't true? I'm the one that intercepted the package containing all the pictures and videos."

"What pictures and videos?" James Creedy asked.

"If you really must know, the guy blackmailing me took pictures and videos of me and are using them to further blackmail me," Natalie answered. "What's worse is he's got pictures of you guys too."

"He what?" Roger gasped. "What do you mean he's got pictures of us? There's no way in hell that's true!"

"It's unfortunately very true," Natalie cried. "And I've got the proof right here. Opening the album, she handed each friend the pages containing their pictures and a copy of the letter that came with it.

"Fucking hell!" Mike gasped as he looked at his pictures. "This can't be happening."

"How in the hell did he get a picture of that? Maria asked to no one in particular. "I wasn't even in the damn country when that happened!"

"Was I with you at the time?" Natalie asked.

"No."

"Then that should tell you right there that I had nothing to do with this. This isn't some sick hoax I thought up for my own amusement so please believe me when I say I don't find any of this amusing."

"Why don't we go to the police then?" asked James. "We don't have put up with this abuse!"

"Because if I go to the police or fail to complete the commandment before the deadline, he'll release everything to every friend and family member I have as well as to Maple Grove and I don't want my family's reputation ruined because of my stupid mistake. And, according to this letter, he'll send your pictures out as well. Meaning your lives will be ruined too."

"What if he films us too?" said James. "What's preventing him from blackmailing us?"

"That's a good question," Roger added.

"He has compromising pictures of all of you, pictures I'm sure none of you would want released to the public. If his plan was to blackmail all of you I'd think he would've contacted you all by now. Has he?"

"No," they all answered.

"The gang bang will happen here," Natalie said. "There are no cameras or other recording devices anywhere in the house and you are all free to search if you'd like. No one will stop you. Look, I know this is all of a sudden and not even close to an ideal situation, but I have two days left before the shit hits the fan and I desperately need your help. Hell, half of you've been trying to get in my pants since we met and I know all of you guys have talked about screwing every woman in this room so what's the big deal?"

"What's the big deal?" asked Maria. "I think the big deal is you're asking us to participate in a gang bang, Natalie!"

"I know, but it's the only way. After it's all over I'll understand if none of you want to be friends with me. Hell, I don't want to be friends with me. All I ask is for you to do this one thing to help me keep all of our families names untarnished."

"Against my better judgment I'll do it," said Jane.

"Me too," said Roger, Maria, and Shane.

"So that we all understand each other here," said James "are we all having sex with just you, or with everyone in this room?"

"You will all be having sex with me, but everyone in this room right now, with the exception of my parents, is fair game if they choose to. My parents will not be home during the...party," Natalie replied. "If you want to have sex with someone other than me please ask them first. We may be forced to do this by an outside source, but that doesn't mean we have to be uncivilized about it."

"Fair enough. I guess I'm in too then."

"What about you, Mike?" asked Natalie looking at the only one who hasn't agreed to participate. Hell, she was surprised even one of them agreed so easily.

"I'm still not convinced this isn't some kind of an elaborate hoax," he replied.

"Why on earth would I call you all here and tell you about my humiliation if it wasn't true? You have the pictures and know t there's no way possible I could have taken them."

"I don't know, maybe you're into kinky sex and want to drag us all into it with you."

"That isn't the case and you know it. You know me better than that."

"Do I? Perhaps if we saw these supposed pictures and videos of you it would lend credence to your story. I mean, so far all you've shown us are our pictures."

"If that's what it'll take for you to say yes then by all means see for yourself." Natalie went to the kitchen and picked up the box of photo albums and DVD's from the table and carried it into the living room, placing it on the coffee table before pulling the flaps open. "It's all in there. Everything I've told you in vivid details. The newest pictures are on top. If that's not enough I'll pop a DVD into the player and you can watch that too. This isn't a joke dammit!"

Mike pulled out a photo album and stared at the picture of Natalie getting fucked in all three holes at the same time on the cover and the title Natalie's First Gang Bang part 1. When he open it, his jaw hit the floor as he flipped through the picture-filled pages. He could feel his cock stiffening in his pants and had to adjust himself to a more comfortable position. Tossing the album back in the box, he looked up at Natalie.

"Are you satisfied?"

"So when is this gang bang supposed to happen?"

"I would like to do it now and get it over with, but if it's too soon, we have two more days before everything gets out."

13

"Better to do it now and get it over with," Maria sighed. "If I have to wait I may have a change of heart."

"I second that," Mike added.

"Then Henry and I will leave you to it," Regina smiled. "Come on honey, let's leave them to their gang bang."

As her parents left the house, Natalie went to her bedroom and grabbed her box of sex toys. "In order to make sure I complete the commandment," Natalie said as her friends started to undress "I think it's best if you all fuck me first. To be as thorough as possible I think you should all fuck me in pussy, ass and mouth. And don't worry about being gentle. As you've seen from the pictures I'm, more than capable of handling the largest of cocks."

"And what about taking our fists?" asked James. "Can we do that to you as well?"

"You are free to do everything to me that you've seen in the pictures. I know you're not into women,' she said to Maria, Jane and Susan "but you have to fuck and lick me at least once. The blackmailer didn't say, but I think it best if we fuck and lick each other's pussy and asshole at least once to be on the safe side.

"Um, that's not completely accurate," said Susan. "I never told anyone this, but I've had sex with a few women in the last year. Why do you think I stepped forward so quickly? Since I got into sex with other women I've been dying to have sex with you too."

"Well that's good to hear," Natalie smiled "because today you get your wish. As for the rest of you, you can decide amongst yourselves who's going first. I'll be waiting over here."

After conferring with each other in a tightly huddled group, Roger stepped forward and pulled his shirt off over his head. "We've discussed it and decided that we will alternate between man and woman until we've all had sex with you. For the first round we'll all fuck your pussy. In round two we'll do your ass and then in round three we'll use your mouth. Is that acceptable?"

"Sounds perfect," Natalie said stripping out of her clothes. And I'm dead serious when I say you can do anything you want to me. If any of you have to take a piss just go right down my throat."

"I'm not done yet," Roger interrupted. "After we've all fucked you in each hole, we're going to take you and the other ladies in pussy, ass and mouth at the same time until we can't go anymore. If you want to be used as a fucking whore, then that's exactly what we're going to do. And it had better be enough to satisfy whatever asshole is doing this to us."

"Open up," Shane said offering Natalie his cock. No sooner was in in then he started to piss and he stared down at her in shocked surprise. "HOLY SHIT! She's doing it guys! She's actually drinking my piss!"

Stepping out of his briefs, Roger walked up behind Natalie, repositioning her onto all fours and then sank his dick into her tightly clenching pussy – digging his fingernails into her hips as he slammed into her hard and fast. And the friendly gang bang was under way.

Jane and James got in line behind Shane and when he was finishes, Jane stepped up and nervously looked down at Natalie. So, um, how exactly does this work with another woman? Drinking my pee, that is?"

"Just…uhn…just let me put my mouth over your pussy. When you feel my tongue licking along your slit you'll know it is okay to start."

"Okay. I've never been with another woman before."

"I know. And don't worry, I'll be gentle when it comes time for us to play and I promise to make it as enjoyable as I possibly can for you." Natalie placed her mouth over Jane's bald pussy and nibbled her inner labia for several seconds, savoring her friend's aromas and flavors before extending her tongue and licking. The piss started to flow and her gag reflex relaxed of its own accord allowing the bitter liquid to slide right down.

"WAIT!" Jane yelled. "I mean, um, please don't stop! Will you do what you did before I started to pee?"

"Sure," Natalie smiled. "Why don't you lay on the floor and make yourself comfortable and I'll do my best to lick and finger you to orgasm.

Speaking of which, how many fingers can the rest of you ladies take?"

"Three in each hole, Maria answered first.

"Three in the pussy and two up the ass," Susan added.

"Jane looked incredibly nervous, her face turning red before she answered. "Um, I um, well, the thing is…"

"Please don't be embarrassed," Natalie said. "You're amongst friends and considering what we're doing together I don't think anyone is going to judge you. How many can you take?"

"A small fist," Jane blurted out.

"Wow! Really? In your pussy or ass?"

"Both. I've only done it like a dozen times in the last year, so please don't go ramming your entire hand in me all at once."

"I'd never dream of doing anything so unpleasant," Natalie assured her shy friend. "But with your permission I'd like to work up to it."

"Okay."

"Not that you asked, but I can take four fingers up my ass," Shane offered. "What? You all know I'm bisexual so is it really that big a surprise?"

∞ ∞ ∞

As the hours passed, and the five men and three women had each fucked Natalie in pussy, ass and mouth – the women using fingers, hands and toys, everyone got a bit more comfortable with their forced situation and took things to the next level. While Natalie fucked her hands in and out of

Jane's pussy and ass, Mike did the same to her. To their left, Maria and Susan were doing a '69' with Maria on top taking James' dick up her ass.

Coating his cock with lube, Shane walked up behind James, shoved him down over Maria's back and then shoved his dick right up James' tightly puckered hole in one swift thrust.

"Aahhgghhh!" James yelped in pain as his asshole was suddenly fucked open. "What in the hell do you think you're doing!? Get your dick out of my ass you god damned queer!"

"Oh stop being such a baby and take it like a man." Shane replied, pushing James back down as he slowly pumped in and out of his ass.

James resisted for several minutes, but as the initial shock of taking something up the ass for the first time wore off and pain was replaced with pleasure, he began fucking himself on Shane's cock, as he fucked his own into Maria's ass.

The only one left without a partner, Tyler stood in front of Jane and offered her his big black cock. It took her only a moment to open up and take it into her mouth and although she gagged and her eyes were blurry with tears as he fucked it down her throat, she did not make him stop.

Mike soon added another load to Natalie's already overflowing pussy and Tyler pulled his dick from Jane's throat and shoved it up Natalie's ass. "Mmmm, I've been wanting your fine white ass for the longest time!" WHACK! His large hand came down hard, leaving a red handprint where it slapped against her skin. WHACK! Another slap to the other cheek and Natalie shoved her hips back to take all ten inches of Tyler's cock.

"Spank my!" Natalie purred. "I've been such a naughty little slut and deserve to be punished for my sins!" WHACK! Tyler's hand landed again and she shoved her right fist deeper into Janes quivering ass. Looking up in confusion at how Mike could possibly be ready to go again, she nevertheless took him into her mouth only to find out he had to pee.

The next several hours went by in a blur as dicks went into pussy, ass and mouth and all four women had been thoroughly fucked and filled with copious amounts of potent baby-making seed. And when the gang bang ended at midnight the nine friends were a pile of semen and sweat covered bodies lying on Natalie's living room floor – each of them with a plug stuffing their assholes, but none as large as the one stretching their host open.

"I hope that gets the blackmailer off your back," James sighed. "But if it doesn't, give me a call and I'll be more than happy to do that again.

"That goes double for me," said Tyler pushing back on Shane's cock.

"You are the most amazing friends anyone could ever wish for," Natalie said with tears in her eyes. "I can't believe you all did this for me. I was so afraid you'd turn me down and I'd be ruined."

"That's what friends are for," Susan grinned. "By the way, are you looking for a girlfriend?"

"Actually, I already have one. As of this afternoon I'm dating a woman named Beth. She works at Raven's Hollow."

"The brothel?" Mike asked.

"One and the same."

"Nice," Tyler added. "As much as you love sex, you should get a job there."

"Already did. Or at least I told Beth to tell Lady Raven that I accept the offer.

"Congratulations," said Tyler "do you need a boyfriend too?"

"The way Shane's pounding your ass, I'd have thought the two of you were already dating," Natalie giggled.

And then they all broke out in a fit of laughter that lasted several minutes. And for that brief period of time, Natalie was the happiest she had been in a very long time.

14

"So not only are you letting some asshole blackmail you into being a whore, now you're going to be a prostitute as well?" Henry angrily said to his daughter."

"FUCK YOU!" Natalie shouted in reply. "I didn't have to tell you at all, but seeing as how you and mom are swingers I didn't know if you've ever been to Raven's Hollow. Now that I'm working there, or rather will be working there once I go in and talk to Lady Raven I thought I'd save everyone the embarrassment of finding out the hard way."

"Are you certain this is what you want to do sweetie?" her mother calmly asked, though the tone of her voice was barely contained rage.

"It is. Look, I know the past couple of weeks have been one crazy thing after another, but I've come to the conclusion that I actually like everything the blackmailer had me do and working at Raven's Hollow is the logical choice for me. And before you ask, no, I have no intentions of quitting school. In fact, this is an excellent way for me to pay off my student loans and start building a nest egg while I start my career."

"If you are dead set on working at that place then so be it. You're an adult and capable of making your own decisions. Your father and I have been there a few times in the past, but we'll stay away from here on out."

"God, you are such a hypocrite!" Natalie said to her father. Turning back to her mother, she spoke with more respect. "You don't have to stop going on my account. I'm sure Lady Raven can arrange for you to see any other women you want. Which brings me to my next bit of news. I have a girlfriend named Beth and she works at Raven's Hollow as well. In fact, she's one of the women that participated in my commandment there so you might want to steer clear of her as well. Or don't, either way is fine by me. We are in an open relationship and if you want to have sex with her that's fine."

"What in the hell has happened to you, Nat?" her father asked. "What happened to the shy, innocent college freshman who would rather spend her night's home alone studying that go out and socialize?"

"I was blackmailed into opening my eyes and experimenting, remember? And you know what? If I'm going to be completely open and honest about it, it really boils down to those dildos mom bought me. Honestly, if they weren't there and I didn't use that big black one I never would have had the guts to take that first photo album to the men's room at XTC Toys."

"So everything that happened to you is my fault?"

"No. Yes. Maybe a little," Natalie sighed. "Look, I'm not blaming you for anything I did. No one put a gun to my head and made me use the dildo and no one put a knife to my back and forced me to go into the bathroom stall. I did it and I take full responsibility for my actions. All I'm saying is that I most likely never would have taken the plunge had you not nudged me along with the dildos."

"What about school?" Knock, knock. Someone lightly tapped at the front door "You expecting another delivery?"

"Nope." Getting up off of the couch, Natalie walked over and opened the door to see Beth Standing there looking radiant. "Hey honey, come on in." Giving her girlfriend a quick peck on the lips, she stepped out of the way. "I was just talking to my parents. Mom, dad, this is my girlfriend Beth. Beth, my parents Henry and Regina."

"Pleasure to meet you," Beth greeted them with a smile. "If you're busy I can come back another time."

"Nah, that's okay. We were just talking about me working at Raven's Hollow. I just found out my parents have been there a few times before."

"Cool. If you ever come back ask for me," Beth said with a wink.

"See, I told you we're in an open relationship. I already gave them my blessing to ask for you if they wanted. So, what brings you by?"

"Business, unfortunately. I told Lady Raven that you wanted the job she offered and she accepted of course, but before you start you must go in and fill out the necessary paperwork and then there are a couple videos and a lecture by Lady

Raven that you have to sit through. The whole process will take at least four or five hours if you're lucky."

"Yay me! But if it's what I have to do then it's what I have to do. When does she want me to go in?"

"As soon as possible. If you get done early enough you can start tonight."

"So, why come all this way to tell me that? You could have called, you know?"

"Maybe I was hoping to meet your parents," Beth smiled seductively. "Maybe I was hoping I could keep them company while you were busy with Lady Raven."

"Oh," Natalie replied with mock disappointment. "And here I thought I was the one you loved."

"Oh, I do. More than you can even imagine, but you know me, I'm a horny woman and your parents are pretty damn good looking. And from the bulge growing in your dad's pants I'd say you had better be on your way before things get embarrassing for you?"

"Okay. Have fun and I'll see you guys later."

"Just like that?" Her mother gasped. "Are you seriously expecting us to have sex with your girlfriend?"

"If you want to. You heard her. And she's right about dad, so do whatever floats your boats. Shit, you parked behind me."

"Go ahead and take my car," Beth said as she pulled her navy blue tee shirt off over her head. "The keys are in my purse there on the stand."

Grabbing the keys from her girlfriend's purse, Natalie looked back to see Beth's bra drop to the floor and her parents nervously looking at each other. Pulling the front door closed behind her, she got in the car and pulled out of the driveway.

∞ ∞ ∞

"Is this really happening?" Regina asked, watching as Beth tugged the jeans down her well-tones legs.

"It is," Beth purred. "Unless you don't find me attractive, that is. Do you want me to stop? Shit! The way you were staring at me I thought you wanted me, but I guess I was wrong. How humiliating," she said bending over at the waist and slowly pulling her pants back up."

"WAIT!" Henry said eyeing the nearly naked Beth. "You're not wrong, and you are incredibly attractive. Go ahead and strip naked. Come on, honey, let's join her."

"Are you sure?"

"The dick don't lie," Henry said as he quickly unfastened his pants. Pulling them and his boxers off at the same time, his cock sprang to life and Beth reacted as she had so expertly been trained to do. Dropping on her hands and knees, she looked up into Henry's eyes and took him into her mouth and down her throat – holding it there for a solid ten seconds. Looking to her right, she saw Regina's shirt fall out of her hand as she rose to her feet.

"This feels wrong on so many levels," Regina said as she unbuttoned her shorts "but if everyone else is okay with it then who am I to argue?" Quickly adding her bra and panties to the pile of clothes on the floor, she walked behind Beth, raised her ass so that she was now on all fours and then licked her from clit to asshole. "Are you able to take a fist?"

"In both holes at the same time," Beth answered. "You can work up to it slowly, or ram them in whenever it suits you. I can take it either way."

"Good to know. I'm not that loose so please don't use more than three fingers in either hole."

"What about toys? Do you have any we can use?"

"A whole box of them. Nothing as big as what Nat now has, but I think it'll do. Want me to go get them?"

"Please. And grab Natalie's as well. I love being stretched open nearly as much as she does." Turning her attention back to Henry, she looked up and smiled. "You had better fuck me now while you can enjoy it." Spinning around, she dropped onto her hands and knees and spread her legs open. "Mmmm," she moaned when Henry penetrated her pussy. Though she was not as tight as she used to be, with the help of nearly four years of kegel exercises she had pretty amazing muscle control and squeezed his dick like a vice.

"I don't know what the fuck my wife is talking about," Henry grunted as he worked his cock in and out of Beth's tightly clenching pussy. "You're damn near as tight as a virgin!" and then suddenly she wasn't. Relaxing her pelvic muscles, her pussy opened like a tunnel and be barely felt anything at all. And just as quickly, she was squeezing him again. "What the fuck?"

"Muscle control," Beth moaned. "Now fuck your load into me!"

Regina returned to the living room carrying two boxes of toys which she sat down on the coffee table. Pulling the flaps back, she did a side by side comparison for the first time since buying Natalie the three dildos and one obvious difference stood out. "My god, she has some big fucking toys! Other than the two normal ones I bought her, they're all massive!" Picking up the largest butt plug she had ever seen, she held it out for everyone to see. "Does she really take this thing?"

"Mmm hmm," Beth moaned. "She wore it for nearly a week without removing it other than to shower and use the restroom." Seeing the look on Regina's face, Beth smiled. "I don't know how she does it either. Bring the boxes down here and get on all fours in front of me so that I can pleasure you as Henry fucks his seed in me."

Regina put the plug back in the box and pulled a large dildo from her own and dropped it on the floor next to Beth. "That's the largest I've ever taken in either hole," she said pointing to the eighteen inch long, two and a half inch thick double dildo. I have no plans on going any bigger so remember that."

"You're the boss. But I guarantee if you can take that then a small fist isn't much more. In fact, once I stuff that into your pussy and ass I can have my fists in you in about twenty minutes of you'll let me try."

"Do it!" Henry exclaimed. "I want to see you taking a fist up your sexy ass!"

"You know I don't like being stretched open that much!" Regina protested.

"It's not that much more. Besides, Beth here can teach you excellent muscle control. Please, please let her fist you!"

"Alright, Beth can fist me if she can also fist you. But seeing as how I have two holes and you've only got the one, she gets to put both hands up your ass at the same time. That's my deal and I will not negotiate."

"Fine! Now get your ass on the floor so she can do it!"

"Nope. She gets to stretch your ass open first, or no deal."

"Wait!" Beth panted. "Fill me with your seed and then plug me so it doesn't leak out and then we can move on to gaping that asshole of yours open."

"That's not even remotely fair! Why should I have to take two fists up my ass at the same time while you only take one?"

"I just told you why," Regina grinned. "That's my deal, take it or leave it. But she puts both hands up your ass before she ever touches me. That doesn't mean, however, that I won't be touching her," she added, her grin broadening."

"You two are amazing!" Beth moaned, rocking her hips back to meet Henry's herd thrusts. "I can see where Natalie gets her open-mindedness from."

15

Wondering how her parents and girlfriend were getting along, Natalie parked her car and entered the large Victorian home locally known as Raven's Hollow – Maple Grove's one and only legal brothel. She saw the familiar faces of every woman that had participated in her first ever lesbian gang bang and offered them a smile as she approached Lady Raven whom was sitting behind a long counter. "Hello, Lady Raven," she greeted her friend and new boss. "Beth said you needed me to come in?"

"Yes. If you're going to be working here then there are several forms you need to fill out and sign, instructional films you need to watch and then a rather lengthy and boring lecture from yours truly. Where's Beth? Didn't she come back with you?"

"No, she stayed at my house to have sex with my parents."

"Ah, I see. And you are okay with that?"

"I am. One more thing before we get started, my parents have visited several times in the past and will probably do so again. I just want to make sure they don't get sent to my room by mistake."

"Not a problem. I'll just need a picture of them to put on file. What about Beth?"

"They can fuck her all they want. And seeing as how she's not here and she didn't call wanting her car back, I can only assume they are getting along famously."

"You really are something else, you know that?"

"No more so than you, or anyone else working here. Which is something I've been meaning to ask. Do you actually see clients, or just work the counter and do the commandment?"

"I see a few very select clients whose privacy is of utmost concern, but never here. Come on, let's get the boring stuff out of the way. Cindy," she hollered at one of the women strolling around looking pretty "mind the counter while I bore our newest member to death with paperwork."

"Yes, Lady Raven," the bubbly brunette replied. "And before I forget, welcome aboard, Natalie. You won me five hundred bucks!"

"Cool. How did I do that exactly?"

"We took bets to see when you'd take the job and I won the office pool. To thank you I'd like to pay you a visit later if that's okay."

"Fine by me."

"You know the rules, Cindy."

"Yes, Lady Raven."

"Rules? What rules?" Natalie asked.

"The girls are allowed to play with each other here, but only as worker and client. If she wants to pay you a visit it'll have to be after her shift ends."

"I see. You don't want to lose money while she's off with me or someone else. I guess that makes a lot of sense."

"Yes, it does. Next to Beth, Cindy is one of my best girls, but between you and me, I'm hoping you'll put them all to shame," Lady Raven said as she led Natalie through the bottom half of the house towards the back where her office was located. "I have a confession to make," she said opening the door and ushering her newest employee in. "While there is a lot of paperwork to fill out, we can forget about the films and boring speech. The truth is, I already have a client lined up for you."

"Really? But how?"

"Because Beth told me you were going to take the job and I lined one up for you." Going to the desk near the back of the room, Lady Raven opened the bottom right drawer and withdrew a folder from a pile and plopped it down. "Go ahead and take a seat here at the desk and read everything thoroughly. If you have any questions whatsoever don't hesitate to ask."

"So, who is this client I'll be seeing? And what will I have to do with him?"

"What makes you think it's a man? And you'll see as soon as you fill out the paperwork and we set you up in a room."

The first ten or so pages had to do with the dreaded taxes and once filled out, Natalie moved on to the waivers and consent forms. One stated she would not sue Raven's Hollow or Lady Raven for anything that happened during a session with a client, while another absolved the brothel of responsibility should pregnancy occur The next two pages were stapled together with the top sheet listing every possible kink that it was legal to perform, while the bottom one was divided into three columns.

The first column was labeled: WILL DO WILLINGLY. The middle was labeled: WILL DO WITH ENCOURAGEMENT and the last column was labeled: WILL NEVER DO. "Um, what am I supposed to do with this?" Natalie asked, holding up the stapled pages.

"That is your limit list. Once filled out, it will go into the system to make it easier to pair you with the right clients. In the first column put those things you will do without hesitation. Place the things it would take the right amount of convincing for you to try them in the second, and those things you'll never do in a million years unless you've got a gun to your head go in the last."

"What if I'd do everything on the list without hesitation?"

"You might want to give it a read first before making such a rash decision. This can take some consideration so I'll give you a couple of hours to mull it over. Please do think about each fetish before adding it to one of the columns. It'll save you a lot of humiliation and possible discomfort down the line."

"Okay." Tapping the pen against the desk, Natalie read down the list starting with anal and one by one added then to the lists. She paused at a few of them, wondering if people really enjoyed such things as needle play and hot wax as much as she loved gang bangs and drinking piss – two fetishes that immediately went into the willing column. When she had added the last kink, Lady Raven still had not returned, so she gave it another going over, followed by a third to make damn sure she got it right the first time.

Lady Raven returned to her office after two hours and walked up to her desk. "Finished?"

"Yeah. I'm pretty sure I put everything in the right place," Natalie answered, holding the paged out for her new boss to take.

"Interesting. I don't see a single fetish in the no way in hell column."

"That's because after careful consideration I didn't see anything outright forbidden. I'm willing to give pretty much anything a try at least once. Besides, you said I could change it later, right?"

"That is correct. And I love your attitude towards sex. Not many women are as open-minded as you even working here. Okay, everything seems to be in order here. Let me finish showing you the house and you can get started with your first client if you're up for it."

"Hell yes I'm up for it. I haven't been this excited since getting my last commandment. So, does everyone working here get their own room or something?"

"No. I suppose that can be easily misunderstood. So, there are twenty-three rooms in the house each catering to various kinks. When a client comes in it is my job to match them with the perfect woman and send them to the appropriate room. When I say I'm going to set you up with a room it doesn't mean one of your own. At least not yet, anyways. If you are here long enough and build up a reputation you may end up with a private room, but so far only three women have that honor. Beth and Cindy are two of them and the third is Brianna. Do you remember the purple-haired woman from your commandment?"

"Yeah," Natalie thought back to the night. She recalled a woman entering late in the game, but making up for lost time in the best possible way. "How can I ever forget the first woman to double fist me while fucking me with a huge dildo at the same time? I still have no idea how she pulled it off. So, that's Brianna?"

"It is. She's been here longer than anyone. Actually, she was the first woman I hired and even after all these years is a house favorite. You have a lot of work ahead of you if you ever want to dethrone her."

"That's not why I'm here. I have no interest in pissing anyone off. All I want is to experiment and enjoy sex to the fullest."

"I think you'll fit right in." Stopping in the mail lobby, Lady Raven turned her attention to Cindy whom was still standing behind the counter. "Cindy, would you be a dear and make sure Natalie here showers and dresses sexy?"

"Yes, Lady Raven."

"When she is done put her in room seventeen for her first client."

"Yes, Lady Raven."

"I thought you were going to show me around?" Natalie said to her new boss.

"I was, but then remembered I need to put your information into the system and call in your client. Unfortunately, the only other person with access is having sex with your parents."

"I wonder how they're getting along."

"If I know Beth? Famously," Lady Raven smiled. "And rule number one while at work, you will always refer to me as Lady Raven as you've no doubt heard every other woman do. Is that understood?"

"Yes, Lady Raven," Natalie replied, her clit tingling with excitement for reasons unknown.

16

"Uhn…uhn…oh god!" Henry grunted and groaned as the dildo worked deeper into his ass. "P-Please take it easy back there! I've taken it up the ass before, but never by anything so fucking huge!"

"Oh, simmer down," Beth giggled. "Three inches is not that thick. Another few minutes and I'll use the next biggest toy and then I'll be able to fist you with one hand. I think I'll do that while Regina sucks you off. Then to be fair, I'll work my fist up her ass while you take a break."

"No way! That wasn't the deal!" Regina balked even as she worked her right arm up Beth's ass nearly to the elbow. "He takes two up his ass first."

"That's hardly fair for him," Beth said looking back over her shoulder. "After all, what's stopping you from changing your mind once he lets me stretch him open that far? No, you will take my fist up your ass next and then I'll work on double fisting his ass. When that is done I will work on fisting your pussy and then both holes at the same time. That is a much fairer deal all around. Don't you think?"

"Absolutely!" Henry exclaimed as the fat toy slid deeper into his ass. "How fucking far are you going to shove that thing in me? I can feel it tickling my damn tonsils for Christ's sake!"

"Well, it's an eighteen inch long double dildo, so I'd guess about fourteen inches are now up your ass. I'd shove more in, but I have to have something to hold onto or it might get lost. Now relax and remember to take slow, deep breaths. And a bit of warning, the next one is two feet long so you'll feel it at least six more inches deeper. But don't worry, yours isn't the first ass I've stretched open and when I'm done, your wife will be able to go in to her fucking shoulder!"

"HOLY FUCKING HELL! Are you serious?"

"Very. You'll be able to do the same," Beth said once again looking back at a very stunned Regina. "It won't happen overnight, but I plan on coming back again and again to play with the two of you so we'll have plenty of time to work on it." Pulling the long, fat double dildo from Henry's asshole, she grinned at the way it remained gaping open for several seconds before almost closing again. Applying more lube to the toy and her left hand, she shoved it back in, fucked it in and out hard and fast and then dropped it onto the floor as she scrunched her fingers together and pushed her entire hand in.

"Aahhgghhh! Oh my fucking god!" Henry yelped. "H-How big is the new toy?"

"As big as my fist!" Beth exclaimed. "You're doing it, Henry! You've got my fist up your ass!"

"No fucking way!"

"Yes way, dear," said Regina. She had pulled her arm from Beth's ass and moved around to see for herself. "Dear lord! She's nearly in to the elbow! How does it feel?"

But her husband was in no condition to reply as his brain was temporarily taken offline. His elbows buckling, Henry's head went to the floor and before his wife could get under him to suck his cock, he was shooting his load all over the carpet.

"Well, I was going to fist him to orgasm, but it looks like he beat me to it," Beth giggled. "So, instead, I'll fist him for say, another fifteen or twenty minutes while you put that big black dildo there up your ass," she said to Regina. "Go ahead and stick the suction cup base to the coffee table and ride it for us. If I don't see all thirteen inches disappearing up your ass by the time I'm done with Henry you'll be sorry."

"Meaning what?" Regina asked with raised brow as she picked up the big toy and placed it on the coffee table as ordered.

"I guess we'll have to wait and see if you've got it up your ass in time. Before you take a seat, put the nipple clamps on and pull them tight. Actually, I have a better idea. Put the clamps on, but take the dildo off of the stand."

"And do what with it?"

"Take it, and this one here," Beth said picking up an equally large purple dildo with suction cup base. Put them on the wall so that you can fuck yourself on both at the same time while down on all fours. How are you at deepthroating?"

"It's not my strong suit," Regina admitted.

"Then take this one and practice. I want to see all of your holes filled in the next three minutes or else. Now be a good little slut and do as you're told." Her thoughts running wild, Beth pulled her left arm from Henry's ass and shoved the right one in, alternating back and forth as she watched Regina place the clamps on her nipples and the dildos on the wall. Out of the corner of her eye she spotted the belt looped through Henry's pants and her grin took on a more sinister appearance.

Regina lubed the two dildos hanging on the wall and then dropped onto all fours. Looking her husband in the eyes, she chewed her lower lip and backed up, easing onto the bulbous heads until both of them popped into place. "Uhn. They're going in," she grunted, pushing back until her ass hit the wall. "Now they're all the way in! Come see if you don't believe me," she said to Beth.

"I believe you. Now fuck yourself on them while you suck the third dildo. I'll be with you in a few minutes." Pulling her arm from Henry's ass, she placed both hands together and pushed in, grinning widely as both hands went in to the knuckles. Balling her hands into fists and placing them close together, she punched one into Henry's ass, pulled it out and shoved the other one in. After thirty or so thrusts, she wrapped her left hand over the right and punched it in.

"Aahhgghhh! Oh my motherfucking god!" Henry screeched as his ass was torn open. "W-What are you doing!? It hurts! Take it out!" Jerking forward in an attempt at easing the pain, he found Beth's hand still up his ass."

"Calm down and relax. I used an old trick to make putting both hands in easier. Can you feel my hands opening up inside of your ass?"

"Y-Yes. It really fucking hurts damn it!"

"Relax your muscles and take deep breaths. Trust me, you are not bleeding and I see no tearing so you'll be fine. Now do as you are told and it'll become a lot easier."

"You hear that honey," henry groaned. "She's got both hands up my ass. Man, that's something I never thought I'd say," he said shaking his head in disbelief. "Now she gets to fist your pussy and ass!"

"We'll get to her in a little bit," Beth said as she rotated her hands in Henry's ass. "I'm not taking my hands out of you until it no longer hurts and I see you pop another load on the floor. So, how are you enjoying your first fisting now?" she asked, pulling one hand out and pushing it back in.

"It's getting better. It still hurts, but not nearly as much."

"You're doing very well for a first timer. You must really want to see your wife's holes getting fisted."

"More than you can imagine."

Leaning down on Henry's back, Beth whispered in his ear so that only he could hear what she had to say. "Don't worry, sexy, she doesn't know it yet, but I'm not just going to double fist her, I'm going to do to her pussy and ass exactly what I'm now doing to your ass."

This made Henry's cock throb in excitement and anticipation and he looked across the living room to where Regina was fucking herself, her ass slapping against the wall with every thrust back. He figured she had about seven inches of the ten inch dildo in her mouth and could see her eyes watering as she tried to take more.

"I'm going to give your ass a break for a few minutes while I tend to your wife," Beth said removing her hands one at a time from Henry's asshole. Wiping the lube from her hands using his shirt, she grabbed his belt and walked over to Regina. Squatting down, she hooked a finger on the thin chain connecting the clamps together and gave it a hard tug. Regina's head went back and she let out a long groan. Beth grabbed a handful of hair and kissed her hard on the lips. "You will continue sucking and fucking the dildos while I give you a few swats of the belt. If you stop even to yelp, I'll continue going until you're able to get through twenty without bitching. Do you understand me, slut?"

"Y-Yes. I don't suppose it'll do any good telling you I don't want to be swatted."

"Not one bit. I'm not leaving this house until you've honored your end of the deal. If there's one thing you need to know about me other than my incredibly kinky streak, it's that I'm a woman of my word and I don't take agreements lightly."

17

Showered and dressed in a simple white bra and matching thong, Natalie was taken to room seventeen which was designed as a very expensive hotel room with a single red rose and bottle of wine sitting on a table and bed made up with satin sheets and a mountain of pillows she was certain never saw use. The door opened and she watched Lady Raven enter. "Will my first client be here soon, Lady Raven?"

"Very soon indeed. She's already here."

"Lady Raven?"

"I am your first client, Natalie. I've wanted to play with you ever since you participated in the commandment and now that you're working for me I plan on taking advantage of the situation."

"But I thought we weren't allowed to play with each other while working?"

"That rule doesn't apply to me. Few of them do, actually. Call it a perk of the job. So, down to business. One thing you need to learn is to anticipate your client's needs even before they do. You can learn a lot from the look in someone's eyes, or the way they carry themselves. For instance, you put on an air of confidence, but I can clearly see the fear in your eyes. And the way you're tensed up I'd say you're trying very hard not to tremble. Am I right?"

"That about sums it up," Natalie sighed. "So, how do I learn to be less nervous? How do I anticipate what a complete stranger wants from me?"

"The room you are in should give you a pretty good clue. Take this room for instance. What does it tell you?"

"That someone has expensive taste."

"Yes, but what else?"

"I really don't know."

"Expensive tastes can mean one of two things. The client could be a rich executive or someone with a fair amount of money to throw around, or they may be someone with a family who scrimped and saved for this one special fling with a woman that isn't a significant other. The flower and wine tells me they're a romantic at heart and the satin sheets on the bed leads me to believe they prefer to make love than simply have sex."

"You can tell all of that by looking around a room?"

"I can. It helps that I've been at this for a long time, though. In the meantime I'll give you a head's up on what your clients will be expecting from you and how long you'll be spending with them."

"So, you chose this room because you want to make love to me?"

"I did. We've had sex, great sex even, but tonight I'll have you all to myself. No gang bangs. No fisting, piss drinking or blackmail. Just the two of us enjoying each other's company and bodies."

"What if I want you to fist me, or to drink your piss, Lady Raven? You know how much I enjoy that sort of thing."

"I do. But not everyone does. You are not here to please yourself, Natalie. You're here for the pleasure of others and your own desires come second. If you want to live out your fantasies you'll have to do it while you're not working. Understood?"

"Yes, Lady Raven. So, I'm to do what the client wants and nothing more, is that it?"

"Exactly. If they want to watch you masturbate, then that's what you'll do. If they want to piss down your throat and call you dirty names you'll do that as well. There's a lot more to being a good prostitute than fucking one client and moving to the next. If that's what you want then you should probably go to the streets. Here, you are to be the fantasy and muse of every man and woman that wishes to partake of your particular brand of pleasure. Have you ever heard the old saying, opposites attract?"

"Yes, Lady Raven, but what does that have to do with being a prostitute?"

"Absolutely everything, my dear. Sex is so much more than physical attraction, Natalie and the sooner you learn that, the quicker you'll make a name for yourself in this business. Think of it this way, a submissive person will naturally and subconsciously seek out someone who is naturally dominant. Good girls love bad boys not because they truly believe they can change him, but because deep down they relish in being treated like a bitch. Everything else is simply an illusion and those few that do manage to change their man for the 'better' find the passion and excitement gone until they find another to replace him."

Pacing the room, Lady Raven continued. Body language, manner of speech, even something as basic and elementary as your natural odors and pheromones will affect your ability to attract and make love to another. But all that being said, sex is not purely about the physical. It's about anticipation, vulnerability and demeanor. It's about being selfish as well as selfless. In short, emotions are every bit as important as attraction."

Unbuttoning her blouse, Lady Raven draped it over the back of a chair and then unzipped the side of her skirt, letting it fall to the floor. Natalie watched with interest, her eyes drifting from Raven's beautiful face to her ample bosom as it slowly heaved up and down with every breath, and a scene popped into her head that she hoped would make for an interesting time.

"Hard day at the office," Natalie asked, walking over to Raven and gently kissing her on the lips. Reaching down, she picked up her lover's skirt and folded it over the chair and then pulled out another. "Come on, sit down and I'll give you a nice massage."

"Mmmm, that sound divine," Raven sighed.

"No, take off your bra and panties and get on the bed. I can see the tension from here and nothing short of a full body massage will do," Natalie smiled seductively.

"Who am I to argue with an offer like that?" Raven smiled, glad to see her newest employee taking control of the scene so soon. Adding her bra and panties to the back of the chair, she crawled onto the king-sized bed, swaying her ass side to side as she went. "There's some massage oils in the cabinet to your left," she purred.

Silently thanking her lover, Natalie went to the cabinet and drew the doors open, her eyes going as wide as her smile when she saw much more than oils. Lining the four shelves were dildos, vibrators, butt plugs and anal beads in a variety of shapes, sizes and colors. Picking up a small bottle of rose-scented massage oil, she found a lighter in a cabinet drawer. After lighting about three dozen candles, she turned off the lights – the room now a flickering menagerie of light and shadow slowly dancing across ceiling and walls.

Her clit tingling with excitement, Natalie crawled onto the bed and knelt with her knees either side of Raven's ass. Leaning down, she kissed Raven between the shoulders and traced a finger down her spine. "You feel so tense, she said kneading her fingertips into her lover's shoulders. "I've got a lot of work ahead of me if I'm going to ease it all. Now you just try to relax and let me take care of everything."

"Hmmm, you're the boss," Lady Raven sighed. "My body is in your very capable hands."

Hoping she knew Raven as well as she thought she did," Natalie drizzled a small amount of oil on her back and gently massaged it in – starting at her shoulders and working down her back, giving her ass a hard squeeze before moving back and along the legs to the ankles. Bending Raven's right leg at the knee, she rubbed the oil in while playfully sucking her toes. She then did the same to the right foot. As she worked her way back up Raven's legs, she leaned down, using the massage as excuse to spread her ass open. Extending her tongue, Natalie licked from clit to asshole for several seconds before adding more oil into her ass and massaging it upwards to her shoulders.

"God, that feels amazing!" Raven moaned. "I never want it to stop."

"I'm only getting started, lover. Roll over so I can get the other side."

"You're not fooling anyone. You just want to grope my tits."

"Can you blame me?" Natalie grinned, Raising up onto her knees so that Raven could roll over beneath her. "I mean really, those have got to be the most perfect pair of tits I've ever seen in my life," she added. Putting a few drops of massage oil on each nipple, she watched as it quickly heated up and ran down Raven's breasts in all directions. Gently, slowly rubbing it in, she leaned down and kissed the side of Raven's neck – her lips moving lower as did her hands. Taking a nipple into her mouth, she playfully nibbled it, inwardly grinning as it grew firm. Switching to the other, she did the same, the fingers of her left hand now on her lover's clit. When she slipped two fingers in, Raven's back arched and she let out a soft moan, encouraging her to continue.

Lady Raven sat up, wrapping her arms around Natalie's body and drawing her close. Their lips met. Tongues danced. Hands groped – moving up and down as they explored each other in intimate detail. Cupping Natalie's cheek in hand, Raven stared into her eyes and then kissed her so hard their teeth clanked together. Falling back on the bed, she giggled uncontrollably for several seconds. "Well, that was romantic."

"Sshhh, just lay there and don't say a word." Getting off the bed, Natalie went to the cabinet and picked up a feeldoe dildo from the second shelf. Pushing the short, bulbous end into her pussy, she crawled back into bed. The time for pleasantries past, she spread Raven's legs open and pushed them back – holding them as she entered her one slow, pleasure-filled inch at a time.

∞ ∞ ∞

"That was…wow!" Lady Raven panted, rolling over and staring Natalie in the eyes. "Very well done indeed."

"Thank you Lady Raven. Honestly, I just went with the first thing that came to mind."

"Well, you did it just right. And the next time I'm feeling tense I'll take advantage of those magic fingers of yours. I mean it, Natalie. That was the best session I've had in a long time. Either you're a much better actress than I imagined, or you were really feeling it, because the passion was damn near palpable."

"I couldn't act my way out of a paper bag," Natalie grinned. "So, when do I meet my next client?"

"I'll line a few of them up for you. Consider yourself on shift."

"Yes, Lady Raven. You know, every time I say that it makes me feel as if you're my mistress or something."

"That's the whole idea," Raven grinned. "Submissives naturally seek out dominants, and the reverse is also true. Now go get another shower and I'll see who I can get in here for you."

"Yes, Lady Raven," Natalie smiled.

18

The belt landed hard across Regina's back and despite the warning, she jerked back, and then forward, yanking herself off of the dildos as she landed on her ass yelping in pain. "Jesus fucking Christ! You didn't have to hit me so damn hard!"

"Of course I did. Now go get two larger dildos and stuff them in your holes. We'll start over from the beginning."

"What are you laughing at?" Regina glared at her husband who was unable to suppress the laughter.

"You better do as she says," Henry smirked. "That pussy and ass aren't going to stretch themselves."

"You could at least tell her not to fucking hit me!"

"Why would I do that? She's obviously the one in charge here and that's the way it'll be until Nat get home. Now enjoy the bigger toys and the belt, sweetie."

"You're not getting out of this that easily," Beth said turning to Henry. "Crawl over here so your wife can fist your ass and I'm going to swat you both. Natalie tells me you're swingers. How many couples do you have sex with?"

"Eight to ten," Henry answered.

"Do they gang bang you?"

"Yes."

"Both of you?"

"Yes. I take it up the ass by men and women."

"And do you suck their cocks and swallow their loads?"

"I do."

"So, ten couples would mean twenty people fucking you at the same time. I can do that."

"What do you mean you can do that?" Regina asked, placing the dildos on the wall.

"I mean I can have twenty men here to gang bang the two of you. And to make it interesting I'll have them bring along a few more toys. What do you say?"

"We can't do a gang bang here," Regina answered. "We can't have our daughter walking in on us doing that."

"No worries. Once she's done filling out paperwork and all the boring stuff, Natalie will begin her first shift. She won't be home until tomorrow."

"Oh."

"Any other excuses? No? Good. You fuck yourself on those dildos and fist your husband's ass and I'll make the calls."

"My god!" Regina gasped when she saw how stretched her husband's asshole was. "She really did a number on you didn't she? Does it hurt?"

"Not anymore. Go ahead and shove your fist in me, honey. But use some lube first," Henry said handing his wife the large bottle.

Regina squirted a copious amount of lube into the palm of her right hand and then ran a trail up to her elbow. After making sure every square inch had been thoroughly coated, she squeezed some up her husband's ass to be on the safe side. Bunching her fingers together, she pushed them in. And in. And in. And in some more. "Dear lord! I'm up to my fucking elbow!" she exclaimed. "How does it feel?"

"Just go slow and it'll be fine," Henry said reaching back to stroke his already stiff cock.

Beth rejoined the couple with a smile on her lips. "They'll be here in about twenty minutes to an hour. Twenty-nine in total if you're interested." Bending down, she picked up the belt and snapped it in the air. "In the meantime," WHACK! The belt landed hard across Regina's ass. With nowhere to escape to, she jerked forward, her arm going a little deeper into her husband's ass.

WHACK! The next swat struck Henry – the tapered tip wrapping around his side and biting in deep. He let out a pain-filled yelp, but stayed his position. Repositioning herself, Beth swung the belt upwards, catching Regina across the breasts, driving the clamps into her nipples, causing her to leap back onto the massive dildos and her arm to pull free of Henry's ass. This left her wide open for another swat to the breasts which was quickly followed by another to the back when she doubled over in pain.

"Crawl over there and sit on that four inch plug," Beth commanded Henry. "Your wife is now ready to take my fists."

"WHAT!? No I'm not!" Regina protested.

"You have three and a half inch dildos in your pussy and ass. Trust me, you're ready. Now crawl to the middle of the room and suck your husband's cock while I fist you, or I'll really tear into you with the belt."

∞ ∞ ∞

As promised, the men began arriving within twenty minutes. Beth was still fisting Regina's pussy and ass and Henry was kneeling like a puppy waiting for another command from his Mistress. The door opened and seven men entered – three white and four black. No sooner had it shut behind them then they heard more movement from outside and another six black men entered the house without invite.

"Welcome gentlemen," Beth said in greeting. This is Henry and Regina and they'll be your playthings this evening. Feel free to use them as you see fit."

"Any way we see fit?" One of the black men asked.

"Yeah, pretty much. They're a couple of submissive sluts these two."

Unbuttoning his pants, the man pulled out his large black cock and shoved it in Henry's mouth. But when Henry started bobbing his head back and forth, the man held him still and began pissing down his throat. Unaccustomed to such treatment, Henry tried pulling away, but the man's grip on his ears was tight and he was forced to take every last drop of the warm, bitter liquid. When it was over, he ran to the bathroom and emptied his stomach.

The rest of the men laughed as they stripped out of their clothes. "Open up, another of the men said to Regina. "I've been holding it in for fifteen minutes."

"I hope you've got room for two," another added.

"One of you can piss down my throat," Beth offered, opening her mouth as she was so expertly trained to do for any person that wished to use her. When the dick went in, she closed her lips around it and relaxed her gag reflex, allowing it to slide right down. Looking back over her shoulder, Regina could not believe what she was seeing, but the cock pushing into her own mouth gave her reason to worry.

Henry returned to the living room just in time to see his wife running passed in the direction of the bathroom and he could smell the piss that was covering her face and chest. The front door opened and three more men walked in as if they owned the place – two of them carrying some sort of folded up contraption. Taking it to the center of the room, they set it up into a Saint Andrews cross.

"What in the hell is that thing?" Henry asked.

"That is a Saint Andrews cross," Beth explained. "And when Regina returns she'll be strapped to it for the next big surprise."

"Oh? And what will that be?" Regina asked from the hallway leading from living room to bathroom. "And if one more of you pisses down my throat this party is over and I don't give a damn about any deals that have been made. You fisted my pussy and ass so as far as I'm concerned I've held up my end of it."

"Come over here and place your wrists and ankles at the corners," Beth commanded."

"Not until you tell me what you're going to do."

"Then it wouldn't be a surprise, would it? Now do as you're told. Henry, take that plug out of your ass so these gentlemen can use you as the sissy bitch that you are."

"I'm with my wife," Henry said, reaching back to remove the plug from his ass. "There's a bathroom down the hall and another upstairs. Use them or we're done here. Now that that's out of the way, whose dick do I suck first?"

While Henry partook of the many cocks, one going down his throat and two more up his gaping asshole, Regina walked over to the large metal 'X' and placed her hands and feet at the four corners – watching Beth with both curiosity and apprehension. Looking to her left, she jumped as one of the men strapped her wrist tightly in place while another restrained the right. "So, what's this big surprise? You going to shove both of your fists in the same hole? I heard what you told my husband."

"Not yet. First, all of the men are going to fuck their loads into your cunt and then I'm going to cane you front, back and side. After that, I'll work on double fisting each hole. And then finally, I'm going to give you something you are sorely missing. I'm going to pierce your nipples for you. Now, this is going to hurt and there will be a lot of screaming on your part so I'm going to go ahead and gag you so you don't bother your neighbors."

"Are you out of your mind?" Regina gasped. "I don't want any of that done to me! All of you, get out of my houmph…" her sentence was cut off by the large red ball of the gag being shoved in her mouth – the leather strap secured behind her head. Looking to her husband for help, she found none offered as he gladly took three cocks at the same time while leaving her to her own devices.

More men soon arrived and the living room became increasingly crowded with naked men vying for a hole to fuck. One of them walked up to Beth, took her by the hips and shoved into her without form or question. She accepted him without complaint and while squeezing one of Regina's breasts with one hand, shoved the other into her pussy.

And so the party went for hours on end without break. And while Henry lay on the floor panting, semen running from his gaping asshole and open mouth, Regina screamed into the gag as the hundred and fiftieth swat landed hard on her inner right thigh adding yet another wicked welt to the criss-crossing roadmap already covering her naked body. He felt bad for her, but another part loved seeing his wife broken, head hanging in defeat as the men continued to use her as their plaything. She too had semen dripping down her thighs which made every swat all the more painful.

And then, as the last of the men finally fucked his load into Regina's stretched pussy, Beth opened a small black case one of them brought and set up all the tools she would need to pierce the bound and gagged woman's nipples. But there was more – a lot more, and when Regina realized the full extent of what was about to happen, she redoubled her efforts to free herself from the Saint Andrews. But the straps held firm and she watched as Beth put on a pair of blue nitrile gloves and then pluck one of the hollow needles from the bowl of rubbing alcohol.

Beth removed the clamps from Regina's nipples and while they were still numb from hours of being pinched, she ran the needle through, leaving a platinum barbell behind. The left nipple quickly followed as did the clit hood. Though it was not part of the original plan, Beth could not help herself. Next, she picked up an odd-looking device and dipped it into a tiny cup of black ink and brought it to Regina's waxed mound – tattooing her with two words that summed her up perfectly.

"So, what do you think?" Beth asked Henry, taking a step to the left so he could see the work she had done on his wife.

"HOLY FUCK! You tattooed her! Does that say? Oh my god it does!" Henry gasped, moving in to get a closer look. "Can you see it honey? It says slave wife! She actually tattooed slave wife on your pussy mound!" He then spun around on his heels to face Beth. "Why did you tattoo her like that? Don't get me wrong, I think it looks sexy as hell, but she did not ask you to tattoo her."

"No, she didn't," Beth smiled. "That is my gift to her. All I did was write her true self on her mound for all to see and know what she is. And now I'm going to do the same to you."

"Like hell you are!"

"Men, hold him down. And if he struggles, take the cane to him until he's as docile and broken as his whore of a wife."

And when she had pierced Henry's nipples and given him a slave husband tattoo just above his cock, Beth saw the gang of men out, cleaned up the mess as best she could and then took a seat on the couch and waited for Natalie to return with her car.

"You're out of your motherfucking mind if you think you'll ever be welcomed in this house again!" Regina shouted. "And once I tell Nat what you did to us she'll leave you as well!"

"I doubt it."

19

Natalie returned home more than eleven hours later exhausted, but feeling great at the same time. After she made love to Lady Raven, she moved to five other rooms to satisfy the primal urges of her clients. Entering the house, the door closed behind her and she stood there staring in wide-eyed shock at what she saw.

"What in the hell happened here? Where did all of these toys come from? Oh my god! When did you get your nipples pierced, mom?"

"Your insane girlfriend did this to us!" her father answered, his hands covering his naked crotch. "She's home now get the hell out of my house!"

"Beth?" Natalie asked. "What did you do to them? Jesus Christ, it looks like you beat the hell out of my mother!"

"I caned her a hundred and fifty times," Beth answered calmly. "And After I double fisted your father's ass and fisted your mother…"

"I don't want to hear any of this! Why? Why did you do it? I trusted you to get to know them and you betrayed me in the worst possible way!"

"I'm sorry," Beth broke down. "I had no choice but to do as he said."

"Do as who said? What's going on, Beth?"

"Like you, I'm being blackmailed. But not to expose my sex life. He has my sister, Natalie.

And he threatened to sell her to some foreign crime lord if I didn't do exactly as he commanded."

"And he told you to do this to my parents?"

"Yes. I was ordered to have sex with your parents at any cost during which time I would convince them to push their limits. If that failed I was to call over a large group of men to help restrain them as I followed the blackmailer's instructions. I'm so, so sorry but I have no choice. Jenna is only eighteen and has the rest of her life to look forward to and I'll be damned if I'll let it be ruined because of me. I know what I did to you was wrong," she said turning to Henry and Regina, "and I'll never ask for forgiveness, but please understand why I had to do these things to you."

"Is it the same son of a bitch that's blackmailing me?"

"I believe so, yes."

Running to her bedroom, Natalie went into the closet and rummaged through her collection of commandment photo albums, found the one she was looking for and ran back. Flipping it open, she pointed to a handsome man in his late thirties. Is that him? Is this the man that told you to do this to my parents?"

"Yes, that's him."

"Glenn Parker," Natalie sighed. "Or at least that's what he told me his name was."

"He told me his name was Calvin."

"You can untie me any time now," Regina seethed.

Natalie walked over to her bound and welt-covered mother and began undoing the straps when she caught sight of the tattoo. "OH MY GOD! Does that say slave wife?"

"It does. And mine says slave husband," her father replied. "And this blackmail business has gone on long enough! We're going to the police whether you like it or not."

"YOU CAN"T DO THAT!" Beth gasped. "If any of us go to the police my sister disappears forever. Please, you've got to give me time to figure out where he's keeping her. Then we can take the bastard down."

"I am not going to let this continue! I understand you didn't have a choice, but we do. I'm sorry about your sister, but this has ruined or lives long enough and I will not stand idly by while it continues. The police can search airports and prevent her from leaving the country and they can find the son of a bitch a lot faster than any of us. I'm going to the police as soon as I get some clothes on."

"PLEASE! Please don't!" Beth cried. "He's promise to do the same to her as I've done to you and more before selling her off. Please don't go to the police!"

"He's right," Natalie said as she helped her mother to the couch. "It's one thing blackmailing me to have kinky sex, but he's now involving my parents and your sister. Where will it end? What if he tells me to do this to your mom and dad? Or if he commands you to do something even worse. A line has to be drawn somewhere and this is it. I'm sorry, Beth, but I can no longer play along with these commandments."

"Then my sister's life is over."

"Not necessarily. We can't go to the police, but what if we send someone else?"

"I can't take the risk, Natalie. I'm sorry, but until she's safe I have no choice but to do as he commands. And neither do you. Unless you no longer care about everything getting out."

"I very much care, but like my dad said, I cannot stand idly by while the son of a bitch ruins their lives as well. What's stopping him from making you do worse to them? Or me for that matter?"

"I don't know. I don't want to do this, Natalie. I hate feeling so helpless, but it's my little sister. She's like you before this all started. All she wants is to go to college and make something of her life. She's never even had a boyfriend."

"I sympathize, I really do, but when does it end? How long before we're out breaking the law for his perverted pleasures?"

"Please just give me a little more time and if I can't find her on my own we can go to the police."

"Fine, I'll give you a couple of weeks to find her, but if he sends you, or anyone else here to do anything whatsoever, I'm going to the police then and there."

"Thank you. And if he commands me to do anything else to your parents I'll go to the police myself," Beth sighed. "I can't apologize enough for what I've done to the two of you."

"Just go and find your sister," Regina groaned.

"If you need anything please know that I'm always here for you," Natalie said wrapping her arm around Beth's waist and guiding her to the door.

"Thank you. I'll let you know if I figure anything out."

20

Jenna came to with a groan and an ache in the back of her head where a knot rose like a hill from the hit by whatever had knocked her out. A warm breeze like a fan circulating stuffy air on a hot day caressed her front, back and sides telling her two things. First, she was butt naked. And second, that she was standing. A latex hood prevented her from seeing anything. A gag kept her screams for help to jumbled mumbles. And the cuffs at ankles and wrists prevented her from doing anything but thrash about in a futile attempt at escape.

Approaching footsteps told her she was not alone and the aromas of vanilla, lilac and something else she could not place either made her captor a woman, or a man that likes scented bath soaps, she could not tell. Until a hand cupped her bald pussy, that is. A finger hooked upwards pressing dangerously close to the thin flap of skin that was her virginity and she jerked to get away from it.

"I'd keep still if I were you," Jenna heard a woman say. "Unless you want to pop your own cherry on my finger. Ah, who really gives a shit if your virgin or not?" The finger slid out and then two were pushed back in hard and fast – tearing Jenna's hymen to shreds in one swift thrust. "See, now isn't that much better? Now you can call yourself a woman. And all good women love a big, fat cock filling and fucking them senseless, right?"

Jenna screamed into the gag and fought to free herself, but the cuffs and chains they were attached to held firm as the woman's fingers slammed in and out of her harder and faster with each passing second. Her right nipple was pinched and she jerked back, but that did not stop her attacker from holding on and pinching tighter – the feeling of fingernails digging into flesh causing her even more worry. She did not feel the trickle of blood, but not for lack of trying on the woman's part she was sure.

And then it stopped and she heard the woman walking away followed by a whispered conversation with at least four, maybe five men, she could not tell for certain. Though most of it was unintelligible, one bit rang loud and clear. "For fuck's sake Lana, you act as if this is the first time we've ever bred a little white bitch before,' one of the men said.

"I just want to make sure she has as much of your potent black seed in her womb as possible before her idiot sister and Natalie finish the commandment in two weeks."

"As long as we're not disturbed you can guarantee she'll have at least a hundred and fifty loads in her by then. And since you've had us yourself more than once you know damn well we'll fuck our loads right into her womb."

"Then have at it boys. But don't get in my way because the cane and flogger stop for no one."

And then there was a group of footsteps coming her way and Jenna knew that Lana fingering her was just a prelude to repeated gang bangs and beatings. Tugging as hard as she could and nearly dislocating her shoulder and wrist in the process, Jenna could feel the cuff around her right wrist starting to give.

"Oh no you don't," said Lana.

WHACK! The cane slapped across Jenna's nipples hard and fast, knocking the wind from her lungs and rendering the scream mute. THWACK! Lana swung the flogger with precision – three of the tassels biting painfully into Jenna's clit as the rest wrapped around her inner thigh.

"Marcus, go get the metal cuffs for this stupid little slut." Jenna felt a finger trace from the base of her neck down between her heaving breast and to her painfully throbbing clit and back up to pinch her nipples. "There is no escape for you my dear. Your sister sold you to me and I'm going to get my money's worth out of you before you are safely returned home. And by safely I mean broken and impregnated by one of the five black men with me here today. But first, for attempting to escape, you will receive fifty swats of the cane and flogger all over that pretty body of yours."

WHACK! THWACK! The flogger came down hard on Jenna's breast about an inch above the nipples while the flogger tore into her back. Lana quickly switched the implements of torture to opposite hands and struck again. This time the flogger hit across Jenna's belly – the tips digging painfully into her right side as the cane tore into her ass. And on it went, one swat after another to back, arms, legs, belly, breast and pussy until fifty had been delivered as promised and Jenna was reduced to a sobbing mess – her head hung in shame and defeat.

"She's all yours boys. And remember, cum only in her womb and stretch her open as much as you can front and back. I want her holes wrecked before she goes home."

"Don't worry, when we're done she'll be taking two big fat fists at the same time. Now sit back and enjoy the show or we'll be popping a baby in you as well."

"I let you give me one," Lana scoffed "I don't want another."

"Shit, before you get started, change those leather cuffs for the metal ones and put the collar around her neck so we're sure she can't go anywhere."

One of the men held Jenna's left arm firmly as the leather cuff was removed and replaced by cold metal that locked tightly in place with no chance of stretching, or room to wiggle free. Her right wrist was secured next followed by her ankles and then a sleek metal collar was placed around her neck and attached to another thin chain hanging from the ceiling. Hands groped her front and back. Her ass was spread open and she felt something big, hard and wet pressing against her asshole and she tensed up, knowing that she was about to be taken up the ass for the first time.

"I'd relax if I were you," Marcus whispered in Jenna's ear as he eased the bulbous head of his cock into her ass.

Another cock slid along Jenna's slit and thumped against her clit several times before being pushed in until it slammed against her cervix. But the man did not stop there. As Marcus pushed more up her ass, Hank applied steady pressure until he felt the muscle finally relax and dilate allowing him into her womb. Jenna's head went back as she cried in agony, but the men did not stop their assault.

Mere minutes into her first sex and gang bang, Jenna felt a huge load of semen being shot deep. It was followed two minutes later by Marcus and then two more men took their turn. When the last man finished unloading in her pussy, she felt something even thicker than their dicks being pushed into her pussy and ass.

"Since you can't see what we're doing, we just put two and a half inch plugs in your pussy and ass. Enjoy the stretching, slut." Marcus laughed. He then leaned in and kissed her hard on the lips. "We'll be back in a couple of hours for round two. She's all yours," he said to Lana. "Try to leave her in one piece."

"I'm going to remove your gag so you can breathe better and talk. Feel free to scream your pretty little head off if you want, but no one will ever here you down here." Reaching around Jenna's head, Lana unbuckled the leather strap and pulled the large red ball from Jenna's mouth.

It took Jenna several minutes to be able to work the pain and stiffness from her jaws. "Why are you doing this to me? Please let me go. I haven't seen any of you and I swear I'll never tell anyone what you did to me," she pleaded.

"Don't worry, you'll go home in two weeks and not a day sooner. That is the deal your whore of a sister agreed to and I fully intend to hold up my end of the deal."

"What deal? My sister would never do this to me! PLEASE! Please just let me go home!"

"You know your sister is a prostitute, right? And before you answer you will call me Mistress. Fail to do so and I will have to punish you with the cane and flogger again."

"Y-Yes M-M-Mistress," Jenna sniffed back the tears.

"And you know she is dating another whore named Natalie?"

"Yes Mistress."

"Well, it seemed your slutty sister wanted to have her way with Natalie's parents in a most humiliating and degrading way. I gave her permission to do so and she gave me you as payment."

"BULLSHIT! My sister would never do something like that! Mistress," she added at the last second.

"Oh, but she did. The deal was simple. For permission to use Natalie's parents she could either serve as my slave for life, or allow me and my men to gang bang a baby in you. Guess which option she chose."

"WAIT! So you're the one responsible for all this commandment stuff I've been hearing about, Mistress?"

"That's right. Those morons are chasing a smoke of a man I hired to throw them off the trail. You sister, Natalie and her parents are all now under my control and will do everything I command of them or their lives will be ruined. Just as you will once you leave here in two weeks."

"You're out of your mind if you think I'll do anything you say once I'm let free."

"Everything happening to you is being recorded and photographed and will be compiled to use in your eventual blackmail so, you see, you will do as I say or everything gets out and your life is over."

"I'm hooded, no one will know it's me."

"You won't be hooded the entire time. Now, we need to talk about your mark. Where would you like it?"

"My mark, Mistress?

"Did I stutter? Yes, your mark. I'm thinking on your breast, but the pussy might like nice as well.

"What do you think?"

"Oh god! What are you going to do to me, Mistress?"

"Just put a little brand on you so that everyone knows what you are. Hmm, now that I think about it, the pussy is the obvious choice. I'll be right back so don't go anywhere."

21

Two weeks later...

Nineteen year old Natalie Holt's life went from boring to crazy and then skyrocketed to insane in just a few short weeks after a strange man ran into her at the park while she was walking home from classes at Maple Grove College. She was jogging through that same park now, thinking about how her life had changed and where things were headed for her and her family and all the friends who were now involved with the commandments in one way, shape or form.

It was noon, and the sun was bright in the sky, but the trail Natalie jogged was somewhat dark – shaded by the canopy of trees lining either side of the narrow dirt path. It wasn't well-used, in fact Natalie rarely ever saw anyone when she jogged or ran the two miles from one end to another and for the life of her she could never figure out why. At about the halfway point, she felt a cramp creep into her left leg, so she stopped and leaned against a black cherry tree – the sports bra she wore doing nothing to prevent the rough bark from digging into her naked back with exquisite pain.

Looking around to see if anyone was hiding in the shadows, she tugged her tight spandex shorts down, and pulled the fat plug from her gaping asshole. Feeling naughty, she brought it to her lips and flicked her tongue over the lube-coated tip before pushing it back up her ass. Out. In. Out. In.

Working up to a faster pace, she turned around and placed her free hand on the tree for support as she fucked it in and out harder and faster until she felt the orgasm approaching. Shoving it in hard one last time, she pulled up her pants and moved to the middle of the trail – denying herself the pleasure building within.

Spreading her legs wide apart, she bent over at the waist and reached back to place her hands on the back of her legs just below her ass as she slowly bent further down. Now, although this is a standard stretching exercise it looked like something totally different to the man approaching from the rear. To him, it looked as if she was offering herself in the most obvious and pleasing manner possible. He watched her bob up and down, her head getting closer and closer to the ground as she stretched her muscles.

All manner of images poured through the poor man's head and he could feel his shorts growing tighter around the middle as they tented of their own accord. And when he saw the smile on her lips as she looked back at him between her tanned and toned legs, he stopped thinking with his brain and let his cock do the talking. Had he been in his right mind he would have smiled and walked on by, but there was something about her position and demeanor that told him she wanted it.

His dick free of the confining prison of his shorts, the man yanked Natalie's down, stared wide-eyed at the base of the plug sticking out of her ass and then pushed into her pussy – grunting and groaning in triumph. Wrapping his left arm around her waist, he used the right to nudge her to the ground where he took hold of her hips and fucked into her as if she were the last woman on earth. And when he saw her hips rocking back to meet his every thrust he knew he had made the right decision.

Taking hold of the base of the plug, the man yanked it out in the hopes of fucking her up the ass, but when he saw the immense size of it he knew there was no way in hell he would ever feel it and another perverted thought entered his mind. Balling up his right hand into a fist, he shoved it in. And in. And in some more until he was nearly halfway to the elbow. "JESUS CHRIST! I've never seen anything so fucked up in my life! My arm is in halfway to the elbow!"

"Sshhh," Natalie purred. "Don't talk. Just have your way with me and go." Lowering her head onto folded arms, she spread her legs open and moaned as the man's fist slipped a few inches deeper.

"WHOA! What in the fuck are you two doing!?" Another man said as he casually jogged up the trail. "Don't you know this is a family park?"

"And you're the first two people I've seen on this trail in weeks," Natalie replied. "Now either move along, or join us, but please stop talking and let me enjoy my damn day in peace!"

"Is this some kind of setup?"

"No. Fuck your dick down my throat, or go away!"

The man thought about it a moment as he weighed the pros and cons of the situation and inevitably jogged on – missing the chance of a lifetime to have his way with a certifiable nymphomaniac. Natalie wasn't always a nymphomaniac. The five foot seven, 120 pound nineteen year old only started having sex a few weeks ago, but in that short time she realized she loved it more than anything in life and went out of her way to have it even if it meant capitulating to an unknown blackmailer.

Glory holes, gang bangs, men attempting to breed her and women turning her bisexual, Natalie's introduction and indoctrination into the world of sex was anything but ordinary. From the moment she took her own virginity on a fat dildo she was hooked and it has been a roller coaster ride ever since.

"Uuhhnnnn," the man groaned, his arm going to the elbow in Natalie's ass as he emptied his balls in her pussy.

"Mmmm, thanks," Natalie moaned. "I jog these trails every day if you ever want a repeat." Pulling off the man's cock and arm, she pulled another plug from the fanny pack around her waist and pushed it into her pussy to keep the semen in place. The other plug went back up her ass and she got to her feet smiling. Pulling her shorts up, she gave the man a wink over her shoulder and jogged on as if nothing had happened.

∞ ∞ ∞

Regina Holt was vacuuming the living room floor when she heard a knock at the door. Not expecting company, the thirty-nine year old was butt naked as instructed by the now family blackmailer. To hide the fact that they were being coerced, Natalie came up with the idea of making it a no clothing, nudist only home where anyone wishing to visit had to remove their clothes or they weren't allowed to stay.

Peeking out the window, she saw her daughter's girlfriend Beth standing there holding an all too familiar photo album - the look on her face one of excitement and apprehension. Unlocking the door, she let her in. "Hello Beth. Is that the latest commandment?"

"Yes. There are about two hundred pictures in here of you and Henry's gang bang and fisting. But that's not the good news!" Beth boasted.

"Oh?"

"According to the commandment in the back, Natalie and I will be doing some peeping and then Jenna will be returned to me!"

"Well that is good news. I know for a fact that Henry has been itching to go to the police with this so it's pretty good timing on the blackmailers part that your sister will be let go. So, what's the catch? Why would he let her go unless he's blackmailing her as well?"

"I was promised she would be returned home safe and unharmed."

"And you trust him?"

"So far he's been a man of his word and I have to hope for her sake that he remains so. I don't think I can cope if he ever did anything to her."

"Okay, let's see the pictures and commandment. Honestly, just between you and me, I loved everything that twisted bastard made you do to us except for the tattoo. I can't wait for the son of a bitch to finally see justice so it can be removed."

"I don't know, I kind of like it," Beth said handing Regina the photo album. "And your nipples are constantly erect from the rings. I could suck them all day," she said leaning in and taking the left one into her mouth – tugging at the ring with her teeth.

"Henry likes the piercings as well. Actually, I do as well. But I think the tattoo has to go."

"Is he home? I'd like to feel that dick of his in me while you look at the photos."

"He's at work and won't be home for another hour or so. Why don't you kneel between my legs and fist my pussy instead?"

"My pleasure." Running to Natalie's room, Beth entered the large walk-in closet and grabbed the bottle of lube from the shelf next to the boxes she kept the photo albums and DVD's of previous commandments and her growing collection of sex toys. Returning to the living room, Regina had taken a seat on the sofa with her legs spread wide – the photo album opened several pages.

"Go slow so I can enjoy it while looking at the pictures," Regina said as Beth approached with bottle in hand. "Speaking of which, how in the hell is he even getting them?"

"Your entire house has been wired with cameras. Mine too," Beth answered as she got down on her knees between Regina's legs.

"Cameras? But how? Where are they?"

"There must have been a period of time the house was empty. It had to have happened then," Beth said lubing her hands. "And don't even think about removing them. I made that mistake when I first discovered one and was caned to within an inch of my life." Placing her bunched together fingers at Regina's pussy, she slowly pushed them in to the wrist and then made a fist so she could go even deeper. Regina got comfortable and flipped to another page showing her fisting her husband as Beth fisted her and her clit throbbed with excitement at the memory.

22

The front door opened and Beth yanked her hand from Regina's cunt and spun around to see a very sweaty Natalie. "Hey babe," she smiled. "About time you got home. I have some great news."

"Were you fisting my mother again?" Natalie asked as her sports bra came off.

"She was," Regina smiled "but alas, the moment is gone. You have another commandment."

"What now?"

"We're going out to do some peeping and at the end I'll get my sister back!" Beth exclaimed.

"Unless we get caught and tossed in jail," Natalie scoffed.

"I don't think that's likely," her mother replied, taking the slip of paper from the back of the photo album and handing it to her daughter. "Trust me, you don't want to see what's inside. Suffice it to say, this one belongs to your father and me. Anyways, I don't know the exact houses, but I do know the streets they are on and all of them are remote and seldom traveled except by those living on them and their mailman."

Taking the commandment, Natalie read it with mixed feelings. She was thrilled her girlfriend's sister would be returned, but feared the price they'd have to pay to see it through. "So, something fun and unexpected happened to me at the park today. I was doing some stretching and a man walked up and took me like he owned me."

"OH WOW!" Beth gasped. "And you let him?"

"Hell yeah I let him. Not only did he fuck a load into me, but he fisted my ass to the elbow."

"Nice! But you know you're going to run out of luck and end up pregnant if you don't go on birth control, right?"

"Too late," Natalie confessed.

"WHAT!?" Her mother shrieked. "Are you telling us you're already pregnant?"

"Yeah. I wasn't going to say anything until I got the results back from the doctor, but I've taken five different home tests and they were all positive so chances are pretty damn good I'm now with child. And before anyone makes a fuss, I'm keeping it and will raise it with all the love and nurturing it deserves."

"I'd expect nothing less," her mother smiled. "Though I suspect your father won't be too pleased about the news. I don't suppose there's any chance you know who the father is?"

"No idea. And even if I did I wouldn't want him in my life. The only men to have fucked me were at glory holes and gang bangs so not exactly father material in my opinion. Not that I have much room to talk, all things considered." Staring back down at the paper, Natalie read it from top to bottom.

Fifth Commandment: Thou shalt watch thy neighbor.

You and Beth shall embark on a journey of discovery that will take you across town. The goal of this commandment is to show that you are not alone in the kinky things you do, though I suspect you know that already. The four addresses at the bottom of this page are your targets for tonight. Do them in order or Jenna will pay the price for your failure. Do as you are told and you will get her back at the end of the night. Follow these rules to the letter:

__Rule #1:__ You and Beth will wear the largest butt plug you can fit in your asses.

__Rule #2:__ You and Beth will wear cloverleaf clamps on your nipples and pussy.

__Rule #3:__ You and Beth will wear the following clothes. If you are missing anything I suggest you buy it before you go out tonight. Sheer top, latex mini skirt, choker collar, thigh high latex boots, and elbow length latex gloves. If you are missing anything go to Purple Passions to purchase what you need.

__Rule #4:__ You and Beth will take pictures of each other at each location clearly showing your face to the camera as you rub your own clit.

__Rule #5:__ You and Beth will watch what goes on at each location and then perform the same activities with each other before moving on to the next.

Remember, eyes will be on you so don't think you can skip out on your commandments.

"What a smug fucking asshole," Natalie cursed. "I swear to god if I knew where he was staying I'd bite his damn dick off and feed it to him for what he's doing to us and our families!"

"That makes two of us," Beth sighed.

"How do you get these photo albums? Can't you follow him back to his house or where ever?"

"No. I get a call telling me to go to a certain location, usually a bus or train station, but sometimes it's the local 'Y'. He tells me what locker to go to and the combination for the lock and the albums are there for me to take. Other's you've gotten in the mail. The son of a bitch knows how to cover his tracks. I even used fingerprint dust in the hopes of finally figuring out who he is, but he leaves nothing behind."

"Maybe Jenna will be able to tell us more," Regina offered. "Assuming he keeps his word and lets her go."

The front door opened and Henry stepped in. No sooner had it closed behind him then he started removing his clothes.

"Now that you're both home, I have something to tell you," Regina said looking down at Beth who was still kneeling between her legs. "Beth informed me that our entire house has been wired with hidden cameras. That's how the blackmailer's been able to get pictures and video of everything we do. And if we attempt to tamper with them we'll be severely beaten."

"Great!" Henry huffed. "So it doesn't matter what we do he'll have something on us? Like this fat fucking plug I've been wearing up my ass all damn day!"

"In slightly better news, I'm pregnant," Natalie told her father.

"I was wondering how long it was going to take. We'll fix the spare bedroom into a nursery."

"Wait, what? You're not mad at me?"

"The only way I'll be mad at you is if you don't love him or her with all of your heart. It can't help the way it was conceived."

Overcome with joy, Natalie wrapped her arms around her father's neck and hugged him tight, but quickly stepped back when she felt his growing cock pressing dangerously close to her slit. "Dammit dad! You really need to learn some self-control!"

"Hey, I can't help it with three beautiful women running around the house naked," Henry said in his own defense. Is that another photo album?"

"It is," Regina replied. "It's of us being used by Beth and all those men."

"Natalie and I have another commandment and I'm getting my sister back tonight," Beth said with so much enthusiasm Henry could not tell which part she was excited about the most.

"Well, at least there's that. But I'll bet my left nut he's not going to let her go before adding her to the growing list of people he's blackmailing."

"You and mom go ahead and look at the pictures, Beth and I have clothing options to discuss before tonight's commandment," Natalie said, offering her girlfriend a hand up.

∞ ∞ ∞

"How long do you think this is going to go on?" Natalie asked as her bedroom door swung closed. "Is he ever going to stop or can we expect to make this a permanent part of our lives?"

"I really wish I knew the answer to that question." Beth sighed "but I honestly don't know. If Jenna isn't able to give us anything on him we'll go to the police and everything getting out be damned. We may be professional prostitutes at Raven's Hollow, but there's a limit to even what I can handle and it's quickly approaching."

"Amen. A gang bang and glory hole are great once in a while, but not every day of the week. And now I have a baby to worry about. I'm with you one hundred percent no matter what happens. If everything gets leaked as a result of us going to the police then so be it. We'll get over it and move on. And at this point I really don't care anymore. So, what about the clothes we're supposed to wear tonight? Do you own any of those things?"

"A few items, but I'm not above owning more. They have everything we need at work, but we're not allowed to wear it out of the brothel."

"Then to Purple Passions it is."

23

Purple Passions turned out to be the only fetish clothing store for a hundred miles in any direction and despite having driven by it a million times, neither of them had ever really noticed the unassuming, out of the way windowless building before.

"This is where Lady Raven gets most of the clothes at work, but I've never been here personally," Beth said as she held the door open for Natalie to enter first.

"WOW! I've never seen anything like this in my life!" Natalie said looking down aisles of skirts, dresses, pants and various tops in leather and latex.

"Why stop at what he wants us to get? Come on, let's make this a real shopping spree!"

"On a student's salary?"

"No, on a Raven's Hollow prostitute's salary," Beth grinned. "Come on, we both know you make more than enough to afford a few new outfits and toys."

"Hello ladies, can I help you find anything today?" asked a statuesque brunette – her narrow-framed glasses, hair done up in a bun and the latex dress giving her the appearance of an incredibly sexy, yet stern principal.

"Um, probably," Natalie replied. "I've never been in a store like this before."

"That makes two of us," Beth added.

"Not a problem. Do you have something in mind?"

Yeah, we have a specific outfit we're looking for, but we're not stopping there. Do you only sell clothing here?"

"No. We sell everything related to the bdsm lifestyle including clothes, toys and furniture if you're looking to buy those as well. My name is Heather, by the way. Sorry about not wearing my name tag, I didn't want to ruin my dress."

"No problem. I'm Natalie and this is my girlfriend Beth. And I do believe we're making this a shopping spree to remember, so we'll look at everything."

Cool. So, if you don't mind me asking, which of you is Dominant and who's submissive? Or do you switch?"

"We switch," Beth answered. "Though we're still pretty new to the lifestyle. Well, Natalie is anyways. We both work at Raven's Hollow. Ever been?"

"A few times, but I don't think I've ever seen either of you there before."

"I've only been there a few weeks," Natalie said as they walked down an aisle of latex dresses.

"I've been there a few years, but I usually work the night shift."

"Oh, I like this one!" Natalie said holding up a short, strapless black and red latex dress.

"Go ahead and try it on."

Thinking she meant right there in the middle of the store, Natalie pulled her tee shirt off and tossed it at Beth. And then she caught the look on Heather's face and her own went red. "Sorry, where's the changing room?"

"It's okay. There are no other customers so if you want to change into it right here that's fine by me," Heather smiled. "Or you can use the changing rooms which are over there along the wall," she pointed behind Natalie's shoulder.

"In that case," Beth said stripping out of her own clothes when a purple bandage dress caught her eye.

"Wow! You two are something else," Heather said shaking her head in disbelief.

"You have no idea," Natalie giggled. Stripped down to her panties, she put the dress on and smoothed out the wrinkles. "Fits like a glove!" Mind if I check it out now so I don't have to take it off?"

"By all means."

A quick trip to the registers and Natalie was the proud owner of her first piece of fetishwear. Beth paid for her dress as well and the three women returned to the aisles. Until the front door opened and another customer entered. "Sorry ladies, I'm the only one working today so I'll have to tend the registers. But if you have any questions don't hesitate to ask. And please use the changing rooms while there are other customers."

"No problem," Beth and Natalie said in unison."

Aisle after aisle, the cart filled with every style of clothing the small store offered from latex bras and panties, to boots, gloves, dresses, spanking skirt, regular skirts, pants, shorts, corsets and shirts. And just before they turned into the toy section, they added a myriad of fetish lingerie.

"This place is fucking amazing!" Natalie said holding up a dildo shaped like an arm and hand with the fingers bunched together. "I think I'll get two of these."

"One for the pussy and one for the ass?"

"No, one for my mom and one for my dad, Natalie giggled, tossing the toys into the cart.

"Yeah, they're going to love you for that. And I'll get them these," Beth said holding up a package of nipple shields that looked like fanged mouths, and another pack containing nipple stretchers."

Stopping at each section, Natalie and Beth added several varieties of gags including Bit, ball, ring and penis to the cart which were quickly followed by alligator, cloverleaf and normal clamps in large and small sizes for nipples and pussy. Next, came several collars from dainty feminine ones to wide leather bands studded with metal spikes, and sleek metal ones with screw locks to prevent removal without the proper tool.

On top of all that went the floggers, canes, blindfolds, candles, needles, cuffs in leather and metal and five different spreader bars."

"Um, why do I suddenly get the feeling I'm going to be calling you Mistress soon?" Natalie asked, holding up a metal collar with the word SLAVE etched and filigreed along the front.

"Don't get me wrong, I enjoyed most of what I've done at work, but I'm not entirely sure I want all of this used on me at home."

"Trust me, we'll put it all too good use one way or another," Beth said adding a bundle of purple and black rope to the cart. We're going to have a lot of fun together, blackmailer be damned. And if we're going to be dating you should know the full extent of my perverted mind. Even if you don't want some of these things used on you, I want you to use every single one of them on me. Hot wax and needles included."

"Well, okay then. I think we've got enough for one day, don't you?"

"Not quite," Beth said adding a pack of degrading dog tags to the cart. "Now we have enough."

24

As Natalie was pulling the short, black latex miniskirt up her legs and plugged ass, Beth was still attempting to get hers in place. It was larger than she preferred, but the commandment did say to use one as large as they could fit. This particular one was 9 1/2 inches long and 4 3/4 inches wide at its thickest point and gave her that well-stretched feeling she so loved once finally inserted.

"About time you got it in. You act like you've never been fisted a thousand times," Natalie grinned.

"You know that I have, but this is a bit larger than what I'm used to wearing."

"You'll get used to it."

"I know. Don't get me wrong, I love being stretched open nearly as much as you do, but it'll take me a while before it starts feeling really good."

"I think I can get used to these kinds of clothes," Natalie said looking at herself in the mirror. The nipple clamps were clearly visible beneath the sheer top and her clitoris throbbed every time the massive plug in her ass shifted position. Taking a few steps around the room, she could feel the smaller clamps attached to her outer labia swinging back and forth and tugging downward. Picking up the commandment list, she stared at the first name. "The first one is Wendy and Ryan Ralston."

"I wonder what we'll see and have to do," Beth said as she slipped into her boots.

"My guess, something sexual. And if I know the blackmailer it'll be something kinky. Just remember whatever we see we are supposed to do before going to the next location. No matter how fucked up it is, I don't want to risk anything happening to your sister because we couldn't do it."

"Thank you. She is such a sweet and innocent young woman with a bright future ahead of her and I fear how she'll respond if he does anything to her."

"You mean like I was when all of this started? I'd like to think I handled it okay. Maybe she will as well.

"I don't want her to handle it okay! I don't want her to handle it at all. I just want her back safe and sound at home where she can hopefully put it all behind her."

"I don't mean to sound insensitive, but how exactly are you going to prevent him from doing anything to her? He's had her for two weeks and if the pictures you showed me are accurate there's no way in hell he hasn't attempted to put a baby in her. I mean, look what he intended for me until I ruined his plans."

"Please don't! I can't think about this right now."

"I understand, believe me I do, but you have to face the very real possibility that the Jenna you get back may not be the same one that was taken from you. I mean, if he had you do that to my parents, can you honestly stand there and tell me you believe he'll keep his hands off of her?"

"I said I don't want to think about it! Let's just get this commandment done and over with."

∞ ∞ ∞

The Ralston home was a one story red-brick ranch set far off the road and surrounded by trees on three sides. Sneaking out of the woods at the rear of the house, Natalie and Beth stopped in their tracks when they saw three lights on.

"Which one do we go to first?" Natalie whispered.

"You take the left and I'll go right," Beth replied. "If neither of those is it we'll meet in the middle.

Natalie nodded and they moved towards the house as quickly and quietly as humanly possible. Halfway there, Beth stepped on a twig – the sound of it snapping in the night was deafening to the two trespassers and they stood motionless for several minutes waiting for someone to come out to investigate. But when no one showed up, they resumed their march as a much slower pace while keeping an eye out for hazards.

Peeking through their respective windows, Natalie looked into an empty bathroom – her eye catching an empty enema bag hanging from the shower curtain rod. Beth's luck was about as good as she stared into a small office. As Natalie turned away from her window, she heard someone enter the bathroom and she could not help but to peep inside again only to see a couple locked in embrace. Motioning to her girlfriend to come over, she continued to watch.

Thirty-four year old Wendy Ralston stepped back from her husband and grabbed his stiffening cock. The busty redhead then knelt down and took Ryan's thick cock into her mouth and sucked him off for several minutes – completely oblivious to the two women watching from outside.

"I wouldn't mind switching places with her," Beth whispered.

"I hope the blackmailer doesn't expect us to do that," Natalie replied. "We might be here a while waiting for one of us to grow a dick."

"I don't know, your clit is big enough it could be mistaken as one."

"Shut up," Natalie said giving her girlfriend a playful shove "you don't seem to mind sucking my big fat clit."

"That's not the only thing of yours I like to suck," Susan said flicking the clamp dangling from Natalie's right nipple.

Back inside the house, Ryan placed his cock between his wife's large breasts. She squeezed them together and lowered her head so that as her husband fucked her tits the head of his cock went into her mouth. This went on for several more minutes before Ryan pulled back and blasted her pretty face with cum. As Wendy wiped her husband's semen from her face and brought her sticky fingers to her mouth, Ryan aimed his cock and let loose a stream of piss. Wendy opened up as if on autopilot and let it fill up before swallowing it down. Several mouthfuls later and her husband was done pissing. After licking her lips, they switched places so that he was now the one to drink the warm, bitter fluid.

"You thinking what I'm thinking?" Beth whispered.

"That we're supposed to drink piss before moving to the next house?"

"Mmm hmm."

"My thoughts exactly."

"Before we forget, take some pictures of me." Beth said dropping down on all fours and pulling her skirt up so that the butt plug and pussy clamps were clearly visible and popping her breasts out of her top to show the clamps dangling from her nipples. Looking back at Natalie's cell phone, she smiled and rubbed her clit. After three dozen pictures were taken, they switched places and then stared back into the bathroom.

Wendy was now squatting over her husband's head, her pussy pressed firmly against his mouth and they could clearly see him gulping. In a daring display of insanity, Natalie pressed her phone to the glass and took several pictures as further proof they were there.

"Are you out of your mind!?" Beth said harshly. "What if they saw that?"

"Well, since neither of them is running out here or calling the police I'd say they didn't."

"Do you have to pee?" Beth asked, shaking her head.

"Not really, you?"

"Yeah, I have to go pretty bad now. I had all that water and haven't been to the bathroom in hours. Are you ready?"

"You know that I am. Get that pussy as close to my mouth as you can and make sure to snap more pictures as you do it. I don't want that bastard making any excuses why he can fuck with your sister."

"I appreciate it," Beth smiled, moving into place and letting the stream flow. And like the true piss slut that she was, Natalie relaxed her gag reflex and let it slid down with ease. She then licked Beth's pussy clean. But she did not stop there. Drawn in by the intoxicating mixture of piss, rose, vanilla and her girlfriend's own natural scents, Natalie wrapped her arms around her ass and continued to lick until she felt Beth go weak in the knees.

"I have to pee now!"

"Damn you straight to hell Natalie Holt! I was right on the verge of orgasm when you stopped!"

"I know," Natalie grinned. "I stopped because I know what a screamer you can be and I don't really want to get caught. Now open up and say ah."

∞ ∞ ∞

As they headed back to the tree line, Natalie's phone began to vibrate. Looking, she saw a series of texts from an unknown number.

Performed like true sluts. Before going back to your car and heading to the next location I want you to shove an even larger plug up your asses. From tapping into the security cameras at Purple Passions I know you bought some as big as six inches and from watching you at home I know you have at least a couple of five inchers in that bag of yours. Put them up your asses like the good anal freaks that you are.

"Guess what we get to do next," Natalie said as she dropped the bag onto the ground.

"What now?"

"That was the blackmailer. He said we are to put larger plugs in our asses. Nothing less than five inches."

"Let me see that," Beth said snatching the phone from Natalie's hand. She read the text twice before handing it back. "There are two plugs in there five inches or larger and they are going to stretch us both out more than ever. I don't even know why I put them in there."

"Maybe something in the back of your mind told you the bastard would want us to really wreck our asses tonight," Natalie said digging through the bag. Looking at the base of the first massive plug it read 5 1/2 inches. The second was 5 3/4 inches. Since I can take it a lot easier than you, I'll use the larger of the two, she said handing Beth a butt plug.

"That's noble of you. Not really much difference between them is there?"

"Not much. Should we wear a gag to prevent anyone from hearing us?"

"Probably. Give me the penis gag and the lube."

25

An inch does not sound like much until you are trying to stretch your asshole open that much more as Natalie and Beth were now doing at the command of their blackmailer. *At least he didn't tell us to shove them into our cunts,* Natalie thought as the plug slipped a little deeper. Lying her head on the grassy ground, she reached back with her free hand and applied more pressure to the base of the toy – nearly biting the ball gag in half when it finally went in. The burning sensation was immediate and intense and she remained still for nearly three minutes for fear of splitting in two.

Beth was having a much harder time of it and was in tears as the toy stretched her open more than she had ever been before. But, with her sister's fate in their hands, she pushed through the agony and it eventually went in – her sphincter snapping shut around the slightly narrower base locking the toy in for the time being. "Come on, let's get the hell out of here before we're caught, "she said after removing the penis gag from her mouth.

"Right behind you," Natalie groaned. "I think I've hit the limit of what my poor ass can handle."

"You and me both. It feels like I've got a football up my damn ass!"

"Well, if yours in a football then mine's a basketball," Natalie cringed. "Seriously, I don't think I could take a millimeter more without bursting at the seams. I hate so sound like a vindictive bitch, but I might just have to fuck your sister silly after going through all of this for her."

"Don't even think about it! You lay one finger on her and we're through!"

"Relax, I'm kidding. But in all honestly, what happens if the blackmailer commands me to do fuck over Jenna like you did my parents? I'll have no choice just as you had no choice."

"I was assured that would never happen."

"We've been assured of a lot of things that somehow keep creeping up on us. Come on, it's a fifteen minute drive to the next location. Ever hear of a Tabitha Channing?"

"Nope. You?"

"Nada. I wonder what we'll have to do there."

"Not stretch our asses open I can tell you that much. I'm glad I didn't bring those six inchers along."

"Yeah, no kidding."

∞ ∞ ∞

Driving down a long dirt road right out of a horror movie, Beth spotted the address – a two-story tan colonial with detached garage. As they did with the Ralston's, they parked down the road and would backtrack, keeping to the shadows as much as possible. Turning the car off, Natalie was just about to open the door to get out when her phone went off.

"What does the son of a bitch want us to do now?"

"We're to take off our tops and leave them in the car," Natalie said reading the text. "We are to remain topless until we come back to leave for the next house."

"Why don't we just strip naked? That bastard is something else," Beth huffed as she removed the sheer top that was not hiding anything to begin with.

"Don't give him any ideas. Besides, it's not as if these things are actually covering anything," Natalie said tossing her top in the back seat.

Making it to the house unseen, they found it dark and silent. "What now?" Natalie asked.

"I have no idea. Maybe we should wait a while and see if anyone turns a light on. Hell, for all I know they may not even be home yet."

They found a nice spot at the far end of the garages where they could remain hidden while keeping watch on the house and no sooner had they hunkered down to wait then they heard noises coming from within. Finding a window with a partially opened curtain, they peeking in to see finished walls and carpeted floors, but it was the woman of about twenty-five standing spread-eagle in the center of the room that caught their attention.

Butt naked, her arms stretched over her head and cuffed in place to hooks in the ceiling, her legs were kept wide apart by way of a spreader bar which was attached to hooks in the floor. Five men and another woman came into view and their eyes went to the riding crop in her hand.

"How much you want to bet the bound woman is Tabitha," Natalie whispered.

"You're probably right," Beth agreed "but you never know. It could be the fully dressed woman."

"With our luck?"

"How does the blackmailer expect us to do what they're doing while out here?"

"No idea. Unless you packed another bag and didn't tell me."

"Nope. Whatever is in that bag is it and I'm seriously regretting packing that one," Beth said shifting her weight in a futile attempt to ease the pain in her ass.

As they continued to watch through the parted curtain, they saw two men approach Tabitha – the one in front lifting her only his cock while the one in back pushed into her ass. "If that's what we're here to do then fine by me," Natalie grinned as Tabitha leaned back against the man fucking her ass. The man in her pussy leaned in ant bit her right nipple – tugging at it painfully and not letting go.

"Aahhgghhh! Not so hard!"

"Keep complaining and I'll tell him to bite it off," the woman said as she placed three tapered candles in a holder and lit them. She then moved to another table where she placed several long needles in a bowl of liquid. When the candles had burned sufficiently, she picked it up and tilted it over Tabitha's naked form. No sooner had the trails dried then she added more – painting her nipples, breasts and belly blue, red and black.

One by one, the five men took Tabitha in pussy and ass as the woman continued to drizzle hot wax all over her body – spreading out form breasts and belly to hit her back, arms and legs as well. She then sat the candle holder on the cart and plucked one of the needles from the bowl and scraped it along Tabitha's right breast.

"Please Mistress Dawn," Tabitha begged "not the needles again. Oh god, anything but that!"

"But you came so hard the last time," Mistress Dawn said, tapping the needle against Tabitha's growing left nipple. You're a dirty pain slut aren't you my little Tabby? You love it when I torture your sexy body don't you?"

"No Mistress," Tabitha wailed, her body visibly trembling in fear and apprehension.

"Are you sure?" Mistress Dawn asked as she took hold of Tabitha's left nipple and pushed the needle through.

"Aahgh!" Tabitha screeched, throwing her head back and clenching her teeth tightly together against the pain. Her legs buckled as another needle pushed through the right nipple.

From outside, Beth and Natalie cringed at what they saw, but like watching a ten car pileup could not tear their eyes away from the show. And then they realized Mistress Dawn was right. If the pussy juices freely flowing down her thighs was any indication, Tabitha was in the throes of orgasm.

"Fuck me!" Beth gasped "I don't think I'll be able to do that."

"Wait, aren't you the one that told me you bought the needles to use?"

"Yeah, but now that I'm seeing it up close I don't think I want to anymore."

"Well, let's hope it doesn't come to that. I still don't see how we're supposed to even do it in the first place. We don't bring the needles."

"That's ok," said a voice behind them "we've got plenty inside. Care to join us?"

The sudden appearance of the man caused Beth and Natalie to nearly jump out of their own skin. Spinning around, they looked up at the smiling man and Natalie felt a little pee escape her bladder and trickle out. "Oh fuck! This isn't what it looks like!"

"Save it. I know why you're hear. And if you've got to take a piss feel free to go in your girlfriend's mouth. Go on, piss down her throat so we can move on."

"You know why we're..." Beth's sentence was cut short by Natalie's pussy and piss filling her mouth. Looking up into her girlfriend's eyes, she swallowed every drop of it.

"Yes, I know why you're here. The question is, will you come in and suffer the same treatment as Tabitha, or will you run away and fail your commandment?"

"What do you know of the commandments?" Natalie asked, suddenly very suspicious. "Who the hell are you?"

"I know enough to be expecting the two of you and what you're supposed to do here."

"And what exactly are we supposed to do here?" Beth asked.

"You'll both be fucked by me and the other men inside while Mistress Dawn does her work. You'll experience hot wax, the riding crop, and some needle play and when we're done playing with you, you can go on to your next destination."

"And if we refuse?"

"Then leave now, but I think you both know what will happen to Jenna if you do that. And as much as I'd love fucking you both silly, it's your choice to stay or go."

"WHAT DO YOU KNOW ABOUT MY SISTER!?" Beth shouted, jumping to her feet with hands balled into fists.

"Only what will happen to her should you fail the commandment. Now make your decision."

"What do you think, Beth?"

"I don't know. I don't think I could stand the needles despite my earlier claims otherwise. I've done hot wax before and it's not bad, but I think needles being pushed into my nipples is going too far."

"Do you want to do it or not? Remember, everything gets out if we fail and your sister gets used like a fucking whore!"

"Let's get it over with," Beth sighed. "And so help me god, if one hair on her head is harmed I'll hunt every last one of you down and do things not even your twisted minds can conceive."

26

Beth, Natalie and the man entered the garage just as Mistress Dawn pulled the last of the needles from Tabitha's nipples. "The ladies have agreed to continue with their night's activities, Mistress."

"Thank you, Glen," Mistress Dawn replied. "Since there are two of them why don't you go call the rest of the men while I get them prepared?"

"As you wish Mistress."

"Wait! Your name is Glen?" Natalie asked with raised brow. "Is your last name parker?"

"Um, do we know each other?"

"Never met you in my life, but I have heard the name before."

Beth, however, had other thoughts on her mind. "What other men? How many? What are you going to do to us?"

"Everything you saw me do to Tabitha. And you didn't seriously think it was going to be the five of them, did you? No, professional whores like you need at least twenty big black cocks fucking their seed into you."

"If your plan is to knock us up you're a few weeks late," Natalie said indifferently. I'm already pregnant."

"Well congratulations, but no, my job isn't to breed you. It'll take some time for them to arrive so we'll start with the painful portion of tonight's show. I assume you both got a good look at what I did to Tabitha?"

"Yes," Natalie and Beth replied.

"Good. That's what you'll endure as well. Since I already have the needles out and ready why don't we start there? Who wants to go first?"

"I'll go first," said Natalie.

"Strip out of the rest of your clothes and step over here. Spread your legs and raise your arms over your head."

Natalie did as she was told, taking the place Tabitha occupied only minutes before. Mistress Dawn secured her wrists with leather cuffs and then knelt down to place the cuffs of the spreader bar around Natalie's ankles. Once it was locked in place to the floor, she picked up a penis gag from the toy shelf and placed it in Natalie's mouth and fastened the leather strap around her head.

"Are you ready?" she asked Beth.

"Ready for what?"

"Didn't I tell you? You're the one that's going to use the needles on your girlfriend."

"I'm going to do what now?" I can't do that. There's no way in hell I can do that to her."

"You will if you want to complete the commandment," Mistress Dawn smirked. "It's easier than it looks. Just line it up and push it through quickly. If you want to torment her you can go slowly. It's all up to you."

"But I've never done anything like this before. I have no idea what I'm doing."

"No better time to start than now. I'll help you with the first one, but the rest are in your hands."

"The rest? How many do I have to use on her? Where do I put them?"

"Use these on her nipples," Mistress Dawn said pointing to two needles, each about three inches long and hollow at one end. "Push them halfway through and leave them. After that, use that one on her clit hood." The third needle was similar in shape but slightly thinner.

"I'm sorry hun," Beth said as she picked up one of the needles and moved to stand in front of Natalie "but you know what's on the line." Removing the clamps from her girlfriend's rock hard nipples, she lined the needle up against Natalie's left nipple and pushed it through.

"Aaahhgggghhh," Natalie screamed into the gag as the needle pierced her nipple. As the blood flow returned, she wiggled all over the place.

"That's enough of that," said Mistress Dawn with a slap of the crop to Natalie's exposed ass. It took three more before Natalie got it into her head to stand still and let her girlfriend continue working.

Beth pushed the next needle through Natalie's right nipple and then knelt down so she was eye level with her girlfriend's pussy. "Where do I place this one?" she asked Mistress Dawn. "I don't want to fuck up and go through her clit."

"That would be a shame," Mistress Dawn smiled. "Let me mark the area for you." She grabbed a skin marker and a pair of piercing tongs and knelt down in front of Natalie. After finding the perfect location, she placed a dot on either side of Natalie's hood and then clicked the tongs in place. "There you go. Just push the needle through one side and out the other."

Beth took the needle in one hand and the tongs in the other and looked up apologetically. "I'm so sorry I have to do this to you," she pleaded. Placing the beveled tip of the needle against the black mark, she took a deep breath and pushed it through. Natalie jerked back and yelped.

"Don't feel too bad for her," Mistress Dawn said as she set up more needles. "She's going to do the same to you next," she added as she removed Natalie's restraints and gag.

"Oh my fucking god that hurt!"

"I'm so, so sorry," Beth apologized again.

"Don't worry about it. We have no choice, remember?"

"Oh, but you do have a choice," said Mistress Dawn. "You are free to leave at any time."

"Yeah, and what happens to her sister?"

"You really don't want to know."

"Do you know where's Jenna's being held?"

"No clue. My job is to see to tonight's commandment, not babysit. Now get in place so she can pierce you."

"How long do I have to keep these damn needles in me?"

"Until you're done with your girlfriend. Now get to work on her nipples while I mark her hood."

With the needles through Beth's nipples and clit hood, Mistress Dawn stood back and nodded approvingly. "You will both stand there with your arms behind your back and eyes closed," she said dropping several rings into a bowl of rubbing alcohol to sterilize them. "If you move, or open your eyes even a crack, I'll whip the skin from your asses. Do you understand me?"

"Yes," Natalie and Beth answered as they got into position.

Standing as still as statues, Natalie and Beth felt the needles being slowly pushed through one nipple and clit hood at a time. And the feeling of cold metal left behind told them they were now properly pierced.

"You may open your eyes now. They make you look so fucking sexy, don't you think?" she asked Beth. "You are free to go now."

"Free to go? What about the gang bang?" Natalie asked, looking down at the rings dangling from her nipples.

"There is no gang bang planned for tonight. My job was to have you pierce each other's nipples and clit hood and then send you on your way. Now I suggest you go before I give you a dozen more rings."

Natalie and Beth did not need to be told a second time. Gathering their clothes, they ran for the car, waiting to get dressed until they got there. Since they were naked already, they tossed the clothes in the trunk alongside the tops they earlier wore and rummaged through the bags to find something new to wear.

"I guess it's a good thing you bought me all of these clothes," Natalie said as she pulled on another latex miniskirt.

"I guess so. She's right you know. Mistress Dawn that is. The rings do make you look even sexier than before."

"Who ever said being sexy was easy?" Natalie smiled. They both broke out in laughter as they finished dressing and jumped into the car.

They were less than a mile away from their third destination when Natalie's phone went off. Beth picked it up and read the text.

The third destination has been canceled. You will go to the final location and await further instructions.

"Well, it looks like we're getting off easy," Beth said dropping the phone on the seat. "We're to go to the final destination and wait."

"Fine by me. I just want to get this night over with."

27

Pulling onto the road, Natalie was surprised to see it right smack dab in the middle of a bustling neighborhood. Her phone vibrated.

You will pull into the garage and close the door. You, meaning Natalie, will go into the house alone where you will find a bound and hooded woman within.

You will fist fuck her pussy and ass until she has three orgasms and then you will pierce her nipples, clit hood and outer labia with the tools provided. From what Mistress Dawn tells me you'll do fine.

Once she has been pierced you will remove the hood and restraints and take her wherever she wants to go. If Beth leaves the car for any reason you fail the commandment and will be summarily disciplined.

Now do as you are commanded and Beth sees her sister again.

"Who do you think's in there?" Beth nervously asked.

"No idea, but she's going to be fist fucked and pierced if it means getting Jenna back."

"Thank you for doing this for me."

"Hey, what are girlfriends for, right? Stay here and I'll return as quickly as possible."

Entering the house through the kitchen, Natalie found it empty. Walking into the living room, it too was empty. Going room to room, she finally found the bound woman in a back bedroom strapped to a Saint Andrews cross. *Damn,* she thought looking the young woman over – her eyes drifting to the brand on her pussy mound. "No need to be alarmed," she said as calmly as possible. Have you ever been fisted?"

The woman nodded her head.

"Good. I don't want to hurt you, but I have my orders. Can you take a fist up your ass?"

The woman nodded again.

"Glad to hear it. I am to fist both holes until you've had three orgasms and then I must give you some piercings." Looking at the woman's pussy, she saw a series of six black dots down each outer labia and one on either side of her clit hood. Please know that I do not want to do this, but I have no choice. Do you understand?"

The woman nodded a third time.

"Alright, I'm going to lube my hands and fist you now and I promise I'll do my best to make it enjoyable." Her phone went off and she read another text from the blackmailer.

You will put both hands in her pussy and then her ass until the breeding slave has her three orgasms.

"I'm sorry, but that was the blackmailer. It seems I have to shove both hands in your pussy at the same time and then do the same to your ass. Please tell me you can take it."

The woman nodded.

"Thank god. I really am sorry about this. Are you ready?"

The woman nodded.

"You look young. Please tell me you're legal to have sex with."

As if a broken record, the woman nodded yet again. It was all she could do with the long penis gag shoved down her throat.

"I really wish I could take you out of here without doing anything, but more than my life is on the line. Please understand that." Lubing her hands, Natalie knelt between the bound woman's spread legs and pushed the right one in to the wrist, smiling with a great deal of satisfaction at the ease of penetration. Wrapping her left hand around her right wrist, she gently pushed upwards until the hand too was inside of the woman's pussy. "I'm so glad you were able to take them so easily," she said working them in and out one at a time and then together – her knuckles glancing off her g-spot.

"Mmmm, that's one," Natalie purred as she continued fisting the bound woman to three rapid aftershocks. Moving to her ass, she was not in such luck – taking nearly half an hour to bring her off once. Thankfully, her hands went right back into the woman's pussy and orgasm was reached within minutes.

"I wish I could bring you off some more, but I have to pierce you now. I am being commanded to pierce your nipples, clit hood and outer labia. My girlfriend and I just had ours done less than two hours ago. It hurts a little but the pain doesn't last long. Well, the nipples and hood anyways. We did not get any in our labia. I'll try to get it over with as quickly as possible and then we can get the hell out of here." And just as she was picking up the first needle, her phone went off again.

You will use the longest ones first. Push them through the dirty slut's tits until they're all used and then use the cane on her. One hundred swats.

"Jesus fucking Christ! Will it ever end!? I'm so sorry, but I have to do more than pierce what I've mentioned. "I must pushed longer needles through your breasts and then give you one hundred swats of the cane." The way the woman's shoulders slumped told a sorrowful tale of repeated use and it broke Natalie's heart to add to her misery, but there was a lot riding on the line.

Picking up the first needle, Natalie pushed it through the woman's right breast with one quick jab. It was followed by one through the left as the woman screamed in agony. Another in the right. Left. Right. Left. Natalie alternated between sides until all twenty were in place. Next, she pierced the balling woman's nipples, dropping the rings in place before moving to her clit hood. All that remained were the seven piercings in each outer labia, and Natalie stared down at them in confusion. Her phone went off yet again and she thankfully read the instructions on how to properly insert the tunnels.

Everything complete, Natalie removed the long needles from the woman's breasts and then the hood and penis gag combination and what she saw shocked and appalled her. Running down the hall to the bathroom, she threw up in the toilet and rinsed her face before returning to make sure she was not hallucinating.

"JENNA!? Oh my fucking god! Y-You're Jenna, right?"

"Yes," Jenna sobbed.

"Oh my god! Oh my god! Oh my god! I didn't know!" Natalie trembled in fear as she removed her girlfriend's sister from the Saint Andrews. "Your sister is waiting for us outside. She's going to kill me for doing this to you."

"It's okay," Jenna said between slow, deep breaths. "I'll tell her you had no choice in the matter. That fucking bitch ruined my life in the first place."

"Wait, what do you mean? Beth loves you more than anything. Was willing to be used and abused by some sadistic asshole to keep you safe. She was assured you would not be harmed in any way. Who did this to you? Do you know where to find him?"

"Him? It was a woman that did this to me? She used me. Beat me, turned me into her breeding cow for a gang of black men! Oh god! I'm pregnant with their child! Please, please take me out of here."

Beth saw her sister being led out of the house covered in welts and too many piercings for her addled brain to count. Leaping out of the car, she rushed around the car fuming mad. "What in the holy hell happened? Why do you have Jenna? Oh my god! Did you do this to her?"

"It wasn't her fault," Jenna groaned. "I was hooded and gagged and she was ordered not to remove either until the job was done. Now please, for the love of god get me the fuck out of here!"

"I'm so sorry, Beth, I really didn't know it was her. You told me your sister was a virgin. Jenna was bound, hooded and gagged. She had a damn brand on her pussy and her pussy and asshole were stretched to easily take both hands at the same time. How was I supposed to know?"

"Let's just get the hell out of here as Jenna suggested."

∞ ∞ ∞

"How's Jenna coping?" Natalie asked. It had been a week since that horrible night and as much as she'd rather put it all behind her and move on, she knew there was no way that would ever happen.

"She's getting better," Beth sighed.

"Then why the long face?"

"She wants to keep the piercings, brand and the baby she's carrying as a reminder of what

197

happened and our parents are not pleased. They're threatening to throw her out of the house, Natalie!"

"Then she can come live here," Regina offered. Considering everything that has happened to this family these last few months she'll fit right in."

"Thanks, but I'm trying to get them to understand this wasn't her fault. I told them everything, Natalie. I showed them the photo albums you let me borrow, came clean about working at Raven's Hollow, all of it. And like your parents they want to go to the police with this."

"And I think we should!" Natalie scowled. "This has gone on long enough, Beth. How much more are you willing to give…whomever the hell it is? For fuck sake, we don't even know if it's a man, woman or an entire team of blackmailers."

A knock at the door paused the conversation and Natalie opened the door – giving the ups man a full-frontal view of her naked body. "Like what you see?" she winked, signing her name to the digital pad. Unfortunately, the man scurried off in a hurry and Natalie closed the door and tore the box open. Three guesses what this is," she said holding up yet another photo album. "There's more." Putting the first album of pictures on the coffee table, she withdrew another and then three DVD's – all depicting her playing with Jenna.

"I'll take those," Beth said. Those pictures will be destroyed before anyone sees them."

"I don't think so," Natalie protested. "They are mine and they will go in my closet with the rest. I'm sorry, but you know I will not budge on this."

"Fine, but please don't show them to anyone. Present company included."

"I'm not showing my parents pictures and videos of me having sex with your sister."

"And we wouldn't ask," Regina said reassuringly.

"There's another commandment in this one," Henry said taking the slip of paper from the back and handing it off to his daughter. "You're not going to like it."

Taking the commandment, Natalie read it aloud. "Sixth Commandment: Thou shalt submit for training. Unless you wish for these and everything else to be posted on the internet and given to everyone in town, you and your girlfriend will submit to training as sex slaves. Training will begin in two weeks at the Domination Farm in Rome, Wisconsin and last until the Dominants there are satisfied you have been broken and reforged. Further instructions forthcoming."

28

"Come on mom," Kim whined as she paced back and forth in the dungeon "I don't want to wait years for her to be trained. I want to fuck her over now!"

"You need to learn some patience, sweetie," Lana sighed. "We've come this far so why risk it all falling apart now?"

"She'll never know we're the ones behind her commandments and descent into the kinky. Just like she had no idea we've been making a killing on her pictures and videos since she did her first glory hole at the toy shop. Come on, I want to give her a good caning before it becomes old hat at the Farm."

"Fine, have a session with her, but we've paid a non-refundable fee for their training so if she figures it out you'll go to the Domination Farm in their stead. Now, do you think it's still worth it?"

"Absolutely. I'll come up with another commandment so she has no idea we're responsible. If you're going to do another session with Jenna you had better do it soon because I'm going to need the dungeon Friday night."

"I haven't been in contact with Jenna since Natalie 'rescued' her."

"Then I guess it's a good thing we've already made a small fortune on her training so far, huh?"

"No matter to me. It's Natalie and her uppity parents that I want to bring down."

"Speaking of which, why aren't we sending them to the Farm with Natalie?"

"You know why. I want them for myself and seeing the looks on their faces when they realize what their daughter has to do is going to be priceless."

"But didn't you say they loved what Beth and all those men did to them? I don't think they really give two shits if their daughter is a fuck slave as long as they get to join in the action from time to time."

"True, which is why I'm coming up with a plan just for them while their precious never-does-wrong bitch of a daughter is off being trained. Feel free to use the dungeon all week."

"Thanks, mom."

∞ ∞ ∞

"You got a letter in the mail today," Regina said handing Natalie the sealed envelope with her name typed across the front. With no stamp or addresses, there was no way to know where it came from and she immediately knew it came from her blackmailer.

"Probably the instructions the son of a bitch promised to send," Natalie said tearing the envelope open. Tossing it onto the coffee table, she opened the folded piece of paper and read.

Commandment Seven: Thou Shalt Confess Your Sins.

Before you make your trip to the Domination Farm where you will be trained as a sex slave, you will confess your sins to your best friend and beg her to discipline you for being such a naughty woman. You know what happens if you fail to comply.

"Oh fucking hell!" Natalie gasped.

"What is it now?"

"It's not the instructions we were waiting for. It's another damn commandment telling me to confess everything to my best friend and beg her to punish me."

"Kim?"

"It doesn't give any names, but I can only assume so since she's been my best friend since we were little."

"What are you going to do?"

"The only thing I can. I'm going to…hold that thought," she said as her phone began to ring. "Speak of the devil. Hey Kim, what's up?"

"What in the hell is going on!?" Kim asked, her voice panicked. "I got a letter in the mail and it says some really weird shit!"

"Calm down. What does it say?"

"It says I am to expect you on Friday and do everything you ask of me without hesitation or complaint or my life would be ruined! What in the hell is going on Natalie? What is this dungeon I'm supposed to take you to?"

"Dungeon? My letter didn't say anything about a dungeon."

"You got one as well?"

"Yeah, I just finished reading it when you called."

"Well, what in the hell is it? What's going on?"

"What is the exact wording of your letter?"

"It says: Your best friend will confess her sins to you and beg you for punishment. You will do as she asks without hesitation or complaint or your life will be ruined. We have pictures and videos of you performing acts of an incredibly kinky nature and will release it all to the internet and everyone in town if you do not comply. You will take her to the dungeon and teach her a lesson she will never forget."

"Is that all it says?"

"It gives an address for the dungeon but says I am not to tell you or everything will be released."

"I see. And have you participated in incredibly kinky sex? Did they send proof of their claims?"

"Yes. They sent a few pictures and a twenty minute video of me, well, it doesn't matter what I was doing, but it is something that would certainly ruin my life if it ever got out. What in the hell have you gotten me into? What are we going to do? I can't punish you! For fuck's sake Natalie we're best friends!"

"I know, I know, but we don't have much choice in the matter. Look, I'm sorry you've gotten involved in this, I really am, but we have to do what the letters say or else."

"Wait, so, this isn't the first letter you've gotten like this?"

"Not even close. I've been dealing with this asshole for months now and his commandments just keep getting worse and worse. But suffice it to say, they're nearly at an end."

"How can you be so sure? Did you go to the police?"

"No, but a previous commandment mentioned being trained as a sex slave at some place called the Domination Farm so I can only assume that'll be the end of it. Unless he's going to pick up the blackmailing in a few years once I'm trained."

"JESUS CHRIST! You can't seriously be telling me you're going to do it! Are you?"

"I have no choice, Kim. This has gotten way out of hand. He's involved a lot of other people that I care about and I can't see another one dragged down with me. So, when do you want to do this?"

"Um, no offense, but never. I don't want to punish you. Whatever the hell that even means and I certainly don't want to go to some dungeon."

"I don't see as how we have any choice in the matter."

"Well, you may be a coward, but I'm not and I'll be damned if I'll let someone walk all over me like a fucking rug. I'm going to the police."

"NO! You can't do that. This isn't just about you, Kim. He's blackmailing my parents, my girlfriend and even her sister! He's got shit on all of us that will ruin any chance of a normal life. Please, just do as the letter commands and punish me at this dungeon and that'll be the end of it. I'll be going away for a while and everyone can get on their lives without any further interference from me."

"How do you know? I mean, what's stopping him from further blackmailing one of us while you're off being trained?"

"I honestly don't know. I'm sorry Kim, I really am. I've done my best to keep this from you, but I guess he knows everyone I know by now."

"Is this why you've been avoiding me for the past few weeks?"

"Yes. Look, I want to get this done and over with as soon as possible. Are you free tonight?"

"I am, but I still don't think I can go through with it."

"Please at least try. I'll drop by your place in a few hours." Hanging up the phone, Natalie sniffed back the tears.

"Well, that was an intense conversation. What's going on?"

"He sent Kim a letter telling her what to expect with instructions on taking me to a dungeon for my punishment. He's got something incriminating on her as well."

"Oh god! Not her as well!"

"Afraid so. I just hope it all ends when I go in for training."

"I still think it's a huge mistake for you to go to that place."

"We've talked about this, mom. I have no choice."

∞ ∞ ∞

"Ah hahahahaha!" Kim doubled over laughing. "What a stupid bitch!"

"So?"

"She believed every word of it. Come on, someone give me my fucking Oscar because that was the best damn performance in a decade!"

"Don't get too cocky. All it'll take is one fuck up and this whole ruse comes undone."

"She'll be here in a few hours and then we'll be headed to the dungeon."

"I'll make myself scarce and remember to play your part and nothing more. I know how much you want to knock her down a few pegs, but you're going to have to leave that to the Masters and Mistresses at the Domination Farm."

"And Mistress Gwen knows not to let them get collared by anyone else?"

"She assures me that she will collar them so no one else can and then once their training is complete we can pick them up and take over ownership."

"I wonder which one of her friends she'll choose to take with her. Or which one will volunteer. God, I want to dominate her so fucking bad it hurts almost as much as I want to hurt her."

"Nothing permanent. You don't want to give away your skill with the needle, or the cane for that matter. You need to appear clumsy with it tonight."

"I know my part dammit!" Kim shouted. "And I don't need you reminding me or I'll show you just how fucking skilled I am! Now take off before she gets here. I need to concentrate to get myself into character."

"Watch that tone with me, young lady or I'll end this game here and now and you'll have nothing."

"Go ahead. If you do anything to interfere with me teaching that bitch her place I'll just have to release everything I've got on you."

"And I release everything I've got on you."

"Too late. I'm in this to win, mom. I've been posting my stuff to another site for the last three months."

"YOU DID WHAT!?"

"You heard me. You have nothing on me a million people haven't already seen. Now get lost or they'll see just what a fucked up whore you are as well."

29

"I said I have nothing to say to you!" Jenna said through the closed bedroom door. "Now please just go away and leave me alone."

"You've been avoiding me for the last week dammit!" Beth growled in aggravation. "Come on, will you please talk to me. I know what you've been through and want to help."

"Help? HELP!? How exactly are you going to help me, sis? I've been branded, pierced, my pussy and asshole stretched open so far I can park a tank in them and still have room for a car! That sadistic bitch trained me to be her pussy-licking slave and beat me half unconscious every time I refused a command. Can you make it all go away? Can you make me forget it ever happened?"

"You know I can't, but I can at least be here for you. You're not the only one that's been through hell, you know? Natalie did not mean to do those things to you and all we want to do is help you get through this as best we can."

"I know she didn't mean to do it. She didn't even know it was me in there. But that's beside the point. Mistress did these things to me and she wants to do more. She's been calling me and I've been ignoring her, but if I don't talk to her soon I know she'll release everything and my life will be over. Can you make her stop?"

"I don't even know who she is. Natalie and I have been blackmailed by a man, not a woman. What is her name?"

"I'm not allowed to tell. The house is wired and if anyone finds out everything gets released and all of our lives are ruined. So, I either ruin us all, or willingly let her train me as a sex slave. What would you do?"

"I honestly don't know. But if it's any consolation, Natalie and I are going to some farm to be trained as such to make all of this go away."

"You're doing what!?" Jenna exclaimed, her door opening so hard and fast it nearly came off the hinges as it slammed into the wall. "What in the fucking hell do you mean you're going to be trained as a sex slave?"

"I mean just that. Natalie got a final commandment telling me, her and one of her friends to go to some place in Wisconsin called the Domination Farm where we will be trained as sex slaves. I don't want to do it, but if it keeps you and everyone else safe then it's worth the humiliation and degradation."

"You're as gullible as Natalie if you think this is over. With the two of you out of the way Mistress will come after me again. And her parents. OUR PARENTS Beth! Is that what you want? Do you want everyone you love and care about turned into Mistress's sex slaves?"

"Of course not. We have his, her, whomever the hell is doing this, we have their word this is the end of it."

"And you believe that? No, mark my fucking words sis. This is not over by a long shot. I might as well call Mistress back and tell her to go ahead and train me and get it over with!"

"You'll do no such thing! If you would just tell us who she is maybe we can end it once and for all before Natalie and I have to leave."

"I CAN"T! She'll take mom and dad and do ten times worse to them as you did to Natalie's parents. I will not put them in the middle of this Beth. I would rather die than to see them come to harm."

"Fine, but please promise me you won't go back to her."

"If I don't she'll release everything. Her last text said if I wasn't at the dungeon on Saturday night then she's putting everything on the internet and sending copies out to family and friends."

"I can't stop you from going Jenna, so please be careful. I'm trying to make this all go away and all I can do is follow the commandment and go to the Farm for training."

"You do what you must and so will I, but I know deep down that this is a battle that none of us are ever going to win."

"We'll figure it out. Now, is there anything I can do to help? Anything you want to talk about?"

Giving her big sister a long, silent look, Jenna walked back into her bedroom and plopped down on the edge of the bed. "I'm eighteen years old, Beth," she exhaled. "I've been gang banged, fisted, made to drink piss and bred like a god damn animal by thirty fucking black men! I'm pregnant!

I have a baby growing in me and I fear I'll resent it, but I can't give it up. What in the hell am I supposed to do?"

"Did Natalie ever tell you how she became pregnant?"

"No."

"Did she ever tell you how she lost her virginity?"

"No."

"Well, she lost it much like you. She was thrust into this chaos by a man named Glen and when she went to a sex shop to return a photo album she engaged in her first glory hole gang bang. This was only a few months ago when she was still nineteen. She didn't want to do it, but they gave her little choice. And then the commandments started coming and it escalated into constant gang bangs and other kinky sex. I fisted her. My hand was the first to ever penetrate her pussy and ass and even after everything we did to her she still came back for more. She asked me to be her girlfriend and I love her for it."

"So, what, I should go back and love my Mistress?"

"No. All I'm saying is that if anyone understands what you're going through its Natalie. Talk to her, let her help."

"How? What can she do, Beth? So what that she was gang banged and knocked up. So what they we've been through the same shit. I'll ask again: Can she make it all go away? Can she make me forget it ever happened so I can get back to a normal life and put this nightmare behind me?"

"Probably not, but it helps to share your experiences with someone that can honestly understand them. Sure, I've been used along the way, but the two of you have been through so much more and she's willing to go even further to ensure everyone we love and care about remains safe. You can talk to me as well. And her parents. We are all here to help you however we can if you'll just let us."

"I just don't know how you can help me, sis. Talking about it does no good. Writing it down does no good. I have nightmares that she takes me again and again. I wake up in cold sweats after dreaming of armies of men gang banging and breeding me – my holes stretched open beyond even what they are now. I'm not eating right. I'm not sleeping. My schoolwork is slipping and I don't even care if I fail anymore. What's the point when I'll be a sex slave in the end?"

"Then do what Natalie did. Embrace it. Own it. Don't let her get the better of you anymore. Next time she mentions gang banging you don't cringe and balk. Smile and beg for more. Swallow the piss, drink the semen and learn to orgasm from the cane tearing into your flesh. I'm convinced that's how Natalie's been able to remain so strong throughout months of such treatment. Come to Raven's Hollow and talk to Lady Raven about a job. I'll put a good word for you and you can embrace your inner kink to the fullest whenever you want. Have you told mom and dad that you're pregnant?"

"Not yet. How can I tell them I'm with child when I've never even had a boyfriend?"

"Same as Natalie. I swear the two of you could be twins. She didn't have a boyfriend when this all happened either. But back to mom and dad. You need to tell them sooner than later. Tell them you hooked up with someone at a party and it happened. They'll be pissed, but they'll forgive your mistake and when talk of building a nursery comes up they'll forget and shower you with all the love you need. I think you should tell them tonight and I'll be there right by your side throughout the entire ordeal. Okay?"

"If you really think that's the best thing to do, fine."

"I think it is. And please talk to Natalie about it. I know you don't think it'll help, but it will."

"Alright." Suddenly overcome with emotions, Jenna jumped off of the bed and wrapped her arms around her sister's neck and cried into her shoulder. And when she felt Beth's arms pull her tight, she completely lost it.

30

"Hey Nat, come on in. Don't worry, mom is gone for the night. So, what in the hell is going on? What sins are you supposed to confess to me? How am I supposed to punish you? Um, you need a hand with that?" Kim asked, looking at the large cardboard box in her best friend's hands.

"Nah, that's okay. And all of my sins are in this box. I figured I'd bring proof of my claims so there's no doubt I've confessed everything. Are you sure we're alone?"

"Yeah. Mom is out all night with friends so we have the place all to ourselves. Want anything to drink?"

"Nothing for me. I just want to get this over with and move on. I just hope it doesn't interfere with our friendship."

"Why would it? Unless you're going to tell me you killed someone."

"What? No! But it is some pretty fucked up shit I've been doing the last few months and I'm here to confess every single one of them to you."

"Um, okay. So, what are you confessing?"

"All of my sexual exploits."

"Sexual exploits? When have you taken your nose out of a book long enough to have sex? And for that matter when did you get a boyfriend?"

"I have a girlfriend actually, and I've had more sex in the last few months than a hundred women do in a lifetime."

"Whoa, whoa, whoa! Slow down there a minute. What do you mean you have a girlfriend? When did you start having sex?"

"It all started when some fucked up guy ran into me at the park. He shoved a package in my arms and begged me to keep it. Anyways, to make an incredibly long story short, the package contained a photo album of some woman getting gang banged by a group of men. In the back were instructions on where and when to return it and when I did it turned out to be the XTC Toy shop. I went to the men's room to put it in the middle stall and the next thing I knew there were dicks sticking through the walls."

"HOLY SHIT! Tell me you didn't."

"I didn't want to, but I thought about the woman in the pictures and one thing led to another and I did it, Kim. I sucked them off and let them fuck me."

"Oh my god! H-How many?"

"More than two dozen."

"JESUS CHRIST NAT!"

"Oh, it gets better. After that I went to Ravens Hollow where I was gang banged, fucked and fisted by all of the women there. I did some more gang bangs, public sex and a million other things as commanded by my blackmailer. After each commandment I received another photo album and DVD and another commandment to complete if I didn't want everything released to the internet and everyone I know."

"Whoa! What are you doing?"

"Taking my clothes off so you can see the piercings I got," Natalie said pulling her shirt off. "I was commanded to take my girlfriend Beth out peeping and we were looking in on a woman getting tortured in a garage when we were caught. Beth had to pierce me and I had to pierce her."

"My god! You're not kidding are you?" Reaching out, Kim hooked a finger on the ring through Natalie's right nipple and gave it a gentle tug. "They're really real. You actually got your nipples pierced. WOW!"

"My hood as well. You can play with them if you want."

"Um, you know I'm not into women," Kim lied, keeping her best kept secret to herself.

"Neither was I until commanded to do so. Now, I can't get enough pussy."

"And you can really take a fist?"

"In both holes at the same time. Go ahead," Natalie said spreading her legs open. "Just ball your hand up and shove it in. No need to be gentle as I actually love it rough."

"I'M NOT FISTING MY BEST FRIEND!"

"Go ahead. I have to confess my sins and how will you know if I'm telling the truth unless you test it out for yourself? Go on, fuck your fist in and out of my pussy a few times and then shove it up my ass. I can take it."

"I believe you."

"Please fist me, Kim. I don't know how, but the blackmailer always seems to know if I do the commandments or not and I don't want to risk everything getting leaked to the internet and the rest of my family and friends, so please shove your fists in me so you know I'm telling the truth."

"Um…"

"Please. I know you're not into women, but I need you to do this for me."

God, you're such a fucking idiot, Kim thought as she nervously chewed on her lip. "Okay, but only for a minute. I don't like this, Nat." Taking a deep breath, Kim dropped onto her knees and stared at her friend's already moist pussy. "So, you really want me to just ram it in there?"

"Yep. Trust me, I've been fisted more times than I can count and I can easily take it in both holes. Go ahead, make a fist and shove it in."

Forcing her hand to tremble, Kim balled her fingers tight, placed them against Natalie's pussy and then pushed hard. "Oh my god!" she gasped when it slid right in. Pulling out, she rammed it in again. Out. In. Out. In. Harder. Deeper. Her knuckles pressing against her friend's cervix.

"Don't go any deeper," Natalie moaned, bracing her hand on the back of the chair to support her weakening knees. "I'm pregnant."

"You are?"

"Mmm hmm. About two months now and I have no idea who the father is as it happened at one of the gang bangs."

""What in the hell has happened to you?" Kim asked, pulling out of Natalie's pussy and pushing into her ass, her other hand replacing the first.

"I learned how great sex was."

"So, you lost your virginity to a bunch of men in a bathroom?"

"Actually, I took it myself on a huge dildo my mom bought me."

"HOLY SHIT! You're mom actually bought you a dildo?"

"Three of them. I was horny looking at the pictures of that woman and I grabbed one. It happened to be the largest of the three, a big black one nearly three inches thick. It took forever, but I finally managed to work it in and I was hooked. After you fist me I'll continue confessing my sins to you and then we can go to this dungeon so that you can punish me."

"But I don't want to punish you, Nat. I don't even want to fist you," Kim said pulling her hands free. "This is some seriously fucked up shit!"

"I know, but I don't have a choice. And if the blackmailer has something on you then you don't have a choice either."

"Then beg for it."

"What?"

"Beg for it. You said the letter told you to beg me to punish you so beg for it. I don't like this Nat. You're pretty and all, but I'm not into women. I don't want to fist you, or fuck you, or do anything else sexual with you. I just want this all to go away."

"No more than I do. And it will soon enough. I'm just waiting for instructions and then I'll be heading off to be trained as a sex slave with my girlfriend Beth. Speaking of gang bangs, under normal circumstances I'd never divulge their secret, but for one of the commandments I did a gang bang with Jane Filmore, Maria Kimball, Susan Galloway, Roger Blakely, Mike Suffield, James Creedy, Tyler Beck, and Shane Gosselin."

"HOLY FUCK! Are you serious?"

"Yes and I have the photos and videos to prove it."

"I can't believe they would participate in a gang bang!"

"You and I both, but I told them everything and they agreed to do it to keep me and my family from being ruined."

"Is there anything you haven't done?"

"Not much. Oh, and I can take two fists at the same time in either hole."

"You mean like both of my hands up your ass or in your pussy at the same time?"

"Yep. Go ahead and do it. Like I said, I've been stretched so far open I can easily handle it."

"I can't believe you're the same Natalie I've known for twelve years!"

"I know, but it's me."

"You seem like you're actually enjoying what this blackmailer is making you do."

"Some of it. I don't like that he's involved my parents, but they're taking it better than I thought. They're swingers, you know?"

"Your parents? Dear lord, Nat! Do I even want to know?"

"Probably not, but I have to confess it to you anyways. While I was at Ravens Hollow for a job interview, Beth had sex with my parents. She was commanded to gang bang them and then to pierce and tattoo them."

"HOLY SHIT! And they let her?"

"Reluctantly."

"What did they get pierced? What tattoo and where?"

"They both got their nipples pierced and mom got slave wife tattooed on her mound while dad got slave husband tattooed above his dick."

"WOW! I don't even know what to say, Nat. Why didn't you go to the police? Why would you let someone do this to you and your parents?"

"Because I can't have everything leaked to the world. I don't want our lives to be ruined."

"How do you know it isn't already out there? How do you know he'll stop once you go to…where was it again?"

"The Domination Farm. And I don't know. All I can do is hope for the best. I mean, what else could he ask for after that?"

"I have no idea. So, do you like what you're doing?"

"For the most part yeah. Honestly, I really love getting gang banged, fisted and drinking piss."

"Ach! You're kidding right?"

"Nope. Kneeling between Kim's legs, Natalie pushed her skirt up over her hips and tugged her thong down. "If you've got to go you may use me as your personal urinal. Go ahead, piss

in my mouth and I swear I won't spill a drop of it."
Placing her mouth over her friend's pussy, she
extended her tongue and licked, flicking the tip
over Kim's clit as she playfully nibbled her inner
labia.

"W-What are you doing?" Kim gasped,
taking a huge step back. "You licked me!"

"Sorry. But to prove I love having sex with
women I had to do it. Now please piss down my
throat Kim. I know you don't want to do it, but I
need to prove to you that I'm not lying."

"I believe you, Nat!"

"That's not good enough dammit! Too
many lives are on the line to half-ass it now. Piss
down my fucking throat!" Grabbing her friend by
her naked ass, she placed her mouth back over
Kim's pussy and licked again. "I'm going to lick
until you either orgasm or piss down my fucking
throat so you choose."

"I don't have to pee!"

"Then orgasm it is."

Giving her friend the chance to lick for
about two minutes, Kim grabbed Natalie by the
ears and began pissing. "Oh my fucking god you're
doing it! You're drinking my damn pee! How can
you gulp it down like that?"

"Lots and lots of practice," Natalie replied
when the stream had finally stopped. "Now punish
me, Kim. Take me to the dungeon and discipline
my sinful ass! Cane me. Spank me! Whip me until
I've learned my lesson. Please, please punish me
Kim! I've been such a perverted whore I deserve

every swat of the paddle and sting of the flogger. Mark up my skin with bruises and welts!"

"Alright. Come on, let's get this done and over with," Kim sighed. "Um, I've been instructed to put a hood and gag on you so that you can't see where we're going," Kim said going to the desk on the far side of the living room. Opening the bottom right drawer, she removed a bag and withdrew a latex hood and ball gag from it. "These came with the letter. I wasn't allowed to tell you until we left for the dungeon," she lied.

"Fine, but it's going to look awful suspicious driving down the road with me wearing a ball gag and hood."

"We'll take my mom's SUV and you can duck down in the back."

31

Kim drove around town for about fifteen minutes before even starting the nearly hour long journey to the dungeon. Once she hit the dirt road leading up to it, she put the SUV in four wheel drive and made sure to hit every bump – looking in her rearview mirror and grinned every time Natalie bounced around like an unsteady puppy. Another two miles and she turned off onto another dirt road, drove half a mile and parked in front of a lone building surrounded by forest.

"We're here, but don't take anything off yet. My instructions were to take you in hooded and gagged."

Getting out of the vehicle, Kim walked around back and opened the tailgate and hatch. Helping her best friend out, she closed and locked everything before taking Natalie by the arm and leading her into the single room structure. "Wait here." Walking to the middle, she bent down and opened a trapdoor revealing a set of stairs. "Okay, we've got some steps to go down so be careful.

At the bottom of the stairs stretched a long hallway ending in a steel door and beyond that was a shorter hallway with an old elevator leading deeper into the earth. Out of the elevator, they walked a short distance and entered the dungeon.

"We're here. And HOLY SHIT!" Kim said. "You can take the gag out and remove the hood."

"WHOA!" Natalie exclaimed as she looked around the massive, well-equipped room. "Um, why are all of those men here?"

"I don't know. The letter didn't mention anyone else being here."

"Um, are you here to fuck me?" Natalie shouted at the thirty or so black men at the back of the room.

"No, we're here to gang bang both of you."

"YOU'RE WHAT!" Kim gasped.

"You heard me, cunt! After you punish that worthless whore we're going to fuck a baby in both of you."

"Too late," Natalie smirked. I was knocked up at another gang bang, but by all means fuck as much of that seed into us as you want!"

"Speak for yourself! I am not getting gang banged!"

"You will, or you'll be chained and punished ten times worse than what you're giving your perverted friend. Speaking of which, you are to give her three hundred swats with the cane, flogger, paddle and belt to her entire body below the neck. To make myself perfectly clear, you will strike her back, ass, belly, breasts, pussy, sides, arms and legs a total of three hundred times. When that is done you will strip out of your clothes, crawl over and beg us to gang bang you."

"You're out of your mother fucking minds if you think I'm letting you get anywhere near me!"

You're going to get fucked so you might as well accept it. Remember, ten times her punishment. Do you think you'll survive three thousand swats?"

"Come in me all you want, you'll never knock me up because I'm on the pill."

"Were. We've been at this a long time, whore. We replaced your birth control with placebos. You will be fucked and you will be knocked up like the whore that you are. Now place the handcuffs around her wrists and then secure her ankles to the ones in the floor."

Her mind racing a million miles an hour wondering what game her mother was playing, Kim did as she was told. "Take your fucking clothes off so we can get this done." When Natalie was naked, Kim cuffed her in place and then went to a pegboard and picked up a cane. "I'm so sorry for this, Nat," she lied.

"It's okay. You have no choice and I accept the punishment in full. Don't hold back for even a single swat or they might make you start over from the beginning."

"After each swat you will count it and say thank you Mistress for teaching me this lesson," said the apparent leader of the gang. "If you fail to do either it will start over from the beginning until you get it right three hundred times. As for you, Kim, I think you should go ahead and strip naked now. I want to see what we're getting our dicks into."

"You can all rot in hell!"

"And we probably will, but that's not going to stop us from fucking your brains out. Now strip naked and get on your hands and knees."

"WHAT! WHY?"

"Because I command it. Now do as you are told."

Seething, glaring at the group of smirking men with the flames of hell burning in her eyes, Kim took her clothes off and dropped down onto her hands and knees. Watching the man walk over to a shelf, she gasped when he picked up a large butt plug with what looked like a fox tail coming out of the flanged base, and a bottle of lube and approached her. "W-What are you going to d-do with that?"

"I'm going to push it up that sexy ass of yours."

"LIKE HELL! I've never taken anything that big!"

"First time for everything. Now shut your fucking mouth or I'll stretch you so far open you'll be able to take half a dozen fists up there at the same time!" Plucking a leather belt from a hook on the wall, he brought his arm back and with a skillful flick of his wrist slapped it across Kim's naked back.

"Aahhgghhh! What the fucking fuck! I'm doing as you command why are you hitting me?"

"Because I can and want to. Now shut the fuck up and get back into position. And since you forgot to count and thank me that one doesn't count."

"H-How m-man times are you going to hit me?"

"If you do as you're told only twenty times. Now get back in position or it'll be a hundred."

Moving faster than a cat on a hot tin roof, Kim was back on her hands and knees and biting her lip. The belt struck her back again and she yelped in pain.

"ONE! T-Thank you M-Master for teaching me this lesson!"

WHACK! This one landed on her ass and she counted and gave thanks. The next bit into the backs of her legs. It was followed by strikes to her back, ass, and legs. The man then grabbed a handful of hair and yanked her onto the heels of her feet so that he could swat her belly, breasts and pussy.

"Very good, slave," the man said placing the lubed tip of the plug against Kim's red and welt-covered ass. With a powerful push, he grinned as it vanished – stretching her open more than three inches.

Kim yelped and leapt forward like a lion pouncing on a gazelle. Rolling onto her back, she flailed about, reaching down she grabbed the tail and was about to yank it free until she heard the man tell her that if she removed it before Natalie's punishment was complete then she would take an even bigger one as well as two hundred more swats. Reluctantly, she let go and rolled onto her hands and knees to get to her feet.

"You may punish her now. And bear in mind what she said. Do not hold back for even a single swat. If I suspect you're going easy on her you'll get ten times the punishment. And you can be damn certain I would go lightly on you."

Thinking of the ways she could get back at her mother for this injustice, Kim picked up a can and approached Natalie. Without word, she brought it down on her friend's ass.

"One. Thank you Mistress for teaching me this lesson," Natalie said through clenched teeth. Having learned at Raven's Hollow how to properly take a punishment. And the swats continued one after another with Natalie counting and giving thanks until all three hundred had been administered and she was barely conscious.

"While your whore of a friend recovers from her punishment you will crawl over here and let us gang bang you," the black man said to Kim.

When Kim was in front of the man, she looked up at him and scowled. "Why are you doing this to me? The letter I got said nothing about getting fucked over."

"We're doing it because we can," the man replied. "Now be a good little slut and suck my cock or the needles come next. Men go ahead and take the slut but remember to only shoot in her pussy."

"Well, with that sexy ass plugged I guess we'll have to double penetrate that tight cunt of hers," one of the men said as he stepped forward, grabbing Kim around the waist and twisting her on top of him. No sooner had his big black cock slammed into her then another worked its way in and she screeched in pain. "Don't worry," the man said thrusting his hips upwards "you'll loosen up soon enough.

Slipping in and out of consciousness, Natalie waited and wondered when the men were going to release and gang bang her, but it never happened as they seemed content with fucking their seed in Kim alone.

∞ ∞ ∞

"What in the fuck!" Kim growled at her mother. "I mean, what. In. The. Actual. Fuck! Do you know what those men did to me in there?"

"If they did their job I do."

"What in the hell were you thinking? I swear to god if they knocked me up I'll fucking kill you! You had no right to do this to me. NONE!"

"Sure I did. I had to make sure there was no way in hell Natalie was going to figure out we're responsible for all of this. Seeing you reacting naturally to being whipped, gang banged and bred like the little bitch that you are was the best route to take so shut your mouth or I'll pay for you to join her and Beth at the Farm."

"You wouldn't!"

"Do I look like I'm kidding?"

"No."

"Then be quiet and trust that I have our best interest at heart. After that show there's no way in hell she'll ever consider you a candidate for blackmailer. Hell, she and her girlfriend still think it's a man behind it all."

"Actually, Jenna told her sister it was a woman."

"Did she give her my name?"

"No. Even after Beth insisted, Jenna refused for fear you would release what you have on her. And I'm pretty certain she's going to be calling for more training before the Saturday deadline."

"I'll use her for now, but what good is a used up whore like her?"

"Send her to the farm."

"Not a bad idea, but I think using her here away from her sister would have a much larger impact."

"What about her parents?"

"Oh, I fully intend to use them as well. All in due time, sweetie. We'll break them one at a time until they're nothing more than obedient sex slaves performing every perverse sexual act commanded of them by whomever wants to pay for their usage. We'll make as much as possible before tossing them aside to make room for someone else. I know you've had your eyes on Susan. How would you like to make her your slave?"

"I'd love that, but I don't want to get rid of Natalie. I want to use her until the day she dies so she knows who broke her, reduced her to something lower than dirt.

32

Natalie lay on her bed looking at the invitation to the Domination Farm located in the small town of Rome, Wisconsin. Moving her fingers slowly along the raised letters, tracing every bump and groove, all she could think about were the final days of freedom before the training began and the nightmare of being threatened with blackmail ended. Opening the small folded card, she read what was written within for the thousandth time since receiving it in the mail two days ago.

You are to present this invitation to Mistress Gwen upon arrival at the Domination Farm where you, Beth and one lucky friend will be trained as the lowest, kinkiest and most obedient sex slaves in the history of sexual slavery. Failure to do so will result in all of the pictures of you and your family and friends being released over the internet, at college and to those friends and family still in the dark about your already remarkable transformation.

When your training is complete, two of you will be sold at auction while the third returns home to serve as my slave for the rest of their life. And while you are off being trained at the Domination Farm, know that all of your parents will be trained here at home. That's right, your parents, Beth's Parents and the parents of whomever you decide to take along for the ride will be trained as sex slaves. And to make things even more interesting, two sets

*of parents will be auctioned off to the highest
bidder with the third remaining as my loyal and
obedient servants.*

*I must say I'm very surprised at your
determination to keep your family's name from
being smeared in the mud. That being said, you
should not travel alone. Here are your orders,
enclosed with this letter are nine invitations to the
Domination Farm in nowheresville Rome,
Wisconsin. There is one for you, one for Beth, and
one for each of the friends you so love to gang
bang; one of which must go along with you for
training.*

*If none of your gang bang friends go,
everything gets released. Not only to your family
and friends, but to all of theirs as well. Complete
your training and become a sex slave and your
ordeal is over. Enjoy your training and I'll see you
in a few years. Or maybe not. Either way, I've
gotten what I wanted so I really don't care if
you're the one I get back or not.*

Natalie's eyes welled with tears and she
shook so terribly it looked as if she was having
convulsions. Slamming the card on the nightstand,
she rolled out of bed and paced the floor – her mind
going over the myriad sexual acts she's performed
over the past few months and how she went from
shy, innocent nineteen year old Natalie Holt who
had a bright future ahead of her, to twenty year old
slut with a life of sexual slavery and servitude to
look forward to.

She recalled with vivid detail and clarity of mind that first night she opened the present from her mother and her initial reactions to seeing the three dildos before looking at pictures of Fiona Delmarco, getting turned on and taking her own virginity on a monster black sex toy. She remembered the scared young woman who had entered a sex shop for the first time, and the feel of a cock in her hand while locked in the stall of the men's room where she gave in to curiosity and allowed herself to be gang banged and eventually knocked up.

A tingle of excitement involuntarily going up her spine, Natalie recalled the night she went to Raven's Hollow where she allowed nearly forty women to use her as their plaything and how she felt the first time Beth's hands so expertly worked their way into her pussy and asshole, and how, while walking home through the woods, she met up with Beth and asked her to be her girlfriend. And then her thoughts turned dark, her mood souring even more as she thought about what she had done to Beth's younger sister Jenna.

"I did what I was told because I had no choice," she said, her voice barely a whisper. "Our lives would have been ruined." Walking over to the nightstand, she picked up the invitation and stared at it for several long seconds. "And that's why I have to do this." Letting out a soft sigh, she dropped the invitation back into the large envelope alongside others, slipped into a pair of shorts and a tank top and then went downstairs to wait for her girlfriend and friends to show up.

"Everything okay?" her mother asked. "It looks like you've been crying again."

"That's because I have," Natalie shot back.

"The Domination Farm again?"

"What else? It's one thing to demand that I go, Beth even, but one of my friends as well? And what he plans on doing to you and dad and the other parents is unthinkable."

"What about your father and me? You never mentioned anything about us. Oh god, tell me he isn't sending us to be trained as sex slaves as well!"

"No, you'll be trained here at home," Natalie said, her shoulders slumping in defeat."

"WHAT!? What in the hell are you talking about?"

"I'm sorry mom, I should have told you sooner, but there was more to the letter than what I read to you before. While the three of us are away being trained, he plans on training you, dad, Beth's parents and the parents of whomever is going with us. And when the training is complete, two of us, and two sets of parents will be auctioned off to the highest bidder and only one of us and one set of parents will remain to serve as his slaves for life."

"Oh, hell no! There's no way your father and I are going to even entertain that bullshit, Natalie! You can go off and be a sex slave all you want, but demanding us to do the same is stepping way over the fucking line! We're going to the police whether you want to or not!"

"And then this was all for nothing. Our lives are ruined and we'll be pariahs no matter where we go. We'll have nothing. No family, no friends, no home to call our own. We'll have to move every few months once someone recognizes who we are and the horrible things we've done."

"It's no worse than some porn stars do and you don't see them crying about it do you?" her mother asked.

"Are you saying you want to become a porn star?"

"No, that's not what I'm saying at all. I'm just saying that there are plenty of people out there doing the same shit we're doing and they're not making as big a deal out of it as you are. So what that people find out the truth? We move on, and deal with it. I know you love being a kinky little slut, and to some degree so do I, but we have to draw the line somewhere or this will never end. Who's to say he doesn't do this to all of your friends? What's stopping him from targeting other members of our family and doing the same to them?"

"Nothing, mom. Absolutely nothing. But we don't even know who this man is so how are the police even going to find him? The name Beth and I were given was fake, and we don't even have a reliable address. Hell, even the albums he's been sending have come from different cities so how are the police going to track him down?"

"I don't know, but we cannot keep doing this, Natalie. Your father and I have indulged this nonsense long enough. We let your girlfriend gang bang us. Pierce and tattoo us. We allowed you to make the decisions in this matter, but I cannot…will not be trained as a sex slave and sold like a piece of furniture. And I'm pretty certain your father will have the same reaction, if not the other parents."

"Let me at least talk to my friends about this. If none of them are willing to go through with it then I will concede and go to the police with everything. But if one of them does volunteer then the three of us will go and you and dad can do whatever you think is best once we are gone. Deal?"

"For now," her mother sighed "but I don't like this one bit. Does it say in the letter how he plans on getting us to cooperate with his demands once you are off being trained?"

"No, but I assume he'll use the same tactics he's been using and threaten to release everything he's got on us."

"And at this point I honestly don't care anymore. I'm tired, Natalie. I'm not eating or sleeping right anymore and your father and I are constantly at each other's' throats worrying about what is coming next. I still say the best course of action is to end it here and now and go to the police, but I will let you talk to your friends first."

"Thanks mom. For everything. I know there's nothing I can ever do to make things right again, but I really am sorry you and dad got dragged into this."

"I guess I'm partially to blame for buying you those damn dildos in the first place. Had I not done that, none of this would have ever happened."

"I wouldn't be so sure about that. Sure, I may not have popped my own cherry, but I would have still probably returned that first album to the men's room at XTC Toys and from there it would have all worked out the same. The only difference being I took my own virginity instead of losing it to some stranger. Some small part of me feels that no matter what I did that day I would have gone down the road of the submissive and sex slave. I feel it in my bones mom. I know it sounds insane, but I think this is what I was meant to be."

"You're right, it does sound insane, but what's even crazier is that I believe you. And I now believe that had none if this ever happened you'd still have found a way to become a sex slave."

"Probably."

"Then go do what your heart is telling you and leave the rest to your father and me."

"Thank you mom," Natalie said, wrapping her arms around her mother's neck and hugging her tight.

33

"Did you call us here to do another gang bang with you?" asked Mike Suffield, the bulge already growing in his pants.

"Not this time," Natalie replied glumly.

"So what's going on this time then?" asked Tyler. "What sort of shit are you going to involve us in this time? This does have something to do with the blackmailer bullshit, right?"

"It does, and shit it is," Natalie answered. "What I'm about to ask each of you is a debt I can never repay. We don't have a lot of time to beat around the bush so I'll just spit it out right now and let you decide what happens next."

"This isn't going to be good at all is it?" asked Maria. "I thought you looked bad that first day you told us about being blackmailed, but you look absolutely devastated now."

"That was a very bad day, but at least we can all agree we loved gang banging each other," Natalie replied "but this…this is so far worse I've done nothing but cry for days," she added, handing them each an invitation and copy of the letter she had received. "As you will read in the letter one of you must accompany me and Beth to this Domination Farm in Rome, Wisconsin where we will submit ourselves for training as sex slaves."

"Yeah, and which of us are you going to pick?" James Creedy, the bulge in his pants suddenly diminishing.

"I'm not going to choose any of you," Natalie answered. "This is not something I can, or would force any of you to do. Read the letter. If none of you go then everything is released to your families and friends. That includes each and every one of our gang bangs and what we did during them."

"I thought you said there were no cameras," Tyler shouted. "What kind of sick fucking games are you playing here?"

"I swear I didn't know there were cameras. You all searched the house before every gang bang we've done. I've searched this house top to bottom a hundred times and have never found a camera. I don't know how he got it on video, but he did. He's been sending me copies of the video and pictures if you'd like to see it as proof."

"You're not going to pick any of us to go," said Mike "does that mean you intend for this to get released to all of our family and friends?"

"That's the last thing I want! No, I will not choose such a fate for any of you. I will leave it up to you to decide who goes with Beth and me. And I want to make one thing perfectly clear right now. I will have absolutely no hard feeling towards any of you for not wanting to go and I fully understand if you want to wash your hands of me altogether."

"WHAT THE FUCK!" Jane gasped. "He's going to train our parents as sex slaves as well?"

"Only those of the one going with us. I wish there was something I could do to prevent it, but there isn't."

"Count me out," Tyler said standing up. Tossing his invitation to the floor, he walked out the door without another word.

"That goes double for me," said Roger who followed on Tyler's heels.

The rest of them spent the next two hours arguing back and forth who would voluntarily go and the shouting got so loud and threatening Natalie had to step in and break it up twice. Maria left twenty minutes in, James was gone in forty. By the end of the two hours it was down to three candidates; Jane Filmore, Mike Suffield, Susan Galloway and Shane Gosselin.

"I don't think I should be the one to go," Jane said. "I haven't told anyone yet, but I'm pregnant. I'm pretty sure it happened at the first gang bang we all did together but don't worry, I'm not going to chase any of you for child support. But I'm also not going to have a baby in that kind of environment."

"I don't blame you one bit," Natalie said. "I'm pregnant as well, but my parents have agreed to take care of it for my while I am being trained. Well, they did before I told my mother the rest of the letter. I'm not entirely sure what I'm going to do, but I can't think about it right now."

"Then it's down to the three of us, Susan said looking over at Mike and Shane.

"Sorry, I may like it up the ass, but I don't have to be trained as a sex slave to find a man to give it to me every now and then. I'm out."

"Well then," Mike said standing up "it's decided. I guess I'll be going with the two of you to this Domination Farm. When do we leave?"

"We leave Friday," Natalie replied.

"Hold on a minute," Susan said getting up off the couch. "And what if I want to go?"

"Only one of you has to go and Mike volunteered," said Natalie. "Are you seriously telling me you want to go?"

"No…yes…maybe. Look, I know you have a girlfriend and all, but I freaking love you Nat. Always have, probably always will and I will do anything to be with you even if it means being turned into a sex slave."

"As much as I would like to walk away and let you take my place, I'm the logical choice," Mike cut in.

"How so?" asked Natalie.

"I'm the only one of the group without parents to be taken and trained. By me going, I save two people from having to endure the same fate. There's no one else more suited to go than me."

"You will be trained as a sex slave," Susan said. "Is that what you really want?"

"Not even for a second, but if it saves you and your parents from going through it then I'll take one for the team."

"Look at you being all altruistic," Natalie smiled. "Neither of you wants to go and both of you volunteered, so I will leave it to the two of you to make the final decision."

"I will go," Mike said. "And that's the final decision.

"No, I will go," Susan said. "You may not have parents, but mine are complete and total assholes and if there are two people deserving of being trained as sex slaves it's them. I'll go just to teach them a lesson in humility they'll never forget."

"Damn!" Natalie exclaimed. "Remind me to never get on your bad side. Look, I will not ask you both to go. Hell, I don't want to ask either of you to go, but one of you is going so please make up your minds so we can get this over with."

"I'm going," Mike and Susan said at the same time.

"Dammit, Susan, there's no reason for you to put your parents through that kind of humiliation no matter how dickish they may be."

"You have no idea the hell they put me through," Susan said, her radiant glow replaced with a cloud so dark it threatened to extinguish the lights. "You remember that time I broke my arm skiing? That was a lie. My father came home drunk, was about to attack my mother and I stepped in. He twisted my arm so hard it snapped in three places."

"OH MY GOD!" Natalie gasped. "Why didn't you ever say anything?"

"Because when he wasn't drunk off his ass he was very good to us and mom somehow always convinced me it would get better. But it never did and she was every bit as bad as him, only she went about it in more subtle ways. I'll spare you the details, but suffice to say they are both conniving assholes deserving of a whole lot more than training as sex slaves. And if they're the ones to be sold off? Well, honestly, I don't care."

"If they are that bad, report them to the police and send them to prison where they belong," Mike said.

"Where they'll get a bed to sleep in and three meals a day? Fuck that shit. I want to see them suffer as they've made me suffer." Barely holding herself together, Susan tore her shirt off and let it drop onto the floor at her feet. "You see these?" she said turning her back to them and pointing over her right shoulder at a series of nine blisters. "The ashtray was full so where do you think my father put out his cigarettes?"

"Jesus Christ!" Mike exclaimed. "Send the sick fucker to prison!"

"Don't you think I've tried? I've called children's services a hundred times over the years, but they've talked their way out of trouble time and time again. No, this is my one shot at revenge and I'm taking it. I'm going and that's the final fucking decision."

"Well, I'm going as well," Mike said. If not to keep an eye on you, then because…"

"Because what?" Natalie asked.

"Because maybe, deep down, I get really fucking turned on at the thought of being dominated." Pulling down is pants and boxers, he let his hard cock spring free. "Case in point," he said motioning to his throbbing dick.

"The blackmailer only said one of you had to go, but I don't think he'd give a flipping fuck if you both went. Are you absolutely certain this is what you want to do?"

"Yes," Mike and Susan said at the same time. "When do we leave?" Mike added as Susan dropped onto her knees between his legs and took him into her mouth and down her now well-trained throat.

"We leave Friday," Natalie answered, tearing off her clothes and dropping down onto her hands and knees. "Don't suck him off. I want him to blow his load deep inside of me," she said looking back over her shoulder.

34

"What the fuck, Beth!" Jenna screeched. "You have to tell them."

"I'll tell them what's coming when you've told them you're pregnant," her older sister replied. "You can't keep it from them forever."

"Neither can you. And if you don't tell them, then I will."

"And what will you use as proof of your claim? I have all the evidence locked safely away."

"I'll talk to Natalie. She'll help me."

"No, she won't."

"You're going off to be trained as a sex slave. Mom and dad will be taken and trained. Mistress is training me and I'm knocked up with a black man's baby. What in the hell has happened to us, Beth? Look at me," Jenna said rubbing her belly not yet bulging with child. "I've been pierced and branded and turned into a damn breeding cow. How can I tell mom and dad that?"

"You don't have to tell them the truth. Like I've said a million times already, tell them you hooked up with someone at a party, had sex and are now pregnant. If they ask who it is, tell them you were drinking and you don't know."

"I've been nothing but the perfect good girl my entire life, they're not going to believe that for a second."

"And it's precisely because you've been such the prodigal child that you finally went off the deep end and ended up getting knocked up for your troubles."

"You know I can't lie to them. They'll see through it in a second."

"So, you'd rather tell them the truth?"

"I'd rather tell them nothing at all."

"And when your belly begins to swell?"

"I don't know."

"Look, I can't force you to tell them, but if I were you, I'd do it sooner rather than later. As neither of us knows how long we have with them before they are taken away for training, or how they will be changed because of it."

"We also don't know if we'll ever see them again. What if they're one of the couples sold?"

"All the more reason to let them know now."

"I'll tell them right after you do. And I mean all of it. Raven's Hollow, the Domination Farm, what's about to happen to them. Confess every dirty little detail and I'll tell them what has happened to me."

"I've been thinking about this day ever since Natalie got the letter and invitations and I think I found a way to tell mom and dad without them blowing up in our faces, but you have to play along with everything I say."

"Um, okay, and what is this plan of yours?"

"I'm going to show them a trick I've learned. As in a magic trick. And you are my magician's assistant. Just do as I say and I can guarantee they won't be able to say a word or storm out."

∞ ∞ ∞

"Hey girls," Beth and Jenna's mother said after opening the front door to see them standing there looking nervous. "What brings you by so late?"

"Is dad here?" Beth asked as she stepped into the house.

"Yeah, he's out on the back deck, what's up?"

"I have a trick I've been working on and I want to use you and dad as guinea pigs if you're up for it."

"Trick? What sort of trick."

"Um, well, the thing is, I've sort of been practicing magic," Beth lied.

"Magic?" her mother giggled. "You're kidding, right?"

"It's true," Jenna cut in. I've been helping her out."

"Okay. So what's the trick?"

"Go get dad and meet us back in the living room," Beth replied. And as her mother left towards the kitchen, she followed, grabbing two chairs from around the table and taking them into the living room where she placed them at opposite ends of the room. Their parents joined them a minute later.

"What's this I hear we've got a magician in the family?" their father asked with a bemused look on his handsome face.

"That's right," Beth grinned. "If you and mom would please sit on the kitchen chairs I'll explain the trick I call trading places. Basically, if everything goes according to plan, after a bit of mumbo jumbo, hocus pocus, you will be in mom's seat and mom will be in yours. First, to make it interesting and so the crowd doesn't suspect any foul play, my lovely assistant and I will restrain you to the seat by the wrists and ankles. We will then place a thin sheet over you and I'll begin the hocus pocus and the switcheroo will happen as if by magic."

"And if everything doesn't go according to plan?" their mother asked.

"Then I look foolish and will have to practice some more to get it right," Beth said, reaching into the black duffel bag she brought along. After handing her younger sister a few lengths of rope, she grabbed more for herself. "Just as we practiced. Ankles to the legs and hands behind the back."

"Is this really necessary?" their father asked as Jenna tightly tied a length of rope around his left ankle and chair leg.

"It's all part of the act, daddy," Jenna answered in her sweet, innocent voice.

Once their parents were fully secured to the chairs, Beth pulled her sister into the kitchen and whispered to her. "Okay, this next part is going to piss them off so we'll have to act quickly," she said handing Jenna a penis gag from the bag.

"Oh my god! You can't be serious! You want me to put this in dad's mouth?"

"Do you want him to shut up and listen to what we have to say, or scream at us all night? Don't worry, I have one here for mom as well. And after we've said our piece we'll take it out, untie them and go. Trust me, it's the only way we'll get a word in tonight."

"Let's just get it done and over with."

"While their eyes are closed, quickly ram it into his mouth and around his head. Don't let him spit it out." Poking her head back into the living room, she saw her parents looking around nervously. "Okay, close your eyes and prepare to be amazed," she said, walking back into the room with the penis gag behind her back.

Tied to the chair with their eyes closed tight, their parents had no fighting chance. The gag was in place and tightly secured around their heads and by the time they realized something was wrong it was too late.

"I'm so, so sorry," Beth apologized, but I could think of no other way to get the two of you to sit down and shut up long enough for Jenna and I to tell you what we really came here to tell you. And if you're going to be pissed at anyone for doing this to you, then be pissed at me. Jenna had nothing to do with it. Now, what I'm about to tell you is going to sound insane, paranoid and downright ridiculous, but it's the truth and we have the proof to back it all up." His chair slamming up and down as he fought to get free, Beth stopped and looked over at her bound and gagged father. "Please stop and listen. And when we've said our piece we'll go and never return."

"I'm pregnant," Jenna blurted out causing her father to stop struggling and for both parents to shoot her a look of shock. "Oh god! I didn't want to tell you, but Beth convinced me I should. I was going to try lying about it, but you know how horrible I am at lying to the two of you. I was gang banged by a large group of black men and I got knocked up as a result. But that's not all," she said, too afraid now to stop for fear of never being able to start again. "I've been pierced, branded and am being trained as a sex slave in order to keep everything from being released to you, the world and everyone we know."

"And she is not alone in this," Beth took over. "I too am being trained as a sex slave. Or rather I will be once Natalie and I leave for the Domination Farm on Friday. And up until last night I've been working at Raven's Hollow as one of their legal prostitutes. But it gets even better," Natalie has been blackmailed into performing all manner of sexual perversions and after one thing leading to another, we are finally at the end of the line. While I, Natalie and one of her friends are trained at the Domination Farm, you, Natalie's parents, and the parents of whomever goes along with us will be trained here at home. We do not know who the blackmailer is or we would have gone to the police long ago, but we have DVDs and photo albums of everything they put us through.

Once we are gone, do whatever you must to make it go away, or accept the training if that's really what you want to do, but know that at the end, two sets of parents and two of us at the Farm will be auctioned off never to be seen again."

"And I will be trained by my Mistress," Jenna added. "I wish there were another way, but there isn't. Unless no one cares that our lives will be forever ruined by what gets released, we have no choice but to do as they say. Under the circumstances, I will be living with Beth until she leave for the Domination Farm and she agreed to let me stay at her place while she's away so you never have to see me again if you don't want to. I am so, so sorry," she sobbed, letting the tears flow freely down her flushed cheeks.

"Go to the police if you want, but it will do no good. We have no names, no addresses, nothing on who this blackmailer is or how he even got what he has on us all, so all it will achieve in doing is dragging our names through the mud and hanging our dirty laundry out for all the world to see."

Finally deciphering what her mother had been mumbling for the last two minutes, Jenna removed the gag from her mouth expecting to have her eardrums shattered by screaming. "Your father and I have been visited," their mother cried. "We were warned never to speak of it on pain of torture and worse. They...they did stuff to us," she wailed. "I...I was...w-was pierced and branded."

"Where?" Jenna asked.

"My nipples and down below."

"And the brand?"

"Slave wife on my mound," their mother continued to cry in fear and shame. And they…they branded your father with slave husband and pierced his nipples and penis. They said they would be coming for us soon. Said we would be trained and that I would be used as a breeding cow for black men and if we ever said a word about it to anyone we would never see the two of you alive again!"

"I'm sorry I have to do this, mom," Jenna said just before pulling her mother's shirt up to see the rings dangling from her nipples – little tags reading SLUT hanging from each. Unfastening her pants, she tugged them down far enough to see the piercings and brand and to know she was telling the truth. After putting her mother's clothes back in order, she slumped to the floor and cried.

"Are you going to go to the police?" Beth asked.

"How can we? Like you said, our lives would be ruined and we'd be a disgrace no matter where we went. We have no choice but to comply and hope for a way out somewhere down the line."

"When did this happen?"

"Three weeks ago."

"How?"

"There was a knock at the door. I opened it and there was a young lady who said she was here to see your sister. I let her in and we got to talking and the next thing I know there are more than a dozen black men in the house. I tried to scream and get away, but they overpowered me. I was gagged, bound and helplessly naked on the floor. They stripped and I knew what was coming. They…they…"

"It's okay, you don't have to say anything more."

"And when your father came home they overpowered him as well and they used us all night long, Beth. They made us do unspeakable things."

"I have a pretty good idea what they did to you as I was commanded to do the same thing to Natalie's parents. Did they fist you open enough to take two hands in the same hole at the same time?"

"Yes."

"And they pissed on you and made you drink it?"

"Yes."

"Exactly the same thing I was commanded to do to Regina and Henry."

"W-Who is behind this?"

"We have no idea. The two names we had turned out to be fake and the house Natalie was taken to was actually unowned and on the market. We've done everything in our power to find out who's doing this to us, but they are incredibly good at covering their tracks."

"So we really will be taken and trained as sex slaves?"

"I'm afraid so. I wish I could make it all go away, but I too will be trained and potentially sold. But if it keeps you and dad from losing your jobs and reputation then it's a small price to pay."

"And you really are pregnant?" their mother said looking over at Jenna.

"Yes." Getting to her feet, she pulled her shirt up and pants down to show then the piercings and brands. "And I've been marked as well. Like you, I'll be used as a breeding cow for black men, but unlike you, I'll have to do it for far longer. They are going to breed me for the next twenty years, mom! My life is over and there's nothing I can do about it."

"We'll figure something out. Will you please untie us now?"

"Yes. And then we'll go," Beth sighed.

"Don't. I think we all have a lot to talk about."

35

Five days later...

"So, what do you think we'll have to do to complete the training?" Susan asked as Beth pulled into the large parking lot of the Domination Farm.

"As the only fully trained submissive here, I can say with some certainty that we'll have to do every kinky sexual perversion you can think of whether you want to do it or not. And I for one am not really looking forwards to it as there are a lot of things I'd rather not do."

"I'm into light bondage and a little spanking," Susan said. "Until doing the gang bangs with Beth and our friends, that is. Those were pretty fun to do even if it meant having sex with other women. But I'm not into all that other stuff so I don't think I'm going to like this at all."

"None of us are going to like it," Mike replied "and I did offer to take one for the team to save you the humiliation, but you insisted on coming."

"And I told you I'm doing it to teach my parents a lesson. My only regret is I can't be there to see the look on their faces when they are taken for training."

"I think it's a little too late to be arguing about it now," said Beth. "We're here so let's just get in line and see what we have to do."

"Um, why are most of the people already naked?"

"No idea. Come on, let's get this over with," Natalie said grabbing her purse and getting out of the car.

Beth and Mike got out and were walking behind Natalie when they suddenly realized they were one person short. Turning around, they saw Susan taking her shirt off and tossing it in the back seat. "What are you doing?" asked Natalie.

"I'm taking my clothes off."

"Why?"

"There's a reason most of them are naked. And look, none of the women are carrying purses."

"Get naked if you want, but I'm not," said Mike. "All these naked women are giving me a boner."

"Nothing we haven't seen a hundred times before," Natalie grinned. Hurry up so we're not late. I don't want to risk everything getting out before we even have a chance to walk through the doors.

With Susan now butt naked, the four friends got in the middle line for submissives and slaves. "Excuse me," Susan said, giving the naked woman in front of them a light tap on the shoulder.

"Yes?" the thirty-something brunette said.

"We've never been here before. Is there a reason some people are naked and others aren't?"

"No street clothes are permitted within the Domination Farm," the woman explained. "Once inside we will go on a tour and will be given our submissive clothes to wear while here. Those that have been here before know to leave their belongings in their vehicles."

"See, told you there was a reason they were naked," Susan smugly said to her friends. "The rest of you should strip naked as well."

"And lose our place in line?" said Mike. "We can do it after we go through the line. How long is this going to take anyways?"

"Probably another hour," the woman ahead of them stated. "Those that have been here before only have to have their bracelet scanned," she said holding up her right arm so they could see the silver cuff bracelet around her wrist. "But those new to the Farm have some paperwork to read and sign before entering."

"How many times have you been here?" Natalie asked.

"This is my seven trip to the Farm in the last four years."

"What can we expect inside? We are here to be trained as sex slaves by Mistress Gwen."

"Wow, really? That's some honor."

"Honor?"

"To be trained by the owner of the Domination Farm? I'd say so. How did you manage that one?"

"Long story. Suffice it to say, the four of us are here for slave training."

"I'm only here to sample the many things the Farm has to offer. I've been collared seventeen times, but managed to get it off every time." Leaning in close, the woman whispered into

Natalie's ear. "The trick is to place something non-magnetic between the clasps and give it a good, hard twist."

"Um, thanks, but seeing as how we're here to be trained as sex slaves, I don't think we'll be removing our collars anytime soon."

∞ ∞ ∞

"Welcome to the Domination Farm," the cute, naked blonde standing inside the kiosk greeted Natalie – the name CUMBUNNY tattooed on her right breast. "Have you been here before, or are you a new customer?"

"I'm new, but we have invitations to be trained by Mistress Gwen," Natalie said sliding the card under the kiosk window.

"You are still required to fill out the paperwork. How many in your group?"

"There are four of us."

"Very well. Take these and fill them out and I will get back to you when you are finished," Cumbunny said sliding four clipboards under the glass one at a time. "You may stand over there so the line may progress."

Natalie watched as Cumbunny walked away, her eyes glued to the woman's heart-shaped ass swaying back and forth invitingly. Mike could feel himself starting to get hard and his cock sprang to life of its own accord. *I think I'm going to enjoy this place,* he thought to himself. Susan grumbled under her breath and followed along, getting more aggravated every passing second she had to go through with this craziness. Of them all, only Beth seemed unconcerned, almost at home.

After filling out the paperwork, Natalie, Beth, Susan and Mike were given their bracelets. And while a naked brunette took over her place, Cumbunny led the group towards the door leading into the waiting room.

"Wait," Mike exclaimed. "Can we put our stuff in the car? I don't really want to lose my clothes."

"It's going to be years before we're permitted to leave," Natalie said shaking her head. "Forget the damn clothes."

"Please hurry if you're going to strip. I cannot remain away from my post for long."

"He's right," said Beth. When we do leave we can't exactly drive home naked."

Running back to the car, the rest of them stripped naked and locked their belongings in the trunk before returning to Cumbunny who finally took them into the waiting room, through another door and onto the Domination Farm.

"HOLY SHIT!" they collectively gasped at the sight of so many naked men and women performing all manner of sexual acts. To their left, a raven-haired woman knelt on her knees and sucked off one man while jerking off two more while a row of women locked in stockades serviced lines of horny men. Straight ahead they saw a man on all fours, a saddle on his back as he crawled down the street carrying a fully-clothed petite woman to destinations unknown.

"Come, Mistress Gwen's office is just over here."

Walking to the corner of Domination Drive and Bondage Boulevard, Cumbunny stopped and opened the door to a small building. Dildos and plugs lined shelves while canes, floggers, whips and paddles hung from hooks. "Please forgive this slut's intrusion, Mistress Gwen, but there are guests here to see you."

"Thank you Cumbunny, replied the woman sitting at a large cherry desk. "You may go now," she added without looking up.

"Thank you Mistress."

"You must be Natalie Holt and party," Mistress Gwen said finally looking up at the four people standing in front of her desk. "I've been expecting you. I'm sure you have no end of questions, but that'll have to wait." Opening the top right desk drawer, she withdrew a long box and slid it across the desk to them. "Open it."

Mike turned the box, opened the clasp and raised the lid to see four purple collars nestled inside. "What are these for?" he asked.

"Those are your slave collars. Put them on while I explain things to you. From this day forward you belong to the Domination Farm. You will be trained in every facet of the bdsm lifestyle. You will learn discipline and obedience. You will be taught every form of sex from straight, lesbian, and gay sex to spanking, fisting, and bondage. You will be gang banged, pissed on, and used in ways you can't imagine for the pleasures of anyone wishing to use you and you will smile all the while and thank them for making you their slut."

"We've already done most of those things," Susan said defiantly. "There's no reason to make us do it again."

"Since you are new here I'll forgive that interruption," Gwen replied "but let's get one thing straight right now. If you dare talk over me again you will be punished. I know all about your past...indiscretions. I was shown pictures of your exploits by the one that paid for your training and let me tell you right here and now that watching it through a window a few times does not make you an expert. Nor does doing a few gang bangs with friends. But I can guarantee you one thing. When you leave at the end of your training, those of you that will be leaving, that is, you will be fully trained to perform any and all forms of sex without hesitation or complaint.

"Why must we wear these collars?" asked Natalie fiddling with the strip of leather-wrapped metal with powerful magnetic clasp.

"That collar symbolizes that you belong to this farm, and by extension, me. While you wear it no other master or mistress may claim you as their own, but they are perfectly within their rights to command you to do whatever fits their fancy. You will obey every order given to you by any Dominant wearing a red armband or you will be punished. Before you ask, the red armband indicates they are masters and mistresses, while neckbands of various colors indicate submissives and slaves. And if you see someone wearing a purple armband and matching collar it means they are a switch. Is this all understood?"

"Yes," they all replied meekly.

"That's yes mistress," Gwen replied.

"Yes mistress," Natalie said first.

"There's a few more things you need to know before you go on with your training. First, there is special clothing you must wear at all times. We'll get to that later. Second, you may have noticed the tattoo on Cumbunny's breast. That is required of all slaves. Your next stop will be the body modification building where you will be marked as such."

"No fucking way," Susan yelled. "I'm not getting a tattoo, let alone one like that. You're out of your damn mind if you think you can force me to do that!"

"You *will* get a tattoo and you *will* do as you're told, or you *will* be punished and made to do it anyways," Mistress Gwen said as she hit a button on the telephone. "Cockharlot, come to my office at once."

"Yes Mistress," replied a female's voice. A moment later, a leggy redhead walked in. Like Cumbunny, she was butt naked and her slave name – COCKHARLOT, was tattooed on her left breast for all the world to see. In addition to that were pierced nipples and pussy as well as a slew of other humiliating tattoos and brands. "How may this slut help you, Mistress?"

"Please take these four to the body modification building. Tell Master Jeromy that they are the Holt party. He will know what to do with them. Once Master Jeromy is finished with them bring them back here so that I can finish their registration."

"Yes Mistress. Please follow this slut," Cockharlot said motioning to Natalie, Susan, Beth and Mike.

"Are we really going to let them tattoo us like that?" Susan continued to protest.

"We are here for slave training, Susan," Beth answered. "Slaves do not argue or complain, they do. And need I remind you that you were given ample opportunity to back out and you insisted on teaching your parents a lesson."

"She's right," Mike shrugged.

36

Leaving the main office, Cockharlot led the group of new slaves in training down Domination Drive passed the Puppy Park and Gang Bang Grotto on the left and the Cummypaws Training Facility on the right. At the corner of Ponygirl Parkway, she pulled a door of a one-story brick building open and ushered them in. Along the left and right walls were chairs with one or two dildos attached – nine of them occupied by seven women and two men.

"The Holt party is here to see Master Jeromy at Mistress Gwen's request," Cockharlot said to the slightly chubby woman sitting behind the counter – the tattoo on her breast naming her Foxyslut.

Foxyslut looked up at the four newcomers and then down at the book sitting on the counter in front of her. After searching the page, she found what she was looking for and looked back up. "You may take a seat. Master Jeromy will be with you as soon as he's done with those ahead of you."

"Thank you," Cockharlot replied, taking them to the right side of the room where no one else was seated. "Please, take a seat."

"You expect us to sit on those things?" Susan was the first to complain. "But they're massive. There's no way in hell they are going to fit in me."

"What part of sex slave don't you understand?" Beth asked, picking a seat with two dildos and straddling it. "Is there lube for the one going up my ass?"

"On the shelf behind you," Cockharlot pointed.

"Thank you."

Natalie grabbed a small bottle from the shelf, lubed the back dildo and then straddled them, lowering herself down until she was fully seated. Beth followed and soon Mike too was taking it up his ass.

"I'm not as loose as the two of you," Mike grunted, lifting up and pushing back down.

"Neither am I," Susan griped as the tapered toys slipped into her pussy and ass.

"Why do you refer to yourself as 'this slut'?" asked Natalie.

"Because that is what this slut is. May this slut ask you a personal question?"

"Sure," Natalie answered.

"You don't seem to be here willingly. Why are you here?"

"We are here," Natalie said "because of a big mistake I made and this is the price we're paying for it." And while they waited to see Master Jeromy, Natalie told Cockharlot what led them to this point in time.

"That's a wild story," Cockharlot replied when Natalie finished. "This slut thinks you will make a fine slave. It sounds as if you are already well on the way."

"I wouldn't say well on our way," Susan huffed, the tow going in another two inches.

"You'll do fine," Cockharlot smiled.

"Holt party," said Foxyslut from behind the counter "Master Jeromy will see you now. Please step through that door," she added, pointing to a door to the right of the counter.

"This slut will wait for you here," Cockharlot smiled.

Thankful to be off the dildos stretching her open, Susan was the first through the door and into a small, well-lit room. In the center was a chair much like you would see in a dentist's office next to which was sitting a table and normal wooden chair. Along the back wall were cabinets and shelves lined with a hundred bottles of varying colors and too many plastic packages of rings to count. Gathering up supplies was a large man of about forty with short salt-and-pepper hair and goatee wearing shorts and tank top – every scrap of exposed skin covered in ink.

"I'll start with Susan," Master Jeromy said, his voice deep and commanding. "Take a seat."

Despite earlier protests, Susan felt compelled to follow the burly man's orders and took a seat without opening her mouth. Master Jeromy finished gathering everything he would need and rolled a cart over next to the chair. Picking up a slip of paper, he read it and put it back on the cart. After mixing inks until achieving the desired color – a deep purple that matched the collars around their necks, he got to work tattooing her left breast.

"Son of a bitch that hurts," Susan groaned, wiggling about to the point of almost screwing up the work.

"Sit still or you'll be punished. I will not give you a second warning."

"Easy for you to say. You're not the one getting your god damned tit tattooed."

"And keep your mouth shut. One more peep and you will be punished." Giving her a hard look, he dipped the needle in the tiny paper cup of ink and got back to work. It took her digging her fingernails into the arm of the chair, and her teeth into her lower lip, but she managed to get through it without incurring further wrath and when she was finally permitted to get up, she looked down to see SUGARPUSSY tattooed across her breast.

Natalie was up next followed by Beth and finally Mike – receiving SLUTTYCUNT, JIZZNYMPHO and CUMMONKEY respectively.

"You ladies have some seriously gorgeous bodies," Master Jeromy said, reaching up and tugging the ring through Natalie's right nipple. "You'll be very popular around here. It's a shame you belong to Mistress Gwen or I'd make you my slaves in a second."

"Thank you Master," Natalie replied, remembering her manners.

"And already so polite, unlike that ungrateful Sugarpussy.

"Fuck you, asshole," Susan spit out. And before she knew what was happening, she found herself bent over the wooden chair with Master Jeromy's large hand coming down hard across her ass.

"You'll learn manners one way or another," he said spanking her hard. "Might as well get lesson number one out of the way right now. What do you say after a spanking, Sugarpussy?"

"GO TO HELL!"

WHACK! "Wrong answer. Care to try again?"

"Let me up, you son of a bitch!"

WHACK! Wrong again. You, Sluttycunt, what is the proper response during punishment?"

"You count the swat and say: thank you Master for teaching me this lesson," Natalie answered, recalling what she was made to say during her frequent punishments over the course of the last several months.

"That is correct."

WHACK!

"GOD DAMN IT, LET ME GO!" Susan wailed, kicking her legs wildly in an attempt to hit Master Jeromy in the nuts.

WHACK! "She's a thick one isn't she?"

"Yes Master," Jizznympho answered.

"Well, I can keep this up all night. We're not stopping until you can make it through thirty swats correctly."

∞ ∞ ∞

By the time they finally left the body modification building with Cockharlot, Sugarpussy's ass was beat red, covered in welts and burning hot. "Nice names," Cockharlot smiled. "And really nice bodies. This slut hopes you will be permitted to fuck her with that huge cock of yours," she grinned at Cummonkey.

"You're all a bunch of fucking idiots!" Sugarpussy huffed. "This is most definitely not what the lifestyle is all about. All you're doing is taking something personal…beautiful, and twisting it for your own perverted pleasures. BDSM is supposed to be built on trust, not fear and intimidation. Where is the consent?

"You have a lot to learn about this place," Cockharlot said shaking her head. "Like me, you're all slaves to the farm now and as such can be fucked by any Master or Mistress that commands it. And if you fail to comply you will be punished until you do. The sooner you come to terms with your situation the better it will become for you. What this slut is trying to say is that you might as well try to enjoy your training because it's going to happen rather you like it or not."

"And that, Sugarpussy, is the difference between being a submissive and sex slave," Jizznympho added. "As slaves we have no rights, no control over what happens to our bodies. And if you knew anything about this lifestyle then you would already know that."

"I still don't understand why you're bitching about this," said Mike. "You did volunteer for it after all."

"A decision I am greatly regretting."

"Well, you have a long time to come to terms with it," said Jizznympho. "How long does slave training take anyways?"

"That all depends on the slave," Cockharlot answered. "If you are willing and compliant, training may be completed in as little as two years. Fight it and it can take a lifetime."

At the corner of Domination Drive and Caning Court, Cockharlot took them left and down the paved, single-lane road to a long, one-story brick building with a corset-shaped sign hanging above the door which read: FETISHWEAR. Opening the door, she ushered them inside.

"I thought we were going back to see Mistress Gwen?" Cummonkey asked. "What are we doing here?"

"While you were having your work done I was tasked with bringing you here to be fitted with your submissive clothes and then to take you to the submissive apartments where you will be roomed. And since you are here long-term you will each be given several matching outfits."

"I assume it's what we've seen everyone else wearing?" Sluttycunt asked, referring to the thigh-high latex boots, long gloves and garter belt she saw many other male and female submissives, slaves and bare-necks wearing around the Domination Farm.

"That is correct. That being said, let me give you this bit of advice. Though they may come in a variety of colors, you will be punished if you mix them. Meaning, wear only one color at a time unless you're a masochist looking for a world of pain."

"Thanks for the warning."

37

After being fitted for and getting dressed in their new submissive clothing – Natalie in blue, Beth in pink, Mike in black and Susan in red, they were given rooms at the Farm Submissive Apartments and then taken back to the main office to see Mistress Gwen.

"This is the SRD, or Slave Registration Database," Mistress Gwen said turning the monitor towards the four new slaves in training standing opposite her desk. On the screen was a dossier file with Natalie's picture in the upper left corner. "I'm going to ask each of you some questions. Answer them as honestly as you can. Once registration is complete your training will begin. Since I have your file up we'll start with you Natalie. What is your full name?"

"Excuse me, Mistress, but didn't we already do this before entering the farm?" Natalie asked.

"That was for the main database. This one is specifically for special cases such as yourselves."

"Thank you, Mistress. My name is Natalie Lynn Holt."

"Submissive name?"

"Sluttycunt, Mistress."

"Age?"

"Twenty, Mistress."

"Date of birth?"

"June fifteenth, nineteen-ninety-six, Mistress."

"Hair color and length?"

"Black and long, Mistress."

"Eye color?"

"Green, Mistress."

"And what are your measurements?"

"34C-25-35, Mistress."

"Height and weight?"

"I'm 5'7" and 123 pounds, Mistress."

"Very well, Sluttycunt. Sign your real and submissive name in the appropriate boxes and I am very pleased at your politeness and show of respect."

"Thank you, mistress," Natalie replied, signing her real and submissive names and then standing back for the next person.

"You are now registered in the Slave Registration Database," said Mistress Gwen. "You're up next," she said motioning to Mike. "What is your full name?"

"Michael David Suffield," Mistress."

"Submissive Name?"

"Cummonkey, Mistress."

"Age?"

"I am 21, Mistress."

"Date of birth?"

"April twentieth, nineteen-ninety-five, Mistress."

"Hair color and length?"

Short brown hair, Mistress."

"Eye color?"

"Brown, Mistress."

"Cock length when fully erect?"

"Nine inches, Mistress."

"You'll be quite popular around here then Cummonkey," Mistress Gwen smiled. "Perhaps when Cockharlot is done with you I'll have a go myself."

"Excuse me Mistress," Mike almost choked. "Did you say Cockharlot is going to have a go at me?"

"That's right slave. She asked a personal favor and I granted it. Once we are finished here you will go to her chambers and spend the night with her doing whatever she asks."

"Thank you, Mistress," he smiled. *Yep,* he thought *I'm really going to enjoy it here.*

Susan glared at him, irritated he was enjoying himself so much.

"What's your height and weight?"

"I'm 6'2" and 215 pounds. Mistress."

"And in very fine shape," Gwen replied. "If everything on the screen is correct please sign your name and submissive name in the boxes."

He read everything over and signed the boxes as Natalie did before him.

"And now for the trouble maker," Mistress Gwen said turning to Susan.

"Fuck you," Susan replied. "I'll show you trouble maker when I leap across that desk and kick your ass."

"Bigger and better women than you have tried," Gwen replied unafraid. "I see here that you've already been punished once by Master Jeromy. Once we are finished registering you, you'll be punished again for disrespecting me."

"Go to hell! I don't have to take this shit. You're all a bunch of lunatics. How can you sit there and take this crap?" she asked turning to Mike. "I thought you were a man?"

"I am a man," Mike replied. "I'm a man of my word. We got ourselves into this mess and I agree with Nat. We deserve nothing less. Now shut the fuck up and do as you are told like the slave you've agreed to be." Turning to face Mistress Gwen, he saw her smiling grinning from ear to ear. "I'm sorry for interrupting you, Mistress."

"That's quite alright under the circumstances. What is your full name?"

"Susan Ann Galloway."

"Mistress," Gwen added. "You will refer to me as Mistress when replying, or you will be punished."

"Whatever," Susan said rolling her eyes.

"I'll ask you again. What is your name?"

"Susan Ann Galloway, *Mistress*," she replied, saying Mistress with as much sarcasm as she could muster.

"Submissive name?"

"Sugarpussy, Mistress."

"Age?"

"Nineteen."

"What was that?"

"I said nineteen, Mistress."

"Date of birth?"

"November seventeenth, nineteen-ninety-five, Mistress."

"Hair color and length?"

"Really? You're looking right at me," Susan grumbled.

"Hair color and length," Mistress Gwen repeated the question.

"My hair is long and black as you can plainly fucking see, *Mistress.*"

"Eye color?"

"Green, Mistress."

"Height and weight?"

"5'4" and 116 pounds, Mistress."

"Measurements?"

"36C-25-36, Mistress."

"I see you still have some pubic hair. That will have to be waxed as soon as possible. That goes for you as well Cummonkey. If everything is correct please sign the boxes."

Susan reluctantly signed the boxes and stepped back, feeling more humiliated than ever. It was official. She was now a registered slave. Her life was over. Although she liked the idea of submission, now that she was here and about to experience it for real all she could think about was being shipped off to some foreign country where she would be forced to do all manner of demeaning acts of depravity.

"And finally, Beth. What is your full, real name?"

"Bethany Simone Watson, Mistress."

"Submissive name?"

"Jizznympho, Mistress."

"Age?"

"I am twenty-five, Mistress."

"Date of birth?"

"March twenty-third, nineteen-ninety-one, Mistress.

Hair color and length?"

"I have long blonde hair, Mistress."

"Eye color?"

"My eyes are green, Mistress."

"Height and weight?"

"I am 5'10" and 136 pounds, Mistress."

"And your measurements?"

"36D-26-36, Mistress."

"Perfect. And if everything on the screen is correct you may sign your names in the boxes."

"Yes Mistress."

"Cockharlot is waiting for you in the back room, Cummonkey. You may go to her now."

"Yes Mistress. And thank you," Mike replied with a smile. Although he didn't look back, he imagined the look on his friend's faces and he smiled at what Susan must be thinking and feeling right about now.

Sluttycunt and Jizznympho, you are free to go about the farm as you wish, but remember, if anyone wearing a red or purple armband gives you a command you are to obey them without hesitation or fuss. And feel free to partake in the various activities and events."

"Thank you, Mistress."

"And now to you, Sugarpussy. For disobedience you will be punished accordingly."

"What are you going to do, give me another spanking? You people are pathetic."

"You'll get a whole lot more than a spanking, slave. Master Jeromy was rather soft on you, but I won't make the same mistake. Trust me, when I'm done with you, you'll think twice before disrespecting anyone else."

38

With Mike gone into the back room, Beth and Natalie out on the farm, Susan was left alone staring into the eyes of Mistress Gwen. "Do whatever you want, but you will never break me," she said defiantly.

"Famous last words. Before I get to your punishment, let me give you a little history lesson. I wasn't always a Dominant. I began this lifestyle very much where you are now. Well, not in the same spot, but as a slave in training. It all happened at college, actually."

"Do I look like I really give a shit about your life story? Or is boring me to death your idea of punishment."

"I was trained at the hands of three very sadistic Mistresses who delighted in torturing the students and staff," Mistress Gwen went on. "Like you, I was defiant. I resisted everything they did to me, the only thought crossing my mind, revenge. After my wife and a few others overpowered them, we gave them to Master Joey – the first owner of this farm. And do you know what we did next?"

"No, but I have a feeling you're going to tell me," Susan sighed.

"Three of us came to the farm and submitted to Master Joey to further our training. We gave ourselves to him completely and without reservation. And do you know why? Because he was worthy of being called Master. And after serving him and this farm for years, he granted me the singular privilege of becoming a Dominant myself. I refused at first, wanting nothing to do with it for fear of turning into my former Mistresses, but Master Joey insisted and I eventually caved in and went through the training. And do you know what I learned?"

"Oh, do tell," Susan rolled her eyes.

"I learned that my training as a sex slave gave me an insight into being a Dominant that many others do not possess. One of which was the most effective forms of punishment for breaking hard to control, rebellious little slaves like you...like I used to be. I tell you this not out of any desire to befriend, or intimidate you, but for the sole purpose of letting you know that in more than twenty years I have never failed at training a slave."

"Blah...blah...blah. Spare me the bullshit and just give me my punishment."

"Right this way," Mistress Gwen said motioning to a door to her left.

∞ ∞ ∞

Stepping out of the main office, Natalie and Beth looked up and down the street. "So, um, where do you want to start?" Beth asked.

"I have no idea. I never imagined this place would be so large. How about we go for a walk and get to know the lay of the place before jumping into the sex?"

"Sounds fine to me. So, have you noticed the names of the streets?"

"Yeah, pretty cool given the nature of the place," Natalie said as they rounded the corner onto Caning Court, nearly stumbling over a man getting fucked up the ass by a Dominant woman wearing a large strap-on.

"Watch where you're going, you stupid submissive!"

"Sorry, Mistress," Beth apologized.

"You," the woman said pointing to Natalie "come over here and suck Cumguzzler's cock while I fuck his ass open.

"Yes Mistress," Natalie replied. As far as orders went this was a pretty easy one for her to follow thanks to her blackmailer's commandments. Crawling under the man of about thirty, she took his already hard dick into her mouth and straight down her throat, causing Cumguzzler to moan in pleasure.

"Swallow it all," said the Mistress. "If you spill even a drop you'll be severely punished.

"What about me, Mistress? Is there anything I may do for you?"

"If you have to use the bathroom you can piss all over my slave's face, otherwise you can get on your hands and knees and allow him to ram his fist up your sexy ass."

"It would be my pleasure, Mistress," Beth said, dropping onto her hands and knees in front of the male slave – the first she had seen firsthand. "I am easily fisted so you may ram it in as hard as you like," she said looking back over her shoulder.

"You heard her, Cumguzzler, ram your fist up her ass."

"Yes Mistress," the man moaned. Grabbing a bottle from a nearby dildo seat, he coated his right hand and eased it into Beth's already gaping asshole.

"Uuhhnnn, that's it," Beth moaned. "Ram it in hard and deep! Shove your arm up my ass so deep you tickle my fucking tonsils! Uhn…uhn…Ooohhhh god yes! That's it! Deeper! Harder! P-Please Mistress…please let him fist my pussy at the same time."

"Accept fifty swats and you have a deal."

"I ACCEPT, MISTRESS!" Beth purred, reaching back to furiously rub her engorged clit.

"You heard her slave, fist her pussy at the same time."

"Yes Mistress," Cumguzzler replied. With the pussy juices flowing there was no need for him to lube his other hand so he just balled it into a fist and punched it into Beth's pussy – using her now to balance himself as Natalie took him down her throat and his Mistress continued to fuck him up the ass.

"I can take a fist as well, Mistress," Natalie said, pulling off Cumguzzler's cock long enough to let that bit of information out.

"Good for you. And for taking my slave's dick out of your mouth before he shot his load you will receive fifty swats of the cane to your ass, breasts and pussy."

"Yes Mistress."

"Make that one hundred. Care you make it two?"

Keeping the throbbing dick in her mouth, Natalie sucked and played with his balls until she finally tasted his semen. Relaxing her gag reflex, she allowed it to slide down her throat, savoring every drop as is passed over her taste buds. And then she tasted piss. Clamping her mouth tight, she drank it too before crawling out from under him, licking her lips in satisfaction. "Thank you for allowing me to pleasure you slave, Mistress. Not only did he come down my throat, he filled my belly with piss as well."

"And not a drop spilled. Well done, Sluttycunt, but don't think that gets you out of your punishment. Go fuck yourself on the dildo seat over there and keep your mouth closed except for any Dominants that wish to use it as their personal urinal."

∞ ∞ ∞

Natalie fucked herself to three orgasms on the long, tapered dildos as Cumguzzler fisted Beth through five. His Mistress finally pulled out of his gaping asshole and smirked. "It's a shame you are owned by Mistress Gwen or I'd collar you myself," she said to Beth and Natalie. "Are you here as submissives, or slaves?"

"We are slaves in training, Mistress," Beth answered.

"Do you have training in discipline, slave?"

"Yes Mistress. I am a fully trained submissive now being trained as a sex slave and Sluttycunt has some submissive training."

"Very good. You will sit on the dildo seat with your arms behind your back, hands clasping opposite arms while I swat your breasts. You will then stand with your legs spread open, arms in the same position while I spank your pussy. And finally, you'll get in the punishment position for the swats on your ass. Is that understood?"

"Yes Mistress," Sluttycunt answered.

"Since you have one hundred swats coming, I will give you twenty-five to the breasts, twenty-five to the pussy and fifty to your ass. And you'll get fifteen to your breasts, ten to your pussy and twenty-five to your ass," she said to Beth.

"Yes Mistress."

39

Opening the door and stepping inside, Mike found himself in a bedroom that just screamed feminine – from the light pink paint covering the walls to the pink and red silk sheets on the queen-sized bed where Cockharlot lay wearing her deep purple submissive clothing, a sly grin on her lips.

"Welcome to my bedroom," Cockharlot purred. "I am so glad Mistress Gwen permitted me this favor."

"Not as happy as I am," Mike smiled. "You...you are absolutely stunning."

"Thank you. I want you to fuck me, Mike. I want you to ram that big, fat cock in me until I forget my own name."

"And I...wait, what did you call me?"

"Your name is Mike, right? Please tell me I didn't use the wrong name."

"No, it's my name, but I thought we were only permitted to call each other by our submissive names?"

"Back here, this is my world and the rules of the Domination Farm do not apply."

"Then what is your name?"

"Tawnie."

"That is a beautiful name for a beautiful woman. And if you want me to fuck you silly then that's exactly what I'll do for you. How long do we have?"

"Twenty-four hours."

"Mistress Gwen said I was to follow your every command to the letter, but before we begin I'd like to get to know you a little better if that's okay."

"More than okay. And a welcome relief to be honest. Most men think only of fucking me and care nothing for who I am beyond my status as Farm submissive."

"That's what the blue collar means, right?"

"Correct."

"How long have you been submissive?"

"A little over four years. It started back in college with Mistress Gwen."

"You served her in college?"

"Yes, but that wasn't always the case. It's a long story I'm sure you're not interested in, Tawnie said, her eyes slowly drifting down his chest and stopping at his semi-hard cock.

"As much as I want to climb in that bed and fuck your brains out, I honestly am interested. But you're in charge here, Mistress and I will do whatever you command."

"I am no Mistress."

"No?"

"No."

"Are you in control?"

"Yes, but…"

"Do I have to obey your every order?"

"Yes, but I…"

"I don't know a whole lot about this lifestyle, but I'm pretty sure that makes me the submissive and you the Dominant, Mistress. If you command me on that bed I will not hesitate."

"There was a secret club at the college we attended. It was an all-girl's catholic college so when I heard about the club and that there would be boys there I was immediately interested. Mistress Gwen, however, convinced me that I should steer clear. Anyways, long story short, she investigated and was taken in by three sadistic Mistress that were hell bent on training her as their slave. She kept it from me for weeks to the point I was on the verge of ending our friendship. When she finally told me what was going on I didn't believe her and went to see for myself. I think it goes without saying that what she said was the truth."

"So, what happened next?" Mike asked, his cock springing to full attention.

"I was locked in a dungeon with one of the Mistresses. I was used, abused, my virginity taken by huge dildos until I begged her to make me her slave. She pierced and tattooed me and branded my arm," Tawnie said showing Mike the THSS brand on her right bicep. "Mistress Gwenn has one exactly like it.

"Damn! That's fucked up! So, if you and Mistress Gwen were both being trained as sex slaves, how did she become Dominant and owner of this place?"

"The three Mistresses were ruthless. They trained everyone from students to staff including the Mother Superior. They were a thing of legend, a rumor on the wind no one could track down, or bring to justice out of fear of being exposed themselves. But not Gwen. One day, she had enough of their torture and she devised a plan for bringing them down. And one by one, she did just that. Afterwards, she gave them to the Domination Farm to be trained as slaves by then creator and owner Master Joey."

"What happened to them? Are they still here? What about Master Joey?"

"They are still here serving as Farm slaves of the lowest kind. As for Master Joey, he passed on three years ago."

"I'm sorry."

"Thanks. It was a sad day for us all. After the threat of the three Mistresses was gone from the school, I offered myself to Mistress Gwen I wanted her to train me. At the time she had no interest and in fact, she and Sister Kelly – the woman who eventually became her wife, came to the Domination Farm to be trained by Master Joey. And for a time they were. And when Master Joey fell ill he offered control of the Farm to Mistress Gwen if she would complete training as a Dominant."

"Wow. And you continued to serve as her slave?"

"Not at first. At first I went from attraction to attraction, eventually finding my home with the Petting Zoo. Have you been there yet?"

"Not yet."

"It's out of this world! Men and women dress as various animals and parade themselves around, fucking each other when other Farm patrons aren't. And so here we are. That's enough of my life story, what about you? How did you come to this life?"

"My friend Natalie – the one tattooed as Sluttycunt, got mixed up in a blackmail scheme where she was basically forced into increasingly kink sex acts that were secretly recorded. Whomever was behind it threatened to release everything to her family, friends and the internet if she did not comply."

"That's fucked up. Why didn't she go to the police?"

"She couldn't. If she did, everything got released. In the beginning it was just her, but then her parents got drawn in, followed by her girlfriend Beth, um Jizznympho. They took her sister – Beth's, not Natalie's. Sorry if this is a bit confusing."

"It's okay, I get it."

"After weeks, she was given a commandment to do a gang bang with eight of her friends. Susan and I were two of those friends. There was some argument in the beginning, but once we got into it we started enjoying them. I even started letting the guys fuck me up the ass," Mike confessed.

"Very cool. I love a man who is open-minded. So, how did that lead to you getting into this lifestyle?"

"Natalie's last commandment was to come here with her girlfriend and one of the friends she did gang bangs with. I volunteered because the blackmailer said the parents of whomever went would be taken and also trained. My parents are both gone so I figured I was the logical choice."

"Brave of you. But then why is Susan here?"

"She let it out that here parents were abusive to her and she also eventually volunteered just to teach them a long overdue humiliating and degrading lesson. Since neither of us would budge, here we are."

"So, you weren't submissive or anything before coming here?"

"That's right."

"And yet you were willing to be trained as a sex slave for Natalie?"

"Yes."

"You must love her a lot."

"More than I've ever told her, that's for sure."

"Why not?"

"She has Beth. The two of them are madly in love and what kind of a friend would I be to break that up?"

"So, you love a woman you can never have and are still willing to be trained as a sex salve for her?"

"I am. Don't ask me why because I can't explain it myself."

"I was the same way when it happened to me. And even though I could have walked away I felt deep down that I was meant to serve Mistress Gwen and this Farm. And now, Cummonkey, it's time you serve your Mistress. Crawl between my legs and lick my pussy until I squirt. You are not permitted to use anything but your tongue until I have at least one orgasm or you will be severely punished."

"Yes Mistress," Mike's grin broadened. Climbing onto the bed between her spread legs, his tongue snaked out and teasingly flicked over her clit before being pushed into her as deep as it would go.

40

"You will get on your hands and knees and crawl at my side," Mistress Gwen said to Susan. "And if you open your mouth to say anything but yes Mistress, your punishment will be increased. Do you understand me, Sugarpussy?"

"Yes Mistress," Susan glared at Mistress Gwen before dropping onto all fours.

Going down Domination Drive to the corner of Ponygirl Parkway, Susan knew as soon as they stopped in front of the building what was coming and her first instinct was to run. Looking down at her tattooed left breast, she looked back up to see the door open.

"Inside," Mistress Gwen commanded.

Susan reluctantly crawled into the body modification building without word, knowing deep down that to do otherwise would result in an even more severe punishment than she already had coming. Staying in step with Mistress Gwen, they approached the counter where a thin, small-breasted brunette Farm submissive named Cheerycunt sat.

"Welcome to the body modification building, Mistress Gwen. How may this slave help you today?"

"I would like some more work done to my slave, Sugarpussy."

"Yes Mistress. Master Jeromy just finished and I was going to call another back, but you may go in now, Mistress."

"Thank you Cheerycunt. Come, slave," she added, looking down at Susan. Entering the back room, she saw Master Jeromy washing his hands at the small sink. "Have time for an old friend?"

"For you, anytime Mistress Gwen. Wait a minute, is that bitchy little Sugarpussy?"

"It is. I would like for you to pierce her nipples, clit hood and outer labia and brand her right breast with rebellious slave."

"Your wish is my command. Get in the chair, Sugarpussy."

Her chance for escape gone, Susan scowled at both Mistress Gwen and Master Jeromy as she crawled across the room and into the chair. No sooner was she in the seat then Mistress Gwen began strapping her in place – first around the wrists and ankles and then the waist, shins, thighs, forearms and finally her biceps.

"Don't worry, Sugarpussy, this is only the beginning of your punishment," Mistress Gwen smirked. "It only gets worse from here."

"Fuck you!" Susan shouted, no longer capable of keeping her mouth shut. "I will not be trained by a worthless cunt like you!"

"Add a set of vertical bars to her nipples," Mistress Gwen said to Master Jeromy.

"Yeah, add a set of vertical bars to my nipples! Add two sets…three. I don't give a fuck what you do to me, I will never bend to your will. You're not worthy of the title of Master or Mistress! This is not the bdsm lifestyle! This is a mockery. You're nothing but a bunch of sadistic, insane assholes playing pretend!"

"Make it six tunnels in each outer labia," Mistress Gwen replied.

"Are you sure it was the Mistresses at your school that were the sadists?" Susan snapped back. "From where I'm sitting I think you're the one getting pleasure from my pain. Look at you! Look at how your pussy drips every time you tell him to torture me!"

"Learn to keep your mouth shut and do as you are told and the torture will stop. Well, at least this leg of it. You still have the cane to look forward to."

"And when I get out of here I'll turn this place in to the police! You'll be shut down before the day is over."

"Not likely. We've been investigated by every law enforcement bureau from the local police to the FBI and here we are. This is classified a nudist resort and fetish colony and given the extensive paperwork that all patrons must read and sign, we are breaking no laws. Face it, Sugarpussy, you have nothing but a big mouth. But don't worry, when I'm finished you'll be an obedient, well-trained slave. And you're wrong about me. I gain no satisfaction whatsoever from putting you through this."

"No? Then why is your pussy dripping wet and your clit engorged? And your nipples, they're so hard they could cut glass. If you don't want people knowing that you get pleasure from torturing others then perhaps you should put some clothes on. Face it, you're nothing but a two-faced whore getting off on my pain, Bouncytits," Susan said using the submissive name tattooed on Mistress Gwen's left breast. "Pierced nipples, clit hood and inner labia? Yeah, you're a fucking whore and you know it."

"If you're trying to make me angry you'll have to try much harder than that, Sugarpussy. As I said before, I began as a sex slave-in-training and a good slave obeys orders. But if you really want to know, my slave name was forced upon me, but I overcame and embraced it instead of letting it destroy me as you seem so hell bent on doing."

"I'm ready to get started," Master Jeromy said, rolling the cart over to the chair Susan was strapped to.

"By all means," Mistress Gwen said stepping aside. When you are done, seal her shut and send her to her room. And that is where you'll remain until you are healed," she added, looking Susan square in the eyes. "You will have no contact with your friends, or anyone else on the Domination Farm. When you are healed enough to take the caning I'll return to finish the job. And before you get any bright ideas about leaving, your collar's shock feature will be activated when I return to my office. Step foot beyond the walls and you'll be rendered unconscious."

"So I'm your prisoner then? Holding me against my will is kidnapping and against the law! But before I go to the police I'm going to kick your ass up and down this god damned farm of yours! Mark my words, Bouncytits, you've made an enemy and I will not stop until you're ruined!"

"Better women than you have tried. And no, you are not my prisoner. You entered the Domination Farm of your own free will. You read and signed all of the paperwork and accepted my collar around your neck as a slave in training. But you know what, I don't think you're worth the time and energy required of me to train you. Do the work, Master Jeromy and then escort her off of the premises. You are hereby banned from the Domination Farm for life. Step foot on my property again and you'll be arrested for trespassing."

"You're fucking pathetic!" Susan growled. "I'll have your fucking…AAHHGGHHH!" she yelped as a thick needle tore through her left outer labia making room for the first of the tunnels. "You haven't seen the last…MOTHERFUCKER!" she yelped as the opposite side was done. "You're a dead woman! You hear me? I'll rip your fucking head off and piss down your neck hole you sadistic cunt!"

"Make sure she has a bra and panties to match the rest of her submissive clothing," Mistress Gwen said with an eerie calm. "We wouldn't want her arrested for indecent exposure now would we? And don't worry, I'll let your friends know what happened. Shame everything will be released because you couldn't play nice. And here I was told you were the one into this lifestyle. Guess I was misinformed."

"You don't know the first thing about the lifestyle! This is not bdsm, its torture."

"Did you, or did you not come to the Domination Farm to be trained as a sex slave?"

"Yes but…"

"And did you, or did you not enter of your own free will knowing and understanding what that meant?"

"That has nothing to do…"

"Do you know the difference between a submissive and a sex slave?" Mistress Gwen cut Susan off again.

"Yes, but…"

"Then why are you acting as if you are a clueless bitch? Why are you constantly arguing with everything I say and doing your best to goad me on? What is the point…oh…OH, no, it can't be. Really?" And the knowing smirk that suddenly flashed across Susan's lips told her everything she needed to know. "You're a masochist."

"Yes Mistress," Susan grinned. "I do believe you have work to do, Master," she said looking up into Master Jeromy's eyes.

"Do you still want me to escort her off the premises, Mistress?"

"No. Brand her a painslut and send her to her room. I will personally see to her training. And might I say well-played, Sugarpussy. Well-played indeed."

"Please accept my humblest apologies for what I said to and about you and this Farm. I only said it because it seemed the more I prattled on, the more pain you were going to subject me to. And thank you for allowing me to remain," Susan said, chewing her lower lip when she felt the next needle pushing through her outer labia as the first orgasm approached.

"When you are done, please give her three hundred swats of the cane. Just make sure not to hit the recently pierced or branded areas," Mistress Gwen said to Master Jeromy.

"It would be my pleasure, Mistress."

"I'll call in Mistresses Renee and Amber to see to those still waiting to be worked on."

41

Breasts, pussies and asses covered in nasty red and purple welts, Beth and Natalie remained in the punishment position for several minutes before being able to safely get to their feet without falling back to the ground due to weak knees. Looking down in shock, Natalie could not believe what she was seeing. Not the welts, no, she had seen those many times over the last several months, but the juices running down her inner thighs.

"I can't believe you came from that!" Beth exclaimed.

"That makes two of us. I...I've never done...I don't know what..."

Me thinks you might be something of a pain slut," Beth grinned, slapping her right hand against her lover's red and puffy pussy quick and hard. The reaction was immediate. Natalie jumped and yelped, but the pussy juices continued to flow. "Yep, definitely a pain slut."

"But how? Why? I've never orgasmed from being caned before so why start now?"

"No idea. The mind is a fickle beast and perhaps some wires have been crossed telling it you're feeling immense pleasure instead of pain. I won't even pretend to know what I'm talking about though. That's just what makes sense given my very limited knowledge of medicine. "So, what would you like to do now, little Miss Pain slut?"

I'd still like to explore the farm and get to know where things are and what we'll have to do before our training is complete. But what I could really go for right now is something to eat. I'm starving."

"Yeah, I'm a little peckish myself. Well then, let's go look for someplace to eat, shall we?"

"Let's ask her," Natalie said pointing to a short, slightly chubby brunette Farm submissive fucking herself silly on a dildo seat some fifty feet to their right. "If she's a Farm submissive she should know where to eat, right?"

"Probably."

Walking over to the woman enjoying her ride on the two long, tapered dildos, Natalie sat down on the seat next to her and lowered herself until fully seated. "God I love being stretched open," she moaned. "Shame these aren't a little bigger."

"Bigger?" the woman looked over at her in surprise. "Have you been to the House of Gape?"

"No. We just got here a few hours ago. You been here long, Milkymelons?" Natalie asked, looking at the name branded on the woman's left breast.

"I've been a salve of the Domination Farm for nearly three years."

"So, you know your way around then?"

"I do. Anything I can help you find?"

"How about a guided tour starting with where to get something to eat?" Beth said, sitting on the seat to Milkymelon's left.

"Only the Dominants are permitted to give guided tours. I can show you where to eat but it'll have to wait another hour."

"Why?"

"Because that's how long I have to ride the dildos. I can give you directions to three locations if you want."

"Sure," Natalie smiled, reaching down and pushing four fingers into her pussy alongside the dildo.

"Wow, you really do love being stretched open don't you? If you continue east down Caning Court and south on Discipline Drive to the corner of Bondage Boulevard, you'll find The Dive."

"Wait, is that the place near the submissive apartments?" Beth asked.

"That's the one. And then there's the Cumeaterie located at the end of Anal Avenue. And Rex's Place up on Breeder Boulevard. It's basically a bunch of fast food places in one location. Whatever you do, don't go into the Eternal Goddess. That's for Dominants only and you'll be immediately registered as Farm submissives if you go in for any reason.

"We're already being trained as slaves by Mistress Gwen," Natalie said, pushing her right hand into her already stuffed pussy.

"*The* Mistress Gwen?" Milkymelons gasped. "As in the current owner of the Domination Farm, Mistress Gwen?"

"One and the same. The two of us and two other friends have been sent here to be trained by her."

"You're lucky. Mistress Gwen doesn't train many slaves these days."

"And how long does slave training take anyways?" Beth asked. "And what will we have to do to complete it?"

"It all depends on the person being trained. It can be as little as a year, or as long as a lifetime. As for what you'll have to do? Well, look around. You'll have to go in and complete each and every attraction and event here at the Domination Farm. I see you're both already pierced and tattooed. Well, before your training is complete you'll receive a whole lot more."

"Really?" Natalie purred, her pussy clenching the dildo and her hand tight as the juiced flowed.

"Oh yes. More than a dozen of the buildings require those completing them to get a mark of completion. It can be a tattoo or brand corresponding to the fetish completed within. And before you ask, no, I cannot tell you which buildings."

"I really want to feel two hands in both holes at the same time," Natalie blurted out.

"I think that can be arranged," Beth grinned. Getting up off her dildo seat, she walked over to her girlfriend, knelt at her side and coated her hands with the lube found at every seat. "You sure about this?" she asked, pulling Natalie's hand out and pushing hers in. Reaching around back, she eased the tips of her fingers up her lover's ass.

"Yes! I've never wanted stretched open more in my fucking life. Do it. Shove your hand up my ass, Jizznympho!"

"You really should go to the house of Gape," Milkymelons said. "You'll complete training in minutes.

"What do you have to do there?"

"Exactly what she's doing now. The House of Gape is all about fisting and being stretched open to the max."

"Where is it?"

"At the end of Caning Court across from the Gaper Carousel."

"My hand isn't going all the way up your ass. It's too tight."

"Push it in!" Natalie grunted, leaning forwards slightly as she tried her best to relax her asshole. The fingers slipped a little deeper and she rocked back. "That's it! Shove it up my ass! DO IT! PUSH DAMMIT! Aahhgghhhh YES!" Natalie moaned as Beth's hand finally slipped in.

"You did it! You actually did it! You have dildos and hands in both holes! How does it feel?"

"It hurts so fucking good," Natalie moaned, slowly working herself up and down. "I've taken two fists at the same time before, but I never imagined taking two in both holes at the same time!"

"Well, technically you only have one fist in each hole," Milkymelons said. "Sure, the dildos are as thick as fists at the base, but they are still toys."

"She's right," Beth agreed.

"Then find someone to do it right!" Natalie said, jumping off the dildo seat and dropping onto the ground with her head down and ass up.

"WOW! Your pussy and asshole are wrecked!" Milkymelons exclaimed. "I wish I could get up, but I still have more than an hour to go. Really, you should just go to the House of Gape. You'll have to do it anyways if you're being trained as a sex slave. I guarantee you'll feel two hands in both holes at the same time."

"Come on, Sluttycunt, let's go grab something to eat and then check out this House of Gape."

"Okay. Give me a minute, I don't think I can stand up just yet."

42

"Mmmm," Tawnie moaned, clenching her legs tightly around Mike's head. "You truly have a magical tongue."

"Just wait until I shove my cock into you, Mistress," Mike said as he lapped up the latest jets of pussy juices. "I hope you let me fuck you soon, Mistress. I'm so fucking horny I'm about to explode without even touching myself.

"Assume the punishment position, slave."

"Mistress?"

"You don't know the punishment position?"

"No Mistress."

"Get on your hands and knees." Mike moved off the bed and got on all fours as commanded. "Good. Now fold your arms and place your chin on them. That's it. You really are a good little slave aren't you, Cummonkey?"

"I am doing my best, Mistress," Mike said, the pre-cum leaking from his cock like a dripping faucet.

"And lastly, lift your feet until they are even with the base of your ass. A little higher. Perfect. And that, Cummonkey, is the punishment position."

"Thank you Mistress. Are you going to punish me?"

"That all depends on what you think about taking big black cocks up your ass."

"I've only ever been with one black man before, Mistress, and I loved it. I've let four of my male friends – one of them black, fuck my ass during each and every gang bang we did together. Granted, I hated it at first, but I quickly grew to enjoy it. How many are going to take me, Mistress?"

"Only three. Is that enough, or would you like more?"

"I will take as many as you wish, Mistress. I am here to please you in every regard."

Walking over to the door, Tawnie pulled it open and poked her head out. "Hey Sweettits, could you please go fetch as many black men as you can find and bring them to my room?"

"Sure, Cockharlot. You finally going to let them breed you?"

"Not exactly. They're for my new lover. Tell them to come right in once you get back." Closing the door, she turned to Mike and smiled. "As for you, Cummonkey, get that big, hard cock up here and fuck a load in me. This slave is yours to breed."

"WHOA! You mean you want me to knock you up?"

"That's right. Think you can do that for me?"

"Why me?"

"Because I like you."

"I'm sorry, Mistress, but you don't even know me. I might be a homicidal maniac for all you know."

"Doubtful. Now please breed me, Cummonkey."

"Are you asking or commanding it, Mistress?"

"I am not a Dominant, Mike. Sure, I can play one for the next…twenty-one hours, seven minutes, but I am a slave at heart and I am asking you to breed me," she said looking up at the clock hanging on the wall and then back down into his eyes. "I could always go to the breeding stables where twenty men a day will fuck their loads in me, but I want at least one of my children to be by a man of my choosing and I want that to be you."

"How many have you had?"

"Five so far in the last four years. I had a daughter followed by a set of twin boys and a set of twin girls."

"Where are they now?"

"Being raised by their grandparents. Will you do it? Will you be the father of my next child?"

"How? We only have one day together and then you must return to your Farm duties. Other men will fuck you. I may be able to fuck a load in you three or four times, but I doubt that'll be enough to impregnate you."

"It will be if I ask Mistress Gwen for another favor."

"What favor?"

"I could beg for her to allow only you to fuck me until I am pregnant. The price will be high, but I don't care. I can't explain it, but I felt a connection between us from the moment we met and I feel with every fiber of my being that you are to be the father of my next child."

"What price? What will you have to do for the favor?"

"Whatever Mistress Gwen demands of me."

"Did you have to pay a price to have me for the day?"

"I did."

"And what did you pay?"

"It doesn't matter."

"It matters to me! I don't want you getting hurt because of me and I think I've seen enough of this place to know that whatever it is you agreed to do won't be good or particularly pleasant. If you want me to fuck you, tell me what price you had to pay."

"I agreed to go through training at Cummypaws."

"And that's bad?"

"Depends on your definition of bad I suppose. "Once there I will be unable to leave until my training is complete."

"And what is this training?"

"I will be trained as a puppy and pony slave. But not just any puppy and pony slave. When my training is complete I will believe I really am a puppy or pony – whatever personality my Mistress wishes to keep me in."

"I don't understand."

"Cummypaws uses brainwashing techniques, Cummonkey. They break a slave down both physically and mentally, slowly suppressing their humanity and replacing it with the personality of an animal."

"So, you'll cease to be human?"

"Yes."

"For how long?"

"For as long as Mistress Gwen desires it. Each personality comes with verbal triggers and the only way back to humanity it for her to use the command, or to abandon me which will bring me out of it over time."

"Why would you do that to spend a day with me?"

"Like I said, I felt a connection between us as soon as our eyes met. I know it sounds silly, but I think you're the one, Mike."

"The one?"

"The one I've been waiting for all my life."

Wrapping his arms around Tawnie's waist, Mike pulled her close and kissed her hard on the lips. Holding the embrace, he lifted her up. Her legs went around his waist and she felt the head of his cock penetrate her dripping pussy. The room spun and they fell back onto the bed – him on his back, and she on top, his cock buried deep.

"Then take my seed, Mistress. I will fuck as many loads in you as humanly possible."

"You'll breed me?" She asked, leaning down and kissing him.

"If that is what you want and Mistress allows, but only on two conditions."

"Anything!"

"First, you will not pay any further prices for me. If Mistress Gwen demands it, I will accept the price myself." He felt her pussy clench tighter around his cock nearly causing him to explode.

"That is so sweet of you. And the second condition?"

"Secondly," he said running his fingers through her long, wavy red hair "you'll marry me."

"WHAT!"

"You heard me. If I'm going to father your children then I want you as my wife."

"But we only just met!"

"And yet you want my babies. That's the deal, Tawnie. Be my wife and I'll give you as many babies as Mistress Gwen will permit." Placing his hands around her waist, he could feel the goosebumps and the pounding beat of her heart. Holding her gently, he rolled over so that he was now on top, her legs pushed back, feet up in the air as he pounded his cock into her. "Yes or no, Mistress? Will you be my wife and breeding slave, or will this just be a one night stand?"

"YES!" Tawnie exploded in orgasm. "YES! YES! A MILLION TIMES YES! Now fuck your seed into me! Knock me up! Breed me like a fucking animal!"

The pressure finally building to the point of no return, Mike thrust his cock into Tawnie's pussy and came – splattering her cervix and walls with coat after coat of fertile semen until his balls were drained.

43

"Come in," Tawnie said after hearing a knock at the door. It swung open and Sweettits entered. "I'm back with your black men," she smiled. "I hope he's ready to be fucked because I found seventeen of them for you."

"HOLY HELL!" Mike gasped as he watched the men march into the room. And then he looked over at Tawnie who leapt off the bed, opened the drawer of a nightstand and began placing rings in the tunnels through her inner and outer labia in such a manner as to prevent anyone from fucking her pussy. "What are you doing?"

"I am yours and yours alone for breeding," Tawnie explained. "I will suck them off and they may take me up the ass, but until I am with child no other man may have my pussy."

"But you haven't gotten the okay from Mistress Gwen yet."

"Actually, I have and she gave her permission as long as you were willing to do it for me," Tawnie said with a sly grin. "And to set the rules of the gang bang, you will all fuck Cummonkey up the ass and down the throat until he's able to take your fist with ease. And if you have to use the restroom, well, you have two urinals right here."

"Wait a minute!" Mike protested. "Do you mean us?"

"That's right. In order to be a fully trained sex slave you're going to have to do golden showers. As in letting others piss on you and down your throat. What better time to practice then now? I for one happen to love the taste of piss. Alright, men, we are yours for the taking for the next six hours. And Sweettits, unless you want to partake in this interracial gang bang pissfest, I'd leave before the door closes," she said as one of the men reached out and placed his hand on the door.

Sweettits ducked under a well-muscled arm and spun gracefully towards the closing door, but she was too late. It slammed shut trapping her inside. Looking around the room, her eyes as large as saucers, she felt a powerful hand on her shoulder and allowed it to push her to her knees. A cock filled her open mouth and the rest of the men sprang into action.

"WAIT!" Mike exclaimed, if Mistress Gwen agreed to let me breed you then what was the price you agreed to pay?"

"That's the funny part," Tawnie grinned as a black man lifted her up and brought her down – his hard cock going up her ass "the price I had to pay to be used as a lifelong breeding cow was to marry the man who agreed to do it."

Mike was just about to say something, but the big black dick snaking its way down his throat cut him off. Another went up his ass and he let out a soft moan as his own cock once again sprang to life.

∞ ∞ ∞

Mike spent the next three hours in Tawnie's room getting fucked by seventeen black men –

taking them in mouth and ass and even enjoying
them sucking him off on occasion, but all he really
wanted to do was fuck another load into his new
fiancé. But her pussy was closed for business and
every time he went for Sweettits, he was pulled
back. "Dammit!" he said in frustration. "Stop
yanking me away from her!"

"You're not allowed to fuck Sweettits,"
Tawnie said.

"Is that a command, Mistress?"

"Yes, but not from me. I'm sorry, I did not
tell you the whole truth. Mistress Gwen did say I
could only be the lifelong breeding cow for the
man I marry, but she also said that I am the only
woman he would be allowed to fuck until I'm
confirmed pregnant. That's why I asked for all
these men. You can have sex with as many of them
as you want."

"Nice of you to tell me now."

"I'm sorry. Are you going to back out
now?"

"No."

"Thank you," she said with a smile that
melted Mike's heart. "You have no idea what this
means to me and I will never forget it."

"Put a cork in it!" one of the black men said
just before shoving his hard cock in Tawnie's
mouth.

"You're almost there Cummonkey," the
man shoving fingers up his ass claimed. Adding
more lube, he tucked thumb into palm and pushed

with steady pressure. "You ever been fisted before, sissy?"

"N-No," Mike grunted as his ass was stretched open a little at a time while his cock was being sucked.

"Well, give me five more minutes and my hand will be in. Just relax and don't fight it. That's a good little sissy," he said, feeling the asshole relaxing around his fingers. In. Out. In. Out. Harder. Deeper. Faster. In. Out. Deeper. Deeper. IN! "That's it!" the man exclaimed. "My entire hand is up your sissy ass." Pulling completely out, he applied more lube and then shoved back in again – this time balling his hand into a fist and punching it deeper still.

Three hours turned to four and Mike's asshole continued to be stretched open. After managing one large hand, Tawnie and Sweettits double fisted him to his first ever anal orgasm without his cock ever being touched. Already exhausted, he lowered his head to the floor and panted as the men continued to take him. And then Tawnie moved her ass in front of him and looked back over her shoulder.

"Eat the come out of my ass, slave!" she commanded.

Mike looked up at her and smiled. Getting back onto his hands and knees, he spread her asshole open and began licking and sucking the semen out – gulping it down without thinking where it was coming from. When he was done licking her clean, another cock went down his throat and fed him his seventh load of piss which he immediately scrambled to the trash can to throw up.

Four hours turned to five and Mike's humiliation only increased. Now discarded like a piece of old meat, he was forced to watch the men have their way with Sweettits and his new fiancé Tawnie. And though he had only met her a few hours ago, he felt the pangs of jealousy welling up inside and it made his cock throb painfully to life. Sweettits crawled over to him after six men filled her pussy. Squatting over his face, she squeezed it out and grinned as he gobbled it up like candy. She was followed by Tawnie who fed him another five loads from her gaping asshole.

The last hour was passed with the men resting interspersed with them using Mike as their urinal. And as the final minutes ticked away, they did the seemingly impossible. With both of Tawnie's hands buried deep in his bowels, Mike exploded in orgasm once again as Sweettits worked her right hand in one finger at a time until it too was in.

"You are so fucking amazing!" Tawnie exclaimed, fucking her hands in and out of her fiancé's ass. "I can't believe you have three hands in you!"

"N-Neither...I c-cant...that makes two of us," he moaned.

"Well ladies, our time is up," one of the black men said looking up at the clock.

"Already?" Sweettits sighed. "And here I was just getting used to the idea of being bred by black men."

"That's great news!" Tawnie exclaimed. "I never thought I'd see the day you wanted to be bred, let alone by black men. You should totally go to the breeding stables and ask for the black men only."

"You know, I think I just might do that. But right now, I really need to go pass out." Waiting for the men to leave, Sweettits crawled out after them, unable to safely stand on her own two feet.

∞ ∞ ∞

"You really were absolutely amazing," Tawnie said, snuggling up against Mike. "You'll make some lucky Dominant an excellent slave."

"And you'll make some lucky slave and excellent Dominant," Mike replied, kissing the side of her neck.

"Nah, this is a one night thing for me. Like I said before, I'm a slave at heart."

"That's too bad. Since we'll be husband and wife I was hoping you would continue to dominate me, Mistress."

"You really want to marry me?" Tawnie asked, rolling over and looking him in the eyes.

"Never more. And if that's what being your slave would be like then sign me up. Honestly, I would obey your every command without hesitation. But answer me one thing. Did Mistress Gwen really say you had to marry the man agreeing to breed you?"

"She did. And she also said the one marrying and breeding me could only fuck me until confirmed pregnant. And while I'm pregnant he is free to fuck whomever he wants. I want to get one thing perfectly clear right here and now, Mike. I will never, ever lie to you about anything. Especially a Dominant's command. This entire Farm is wired with cameras and I would have been caught in the lie as soon as Mistress Gren watched the recording."

"Wait, you mean to tell me everything we did was recorded?"

"That's correct."

"So, you're a Farm slave and I'm a slave in training. If we got married where would we live?"

"Here at the Domination Farm."

"I mean, back at my room in the Farm submissive apartments, or here in your room? Also, you need to know that at the end of our training two of us will be auctioned off to the highest bidder. It might be me and we'd never see each other again."

"It's a risk I'm willing to take. And we can live here. My room is much larger than those found at the apartments. But you cannot move in until we are married. Speaking of which, when do you want to do it?"

"Good question. I assume we'll be married on the Farm?"

"Yes. Mistress Gwen can perform the ceremony. I always dreamed of a spring wedding if

I ever got married, but that means waiting until next year."

"I'm not going anywhere, Mistress. And that'll give us a lot more time to get to know each other. Man, the others aren't going to believe this. Speaking of which, I wonder how they're doing."

"I'm sure you'll get a chance to catch up with them tomorrow. For now, I want to take a shower, grab a bite to eat and then lay in your arms for the rest of the time we have together."

"You mean the rest of our lives?" Mike asked, hugging Tawnie tight and licking a stray strand of semen from her shoulder.

"I love you so much, Cummonkey."

"And I love you, Cockharlot."

"There is one more thing Mistress Gwen commanded me to do when our day together is over and you're not going to like it."

"Honey, I'm a slave in training. It doesn't matter what I may or may not like. As Jizznympho stated: a slave does not argue or complain, they do. So, what was her command?"

"You are to be fitted with a permanent chastity device which I will have the only key to, and you will be given two brands."

"What do you mean by permanent chastity device, and what brands will I be getting?"

"Your scrotum will be pierced twice and a ring will be placed at the base of your cock. A chastity device will be fitted and locked in place so that you cannot have sex with anyone except me until I am pregnant. Then it will be removed until I give birth. After I have the baby, it will be put back on. Rinse and repeat for as long as we are married. As for the brands, you'll have fisting whore branded on your ass and cockgobbler branded on your right breast. Before we go in, I would suggest stopping off at the House of Gape. You'll have to go anyways to complete your slave training and it will save you a tattoo or brand."

"How so?"

"The House of Gape is one of the attractions requiring a mark of completion in the form of a tattoo or brand. Instead of getting fisting whore and then fisting king as separate marks, you'll get fisting king."

"Even though Mistress Gwen wants me branded with fisting whore?"

"Yes."

"What will I have to do to complete the training?"

"Take two large fists up your ass at the same time. Something I just happen to know you excel at," Tawnie smiled.

"How much time do we have left?"

"About eleven hours. And remember, when time runs out and we leave this room I am Cockharlot and you are Cummonkey. We cannot call each other by our real names and you must absolutely never call me Mistress. Is that understood?"

"Yes Mistress," Mike grinned.

"I'm serious. If you call me Mistress you'll receive fifty swats of the cane and I'll get three hundred for impersonating a Dominant. You cannot say it even in jest."

"I understand. Now, how about that shower?"

44

Returning to the Farm submissive apartments, Mike went to Beth's room as it was the closest, and knocked on the door. No answer. Next in line was Natalie's and after two sharp knocks it swung open.

"Hey Cummonkey," said Beth. "Come on…WHOA! Is that a male chastity belt you're wearing?"

"It is," Mike cringed, walking into the small apartment. "I've also been branded, but that can wait. Have either of you seen Sugarpussy?"

"She's in her room nursing a hell of a punishment by Mistress Gwen. Want to go over there and talk to her?"

"Yeah, I'd like to catch up and see how everyone's first day went."

"Yours certainly looks to be an interesting story," Natalie said looking down at the wire cage covering her friend's cock.

Not bothering to knock on Susan's door, Natalie opened it and ushered the others inside. "Hey, Sugarpussy," she called out. "It's Sluttycunt and Jizznympho again. We have Cummonkey here with us."

"In here," Susan groaned from the bedroom. "I'm not getting out of bed."

"Don't panic when you see her," Beth warned.

Walking into the bedroom, Mike stopped dead in his tracks at sight of the welt and bruise-covered woman lying naked on the bed. "Holy hell, Sugarpussy, what happened to you?"

"I was punished by Mistress Gwen and Master Jeromy," Susan answered.

"It looks as if they beat you half to death!"

"It's not as bad as it looks. I quite enjoyed it, really."

"Not as bad as it…what did you say?" Turning, Mike looked back at Beth and Natalie. "Did she just say that she enjoyed it?"

"I loved every second of it," Susan purred. "The feeling of the needle tearing away my flesh for the tunnels in my pussy," she said, her eyes glassing over with excitement. "The branding iron searing skin! Every swat of the cane like a thousand orgasms."

"What. In. The. Actual. Fuck?" Mike gasped. "And what is that in your pussy?" he added, looking at the strip of purple leather laced through the grommets.

"It's made of the same stuff as our collars. It keeps me locked up so no one can ever fuck my pussy. I'm a pain slut," she smiled. "I was being such a bitch because I knew it would result in further punishment. I wanted this, my friends. I wanted every piercing, brand and swat."

"Tell them, Sluttycunt," Beth said, poking her girlfriend in the side if the right breast.

"I think I'm a pain slut as well," Natalie confessed. "I never thought myself as such before last night, but when I was being caned by a Mistress we met on the street, I had an orgasm.

And then I orgasmed again when Jizznympho slapped my pussy with her hand. And then again at the House of gape when the men rammed their huge fists into me."

"I was there this morning," Mike cut in, turning to show his friends the brand on his ass.

"WHOA! You were fisted? Double fisted?" Beth gasped in surprise.

"Triple actually. It happened last night with Cockharlot."

"Speaking of which, how did that go? Did the two of you hit it off?"

"You could say that. "We're engaged to be married."

"You're what?" Susan said, bolting upright in bed. Engaged? Did you just say you're engaged to a woman you just met yesterday?"

"What can I say, it was love at first lick," Mike grinned.

"Okay, I'll give you credit for having a truly magical tongue, but she really loved it enough to marry you after one night?" Natalie said with raised brow.

"Correct. To make a long story short, she felt a connection between us long before I ever did. She wanted me from the moment we walked into the main office yesterday. Anyways, she asked me to breed her and one thing led to another and I agreed on terms that she marry me. She accepted. What I didn't know was that she and Mistress Gwen talked about it beforehand and in order to be used as a breeding cow she had to marry the man breeding her, and in order to breed her, the man doing so had to marry her. Anyways, we both agreed and had the most amazing sex of our lives. She was incredible."

"And the triple fisting?"

"I was fucked and fisted by seventeen black men and then Cockharlot and Sweettits fisted me. While Sweettits had both hands up my ass, Cockharlot added one of hers. And then I went to the House of Gape this morning, quickly passed the training and was branded. I was also branded a cockgobbler," he said pointing to the brand on his right breast.

"We went in last night," Natalie said. "I passed the training right away, but it took Jizznympho nearly five hours. Thankfully we were very much into fisting before coming here. We've both been branded Fisting Queens," she said turning around to show her branded ass.

"How many times were you caned?" Mike asked Susan.

"It was supposed to be three hundred, but I begged Master Jeromy for more. I pleaded and cried for him to keep going. I finally passed out at four-hundred-seventy-three."

"SHIT!"

"When I woke up I was here in bed I passed out again and then Sluttycunt and Jizznympho woke me about an hour ago."

"So, you can't take that thing out of your pussy lips?"

"Nope. The ends are magnetic like our collars. Master Jeromy said it required fifteen hundred pounds of pressure to pull apart without the proper tool."

"And you are okay with it?"

"Yes."

"Cockharlot remained closed last night with rings. I wonder if she'll wear something like that."

"Are you okay with wearing a chastity cage? I can't imagine that thing will be comfortable when you get horny.

"It's not. It's nowhere near big enough for my hard cock."

"Then I guess you'll have to learn some self-control," Jizznympho smirked. "And you really can't fuck anyone but Cockharlot?"

"No other women until she's pregnant with my child. But I can have all the men I want."

"Interracial gang bang, huh?" Natalie grinned. "Sounds fun."

"It was absolutely amazing. So many big black cocks. And don't even get me started on all that delicious come. And they…they…they used me as their urinal!"

"REALLY!? They pissed on you?" Beth asked.

"On me and down my throat. They forced me to drink it to begin my training."

"It sounds as if we've all have very productive first days," Susan said lying back in bed. "So, what's on the agenda for today?"

"You're staying in bed as ordered," Beth replied. "You may be a glutton for punishment, but there's only so much you can put your body through in one go. As for Sluttycunt and me, we're going to explore the Farm some more."

"I'll be spending the day with Cockharlot. We're planning a spring wedding, and plan on spending the next several months fucking and getting to know each other."

"No one else is going to ask so I will," Natalie sighed. "I wonder how our parents and Jenna are doing. Do you think they are in training now?"

"I'd rather not think about it," Beth sighed "but I know Jenna will be. She said her Mistress would continue training her the moment we left."

"I could care less if my parents are taken," Susan huffed. "They deserve everything they get and more."

"Well, I'd rather not see my parents trained as sex slaves, but if they are then at least I'll have something to talk to them about," Natalie said with a forced smile. "If I ever see them again, that is."

"I wonder if they'll go through with it to save face, or go to the police," Beth asked.

"I honestly don't know. I wonder if there's a phone around here we can use to call and check in on them."

"If not, perhaps we can go out to the car and use our cells," Natalie suggested.

"We can't go beyond the walls," Susan said. "Our collars have shock features on them that have been engaged. We leave and we're shocked to shit."

"What kind of bullshit is that?" Mike asked. "So, we're prisoners here then?"

"Yes and no. What we weren't told was that we could have placed money on our bracelets to use for buying food and other stuff around the Farm. Since we didn't do that, we're incurring Farm debt which must be paid off before we can leave."

"And how did you learn of this?"

"Master Jeromy told me about it last night. Fortunately, there are attractions we can do to make a small amount of money for ourselves while working off the debt."

"And what are these attractions?"

"I'm not sure of them all, but the cocksucking pillories and dildo bikes are two I remember him mentioning. Oh, and the pony carts. That was one as well. Now, if you'll excuse me, I really need to get some rest. I feel like shit."

"No problem. I'll drop by later to see how you're doing, Mike said, Leaning down and gently kissing her on the lips.

"Jizznympho and I are going to grab a bite to eat, want to come along?"

"I'd love to, but I promised Cockharlot I'd eat breakfast with her."

"Where are you going?"

"A place called the Cumeaterie. Apparently, all the food is covered in the most delicious semen in the world."

"Really?"

"That's what Cockharlot tells me."

"Well, as it just so happens, Sluttycunt and I are going to the same place. Perhaps we could make it a double date and we can get to know this fiancé of yours."

"I think that's a great idea," Mike smiled. "She really is a beautiful woman and I think you'll really like her."

"What do you know about her? What's her real name, her favorite food? Color?"

"We didn't exactly get into that part of her life, but she was forced into training as a sex slave while at school with Mistress Gwen. There were these three sadistic Mistresses that terrorized the campus and…"

"As interesting as this all sounds, I really do need about another thirty-nine hours of sleep," Susan groaned. "Why are you three still here?"

"Sorry," Beth apologized. "Come on, you can fill us in on the way."

"You know what I find funny about all of this?" Natalie said as they walked down the stairs of the Farm submissive apartments. "The blackmailer sent us here to be trained as sex slaves in the hopes of humiliating and degrading us, but after one day we've embraced and made it our own."

"And we're porn stars," Mike added.

"Um, what?" Beth asked. "What do you mean we're porn stars?"

"Cockharlot told me last night that every inch of this place is wired with hidden cameras recording everything we do and broadcasting it live on the internet as well as nearly twenty pay-per-view channels they own. Hell, they have their own television station right here on the Farm. So, in a sense, we're porn stars. Of course we're not getting paid, but still."

"Then what's left to black mail us with?" Beth asked. "If the world already knows what we've done then he has nothing to hold against us. Did the idiot even think that far ahead?"

"Now that you mention it, that's a very good question," said Natalie. "Maybe he didn't know the farm is wired like it is."

"Maybe. So, what do we do about it now? According to Sugarpussy we are unable to leave until we've paid off our Farm debt and we don't even know how much that is."

"I'm not leaving," Mike said. "I know it's crazy, but I really feel something for Cockharlot and I don't think she'd ever leave this place. I'm staying here with her. At least until I figure out if we're a good match or not. And if what Sugarpussy said was true, then I doubt she's leaving either."

"You mean about her parents, or being a pain slut?"

"Both."

"You saw the look on her face while she was talking about it," Beth said. "Trust me, she's a pain slut through and through. And I should know."

"Oh," Natalie said with raised brow "and why's that?"

"Because I know one when I see one," Beth giggled, looking her girlfriend straight in the eyes and giving her a hard slap on the pussy.

"Aahhhh," Natalie moaned, her knees temporarily turning to jelly.

"See, pain slut," Beth grinned, giver Natalie an even harder pussy slap.

"I guess we really do learn something new every day," said Mike.

45

"Hey honey," Mike greeted Cockharlot at the main office.

"Hey yourself, Cummonkey. How's the ass?"

"Stretched wide and burning like I've been branded or something. Oh, wait, I *have* been branded," he said turning to show his new fiancé his freshly branded behind.

"God, that is so fucking hot!" Cockharlot exclaimed. "So, what brings the three of you by today?"

"We were wondering a few things," Natalie answered. First, how do we know if we have farm debt, or any money on our bracelets?"

"You can swipe it at any scanner you find on the Farm. Here," Cockharlot said motioning to the small scanner on the corner of her desk. "Just swipe the chip at the top."

Stepping forward, Natalie scanned her bracelet. "The slave in training known as Sluttycunt owes seventeen dollars and eighty-four cents to the Domination Farm," a computerized female voice said.

"What do I owe that for?"

"According to your purchase history, you ate at Rex's place last night," Cockharlot replied. "Your total was seventeen-eighty-four. And in case you're wondering how I know that, When you swipe your bracelet at one of the scanners attached to a computer as you just did, your personal profile comes up on screen."

"Sugarpussy said there were attractions we could do to work off the debt and earn money for ourselves?" Mike said.

"That is correct. Most of the outside attractions and events are paid. Meaning you are paid for participating in them, and the patrons pay to use you. What else were you wondering about?"

"Are there any phones we can use to call home?" Beth answered.

"We have a phone here in the main office for emergency use. You may make one phone call per day at a cost of fifty swats of the cane split evenly between breasts and pussy."

"DAMN!" Natalie groaned. "It's last night all over again. Before I make the call I have one more question. Is it true the entire place is wired with cameras streaming live on the internet and to nearly twenty pay-per-view channels?"

"That is correct."

"And how many people would you say are watching at any given time?"

"Hundreds of millions worldwide."

"So, in essence, we are porn stars and anyone seeing us will know exactly what we're here to do?"

"Pretty much, yeah."

"Then our enslavement here is pointless. If the world already knows then our blackmailer has nothing on us anymore."

"A better question would be, what are the odds someone saw *us*?" Mike said. "I mean, there are hundreds, if not thousands of people here so what are the chances we even appeared on camera for them to watch?"

"For you? One hundred percent," Cockharlot said looking up at Mike. "Our entire session was broadcast live on three channels with a viewing audience of sixteen million. Same with Sugarpussy. Her trip to the body modification building and subsequent punishment was seen by more than nine million. As for the two of you," she said to Beth and Natalie "You were watched being fucked, fisted and branded by more than eleven million."

"Um, and you know this how?"

"It's my job to keep an eye on all of Mistress Gwen's slaves," Cockharlot answered. "That, and I just got the viewing figures an hour ago from DFTV. That's our television station."

"Then there's nothing keeping us here," Beth said. "The blackmailer has nothing and we can go as soon as our debt to the Farm is repaid."

"That is correct."

"I already told you I was staying for Cockharlot," said Mike.

"And I kind of want to stay as well," Natalie said to her lover. "Are you saying you want to go home?"

"No. I'm already a trained submissive and I've been branded a fisting queen. If you're willing to see this to the end then so am I. Now, about that phone call."

"You know this is supposed to end with us being auctioned off, right?" said Mike.

"That was before we know about our training being recorded and broadcast all over the globe," Natalie replied. "The old rules no longer apply as far as I'm concerned. Tell me, Cockharlot, will the Domination Farm force us to be auctioned off?"

"No. there are strict rules and guidelines concerning the auction block. All participants must be willing and fill out the necessary paperwork witnessed by no less than two Dominants of the participant's choosing. And according to your profile, you have not filled out the paperwork."

"Nor do I plan on doing so. I'd like to call my parents now."

Opening the bottom left desk drawer, Cockharlot plucked out a cell phone and handed it to Natalie. "The price must be paid directly after hanging up."

"Thanks." Taking a deep breath, Natalie dialed her mother's number and listened to each ring in silence.

"Hello?" Regina answered the phone.

"Hey mom it's…hold on a second." Cupping the speaker, she looked at Cockharlot. "Do I have to give her my submissive name, or can I tell her it's me?"

"You may use your real name during phone calls."

"Sorry about that mom. It's Natalie."

"Of course it is. Who else would be calling me mom? Is everything alright?"

"I was about to ask you the same thing. Have you heard anything from the blackmailer yet?"

"Nothing yet. How's the Domination Farm?"

"Interesting. Very, very interesting. I've learned a lot in just one day. I have something very important to tell you and I don't want you to be upset with me, okay?"

"What is it sweetie? After everything this family has been through, you can tell me anything."

"Before I do, I want to tell you some good news. Well, sort of good news. The blackmailer has nothing on us anymore, mom. Nothing. His whole threat relied on our fear of everything being released and that's no longer an issue."

"What do you mean?"

"The Domination Farm is wired mom. They have their own TV station and all. Millions of people saw us performing very kinky acts. We're porn stars, mom. Unpaid, mind you, but porn stars nonetheless. That means you don't have to fear being taken and trained as a sex slave. If you are contacted by him then tell them to fuck off and that you're going to the police the next time they call or attempt to contact you in any way. That being said, we've all agreed to stay for training."

"What? Are you serious?"

"Very. Mike met a beautiful woman, fell head over heels in love with her and is now engaged to be married, and it turns out that Susan and I are both pain sluts. Anyways, with the threat of being sold to the highest bidder no longer looming over our heads, we decided to embrace it and stay to the end."

"Are you absolutely certain that's what you want to do, sweetie?"

"Very. You know how much I enjoyed the things the blackmailer made me do. Now that I can do them on my own terms I want it even more than ever. We are permitted one call per day so I'll try to keep in touch as much as possible to let you know how I'm doing. And can you do me a huge favor?"

"Anything you need, Natalie."

"Can you call Beth's parents and let them know they have nothing to worry about? You'll find their number in my little blue book up in my top right desk drawer."

"I'll call them right away. What about Susan's parents?"

"As much as I hate to say it, don't bother. They have no idea what's supposed to happen and hopefully, with you and Beth's parents no longer fearing him, they'll just go the fuck away and leave us all alone. Besides, Sugarpussy will never forgive me if I warned them."

"Sugarpussy?"

"That's Susan's submissive name. Mine is Sluttycunt, Beth is Jizznympho and Mike is Cummonkey."

"Jesus Christ!"

"And they tattooed it on our breasts for all to see. Actually, other than this phone call, it's the only thing we are permitted to call each other while at the Farm."

"That's some pretty fucked up shit, Natalie. Are you sure you want to remain there?"

"Yes."

"Are your father and I allowed to visit you up there?"

"I'm sure you could, but you really don't want to do that. In order to get in you have to agree to all the rules and that means the risk of being collared, marked as a submissive and put through training. I promise to call as often as I can, but it might not be every day. I love you mom. Tell dad I love him too. And I'll call in a couple of days."

"I love you to, sweetie."

Hanging up the phone, Natalie handed it back to Cockharlot. "I'll take my fifty swats now."

"Here," Beth said holding out her hand, I want to make a call."

"But I told my mom to tell your parents so that you don't have to make a call and get caned."

"That's sweet and all, but I'm sure they'd rather hear the news from me. Plus, I want to talk to Jenna. I will accept the fifty swats to make the call."

"Um, are you going to give us the swats?" Natalie asked Cockharlot.

"No. the only ones permitted to administer swats are the Dominants. Mistress Gwen should be back in a few minutes. She will give them to you then. In the meantime, you may wait over there," she said motioning to the row of dildo seats along the wall to her right.

∞ ∞ ∞

Mistress Gwen entered the main office three minutes after Beth hung up from talking to her parents. "Hello slaves," she said to her four new slaves-in-training. They greeted her in return and she walked over and sat down at her desk. "Anything new this morning, Cockharlot?"

"Yes Mistress, but I think it should come from them."

"Oh? Alright, slaves, start talking."

"After learning we were recorded and our sexual exploits blasted all over the world, we have nothing more to fear from our blackmailer, Mistress," Beth replied.

"But instead of packing up and going home, we've decided to remain at the Farm as your slaves-in-training, Mistress. And since we signed no papers to be put up for auction, we don't have that to worry about either. We are here now because we want to be, and not because we were forced into it."

"Well, that is a surprise."

"Mistress, does the blackmailer know everything is recorded?" Mike asked.

"They do."

"Then why send us here? I don't get it. He had to know we'd find out and that he'd lose all leverage over us."

"She."

"Excuse me, Mistress?"

"The blackmailer is a woman. Or rather two women. And no, I will not give you their names. And all four of you are remaining?"

"Well, the three of us are, Mistress," said Mike. We haven't asked Sugarpussy yet as she's resting after last night's punishment, but I have a feeling she'll stay."

"Your friend is a masochist in the truest sense of the word. No matter what Master Jeromy did to her she begged for more, all the while squirting pussy juices like a damn fire hose. She was pierced, branded, flogged, caned, paddled and had hot wax poured all over her body and she cried for more until finally passing out. In all my years I've never seen anything quite like it. And before I forget, congratulations, Cummonkey and the recent engagement. I have to say it came as a bit of a surprise when I watched the recording."

"Thank you, Mistress. Cockharlot and I are going to take it slow and get to know each other before jumping into marriage, but I have a very good feeling about her."

"She's an incredible woman," Mistress Gwen said with a warm smile. We go way back and I can tell you right now you'll never find a more loyal, loving and honest wife."

"Thank you Mistress," said Cockharlot.

"I meant every word. And I also mean this: if you do anything to break her heart I will do things to you the devil himself couldn't dream up. Cockharlot isn't just my slave, she's also my best friend."

"I can assure you I have no intentions of breaking her heart, Mistress. That is why we are taking the time to get to know each other first."

"You know you are not permitted to have sex with other women until she is pregnant, right?"

"Yes Mistress. And that's a small price to pay considering the life we're considering."

"Why are the two of you sitting on the dildo seats? Do you enjoy being stretched open that much?"

"Yes Mistress," Natalie answered "but we are here because we were waiting for you to get back to cane us. Jizznympho and I made a phone call."

"Then let me get my cane and I'll take care of that for you."

46

One week later...

"Are you sure you're ready to go back out there?" Natalie asked Susan.

"God yes. I've been shut up in this room for a week now and I really, really need some dick."

"Up your ass," Mike smirked, looking down at the strip of purple leather that continued to keep her pussy laced shut.

"Up my ass, down my throat, I don't care. I just want to be fucked before I lose my mind.

"Have you decided to stay at the Farm then?" Beth asked.

"Yeah. I'm here to the end. Also, now that my deep, dark secret is out for all the world to know, I really want to feel the cane biting into my tender flesh again. Have you figured out what we need to do to complete our training?"

"Yeah," Natalie answered. "And you're going to love it. Not only do we have to learn the basics like obedience and etiquette from Mistress Gwen, there are about a dozen events and attractions requiring the marks of completion. In order to complete the training we have to find, complete and receive all those tattoos and brands."

"Nice," Susan perked up at the thought of enduring even more pain and humiliation. "Any idea which ones they are?"

"Nope. We'll have to do them all one by one until finding them. From what I've been able to gather, with the exception of a few areas, this farm is designed so that we train ourselves."

"Pretty ingenious when you think about it," Mike added. "I mean, it's one thing to submit to another for training, but how humiliating is it having to willingly put yourself through the kinky shit there is to find here?"

"How long do you have to go without vaginal sex?" Beth asked out of nowhere.

"As long as Mistress Gwen tells me to wear the lace. It could be another week, a month or a year."

"Or the rest of your life," Mike added. "Can you go the rest of your life not feeling a dick slamming into you?"

"I honestly don't know. But that's enough talking for now. I want to go out and see the damn Farm instead of being cooped up in here all damn day and night. You guys are already a week ahead of me so I have some catching up to do."

"Honestly, we're not that far ahead," said Natalie. "In fact, the only thing we've done in terms of training is getting the fisting out of the way. The rest of the time has been spent roaming the Farm and doing stuff for the occasional, random Dominant. And really, we're on even ground considering you've gotten the pain training done and over with. Anyways, we're not going to train ourselves standing around here all day so let's go."

∞ ∞ ∞

After a light breakfast at the Cumeaterie –
the group's favorite place to eat on the Farm, the
four friends parted ways. Determined to make the
best of her new life, Susan walked down Anal
Avenue looking for sex when she spotted a raven-
haired Mistress leading a male submissive around
on a leash like a dog. And when her eyes found the
cock and large balls hanging between his muscular
legs, her heart fluttered and she knew she had to
have him. Approaching, she hesitated only a
second. "Excuse me Mistress."

The woman stopped, giving the leash a tug
to indicate to her slave to stop as well. Turning to
face Susan, she looked her up and down with mild
amusement. "Are you talking to me Sugarpussy?"

"Yes Mistress," Susan replied. "I'm sorry to
bother you, but I just had to ask," she bit her lip
suddenly becoming very nervous.

"Spit it out. Or do you think it's polite to
waste my time?"

"No Mistress. Sorry Mistress. It's just
that…well you see…I would like permission for
your submissive to fuck me up the ass."

"I see. And why would I allow that?"

"Please Mistress," Susan almost begged "I
would do anything you ask of me in return. I'm
new to this lifestyle and being a slave so if I'm out
of line I apologize. It's just that I've been locked in
my room for the last week healing after being
pierced, branded and brutally caned and when I
saw his cock the first thing that came to mind was
getting royally fucked."

"And you'll do anything I ask in return?"

"Without question, Mistress."

"Then get on all fours like a good little bitch, Sugarpussy."

"Yes Mistress. Thank you," Susan replied, never getting on her hands and knees so quickly in her life.

"Mount, Puppywhore."

"Woof," Puppywhore barked. Moving behind Susan, he stuck his nose in her pussy and ass, gave her several quick licks and then hopped up on her back. The bulbous head of his cock pressed against her asshole for all of three seconds and then all ten, thick inches slammed in.

"Aahhhh fuck!" Susan moaned as the man's cock pushed deeper and deeper. Pushing back on it to take every possible inch, she dug her fingernails into the grass at the edge of the paved street, arched her back and looked up into the clear blue sky – seeing stars as the orgasm quickly approached.

"It looks like Puppywhore is enjoying his new bitch," the Mistress said. "Do you like his cock, Sugarpussy?"

"Yes Mistress. Oh my fucking god yes! I love it. It's only been a week since I had sex, but it feels like a year. Thank you…thank you…thank you Mistress for allowing this worthless slave to take such a big, fat cock."

Puppywhore dug his long fingernails into Susan's hips, raking them along her sides and leaving behind red scratches as he continued to plow into her tightly clenching asshole. Placing his hands on her shoulders, he dug in once more and brought them down her back with enough force to leave instant welts. Susan moaned through it all and clenched his cock even tighter.

"Fuck me harder! Harder...HARDER DAMMIT! Mmmm, that's it. Fuck me like you hate me! Fill my ass with your hot load!" Her elbows buckling, her head went down, barley being caught on one arm as she exploded in orgasm – pussy juices squirting out and running down her thighs as well as Puppywhore's. And still he continued to fuck, his stamina increased thanks to years of training. Several minor aftershocks followed in the wake of the first orgasm, but the volcanic eruption came when she felt his teeth sink into her shoulder as he filled her bowels with semen. The bite lasted several seconds, nearly breaking the skin, but leaving behind a very visible mark. Waiting until his cock was fully limp, Puppywhore finally gave her a few more hard nips on the back and sides before dismounting and assuming the sitting position as he was so well-trained to do, leaving her on the ground panting like a bitch in heat.

"You ready to pay the price now, slave?"

"Yes Mistress."

"Did you enjoy being a bitch for my puppy slave?"

"Oh god yes, Mistress. I loved every second of it. Even the scratching and biting."

"Glad to hear it. You will remain on all fours and follow along my right side next to Puppywhore.

Going east on Anal Avenue, the Mistress led Susan north on Domination Drive to a long wooden building at the corner of Sadism Street. Looking through the open barn doors, Susan could see several stockades – some filled with women being fucked while lines of men waited their turn. Staying at Puppywhore's side, she followed the Mistress in and to a counter where a corset-wearing blonde greeted them.

"Hey Kelsey, have another slave for me to breed?"

"Yes, but she's not mine. She's one of Mistress Gwen's, but she offered to pay whatever price I set for allowing my Puppywhore to mount her and this is what I want."

"Excuse me, Mistress," Susan said looking up at the two women "But my pussy is laced shut at Mistress Gwen's command. How can I be bred if the men cannot fuck their cocks into my pussy?"

"Not a problem slave. You're lacing will be removed while you are here and replaced once you've met the daily quota of men. You will come here every day and remain until you've taken twenty loads. And you will continue to do so until you are confirmed pregnant. Is that understood?"

"Yes Mistress."

"If you leave the Farm before impregnated then you will be automatically registered as a Farm submissive. Is that understood?"

"Yes Mistress. May I make a request?"

"What is it?"

"Can I be bred only by black men?"

"Is that what Mistress Gwen wants?"

"She never said anything about breeding me, Mistress. My mother is incredibly racist and I want to see the look on her face when she sees her grandchildren are mixed race. Not that I give a flipping fuck what the bitch thinks."

"Then black men it is. You may crawl to any of the empty stockades over there in the black cock's only section and place yourself in. Once the bar is locked in place, the black men present will breed you and I'll make sure we have enough here every day to meet your quota."

"Thank you Mistress."

47

With Susan off doing her thing, and Mike headed back to the main office to spend time with his fiancé – a woman he's come to love and respect a great deal in such a short period of time, Natalie and Beth remained together until the former spotted the squirt gun games. Having no interest in being blasted with a high-powered squirt gun, Beth opted out and continued exploring.

Her interest piqued, Natalie walked up to the small booth and got the attention of the man within. "Excuse me, Master, but what's the squirt gun game and how do I participate?"

"It's very simple. You will be strapped spread-eagle to a Saint Andrews. You will have targets painted on your breasts, belly, arms, legs and pussy. As soon as you have a contestant, the timer will be set and the prize won will be based on how many of the targets they can blast off of you."

"When you say blast off…"

"I mean, he or she will be using a high-powered water gun to remove the targets. It's not as strong as a pressure washer, but its damn close. Go ahead and get on a Saint Andrews and I'll get you painted up."

"Yes Master. How long do I have to remain?"

"Two hours or until a contestant manages to remove all of the targets, whichever comes first. You will have to strip out of your submissive clothing."

"Yes Master."

After stripping out of her submissive clothing, Natalie placed herself on the Saint Andrews and allowed herself to be strapped in place. No sooner were her wrists and ankles bound, then the man grabbed her by the hips and pushed his cock into her pussy. Not bothering to protest, she let it happen, moaning here and there when he managed to hit the sweet spot. When he finally dropped a load in her, he went to work painting the targets and then returned to his booth.

Natalie waited a good fifteen minutes before attracting the attention of a twenty-something man strutting around as if king of the world. Placing a bill in the machine he picked, the rifle was released and he took aim as a computerized female voice spoke. "This slave has earned five dollars." The water shot out, blasting Natalie's right breast much harder than she imagined, causing her to screech in pain. Her pussy tingled and she bit into her lower lip as the jet moved to her right arm. In seconds that target too was gone and he was washing away the one on her right leg – making excellent time of it. Or so she thought. The left leg was next followed by the belly, and then the left arm. But before it was peeled away, the timer buzzed and the water stream trickled to a stop.

Panting and groaning on the verge of orgasm, Natalie watched as the man attempted to put another bill into the machine. "Not so fast, Mister," the Master in charge yelled. "You want another go then you'll have to wait until I get her pained up again."

"That's bullshit! This game is fucking rigged. There's no way in hell anyone can get them all in time."

"You did pretty well for your first go. Five targets gets you your choice of five minutes of sex with her, or twenty swats of the cane across her tits. What'll it be?"

"Give me the cane," the man said with a sadistic grin – the look in his eyes telling Natalie that it was somehow her fault he did not get them all and he was about to take it out on her breasts.

WHACK!

"ONE! T-Thank you Master," Natalie said on automatic as the cane tore into her breasts. It was followed by nineteen more equally as hard, and three mind-blowing orgasms before the Master of the event repainted her for the next contestant which happened to be the same man.

Changing tactics, the young man started with the right breast as before, but then moved to the left breast, belly, pussy and right leg. The target on her left thigh was quickly blasted off as was the one on her left arm, but the timer ran out just as he was passing over her breasts to the right arm.

"God damn son of a fucking bitch! What does seven targets get me?"

"Fifteen minutes fucking her, fifty swats of the cane split between breasts and pussy, or your choice of body modifications. On her, of course."

"Give her a second hood piercing and place a clit shield on her so she can't use that route of pleasure."

"You got it. You want to give her another go?"

"Nah. I've had my fill for now." Hanging up the rifle, the young man walked away and the Master of the event went back into the boot – returning momentarily with a small black bag.

"Hold still, you don't want crooked piercings."

"Yes Master." Looking down, she watched the man clean her pussy place a mark where it needed to go to fit the shield and then push the needle through. She grunted slightly, but after already enduring so much, it was nothing and she continued to watch as he removed her ring and placed the decorative curved piece of metal that completely covered her clit. "How long will I have to wear it Master?"

"How long will you be at the Domination Farm?"

"I don't know, Master. I am here to be trained as a slave and I'm only a week in."

"Well, anything added to your body or outfit must be worn every day for as long as you are here. For all intents and purposes, it's permanent."

"So, I'll never feel my clit again?"

"Not as long as you're at the Domination Farm."

"Yes Master."

"And because I saw how being caned made you orgasm, I'm going to go ahead and give you fifty more swats of the cane."

"Thank you Master."

∞ ∞ ∞

After an hour and forty minutes, nine contestants, two-hundred-fifty more swats of the cane and vertical bars added to her nipples, Natalie was exhausted and incredibly sore when a tenth man walked up, placed money in the machine and took aim. As if a navy seals sniper, he shot the targets off in rapid succession starting with her right arm and working his way back around to her right breast.

"Nice shooting," said the Master of the event. For getting all eight targets you have a choice of prizes. You may fuck her to completion, give her one hundred and fifty swats of the cane, order another piece of body modification, or take her to any building here in the Domination Farm whether she wants to go or not, with the exception of the Cummypaws Training Facility. That is by appointment only I'm afraid."

The man looked Natalie over several times, looking at her tattoos and brands. "You been to the animal training barn yet, Sluttycunt?"

"No Master."

"Then that's where you're going now. I hope you love kinky, taboo sex because you're about to get a load of it."

"I love kinky sex, Master."

Removing Natalie from the Saint Andrews, the man order her to all fours and then led her to the huge barn right next to the squirt gun games. Taking her inside, Natalie's eyes went wide as it did not take her brain long to know what fetish she would have to complete before being permitted to leave. A hand pressed on her back and she instinctively lowered her head to the floor and spread her legs as a leggy brunette approached. The Master bringing her in, shoved his cock into her pussy and quickly fucked a load into her before leaving her in the very capable hands of Breedingmare.

48

Two month later...

Every day at the Domination Farm brought with it new challenges to overcome – be it a fetish they hated with every fiber of their being, or learning proper positions, etiquette and how to obey commands without hesitation. And though each attraction and event complete brought them all that much closer to fully realized sex slaves, none of them thought about going home. Mike and Tawnie were madly, deeply in love. Natalie and Beth were as well and met Susan every day at the Breeding Stables where they were fucked and filled by only black cocks.

Seven weeks in and Cockharlot received the good news. Four days later and Beth was with child and a day after that, Susan. But that did not stop any of them from being bred day in and day out. Finally free of his chastity cage, Mike went to the farm fucking as many women as possible – returning to his fiancé's room every night to tell of his conquests. But at the end of two months, Natalie found herself in Mistress Gwen's office with a million questions plaguing her mind.

"How can I help you this evening, Sluttycunt?"

"Please forgive the intrusion Mistress, but I was hoping we could talk."

"I have a few minutes to spare. What is it you wish to discuss?"

"Well, I've been wondering about a few things. Like, how long is the term of our enslavement? Who paid for our training? Things like that."

"I see. You've been here what, a couple of months now? And this is the first time you've thought to ask?"

"Yes Mistress. To be honest we were all so engrossed with training none of us even thought about it until now."

"The length of your training was originally set to be three weeks," replied Mistress Gwen smiling.

"Three weeks?" asked Natalie in shock. "You mean we could have left long ago? Why didn't anyone tell us?"

"Why didn't you ask? When the original time lapsed I was in contact with the one that paid for your training and they so graciously paid for an additional six months. So to answer your question you have another five months of training to go through that has been paid for before you are either free to go, or they pay to keep you here longer. As for who paid for your training I'm afraid that's confidential information. Suffice it to say they want to make sure you're all very well trained sex slaves."

"I know we've asked this already, but how long does it take to become fully trained?"

"That all depends on the slave. Some, like you and your friends are more compliant than others and complete the majority of the training in under a year with only the finer details remaining. And then there are those who fight it tooth and nail. Those are the ones that take a lifetime. As I told you weeks ago, in order to complete the training here at the Domination Farm you will have to get all of the marks of completion on top of the training I put you through. In two months you've taken care of over half of them, but you still have a long way to go."

"And when they are all complete then what?"

"Then you'll have a few options at your disposal. You may remain here as my slave. You may choose another Dominant to serve, or you can even opt to go through the training to become a Dominant yourself. And if you really wanted to, you could go home and forget any of this ever happened and move on with your life."

"I don't think I'll ever be able to forget this happened, Mistress," Natalie replied. "And I've come too far to turn back now. Wait, I thought once registered as a slave it was impossible to become a Dominant?"

"Let's just say there are perks to being the owner's slave."

"And how long does that training take, Mistress?"

"About a year. At the end of the training you will be tested. If you pass, you'll be given the option of becoming a full, red armband wearing Dominant, or a purple armband and collar wearing switch. If you choose to be a Dominant, you may always change and become a switch, but once a switch there is no going back. And if you seriously break the rules and are demoted to Farm submissive, that will be your status for life."

"Thank you Mistress, you've given me a great deal to think about."

"You know there's no rush, right? I mean, sure, there is a limit to the time paid for, but you've already racked up quite a bit working the attractions and could easily pay for another few months assuming your benefactor doesn't beat you to it. You do not have to rush through everything in one go."

"Yes Mistress. I guess given the kinky and taboo nature of some of the fetishes, I'd rather get them done and over with as quickly as possible. I just wish I didn't have to wear this damn clit shield all the time."

"Go through Dominant training and you can take it off."

"But I can't do that until I complete my slave training, right Mistress?"

"That is correct."

"So at least another ten months of wearing it. Sorry clit," Natalie sighed "It looks like you're remain untouched for a while. Can I ask another question, Mistress?"

"You may."

"I've noticed many on the Farm that have completed some of the same things as my friends and I, but they are tattooed. Is there a reason we've only ever gotten branded, Mistress?"

"It was the request of the ones paying for your training. All marks of completion are to be in the form of brands."

"So, we have half a dozen more to get, Mistress?"

"Something like that, yes."

"I see. Thank you Mistress."

"I didn't think that would be a problem for pain sluts like you and Sugarpussy."

"Oh, I orgasm every time, Mistress, but I was just thinking about the future and what people would think should I ever leave this lifestyle. Tattoos I can have removed. Brands? Not so much."

"I understand. I have a few brands myself, remember?"

"Yes Mistress. Do you ever regret them?"

"In the beginning I hated each and every one of them, but now, now I've come to terms with them and wear them as badges of honor and survival. Tell me, do you ever see yourself leaving the lifestyle, Sluttycunt?"

"I honestly don't know, Mistress. I mean, I've only been in it for a few months now. I can see myself here years from now, but who knows what the future will bring?"

"Truer words were never spoken. You know you may come and talk to me about anything, right?"

"Yes Mistress. Thank you. In the couple of months I've been here on the Farm, I've seen a wide variety of Masters and Mistress, submissives, slaves and bare-necks and I've learned a great deal about myself in the process, but I still feel this pang of guilt and shame for allowing my life to spiral out of control to the point it landed me here in the first place and I'm afraid I'll never get over it, or what it has done to my family and friends."

"You know my story, so you know I understand where you are coming from. It took me a long time to come to terms with it even after taking down the three Mistresses and voluntarily submitting myself for training under Master Joey."

"Does anyone in your family know, Mistress? Friends?"

"My mother knows about it and all the friends that know have either been trained by the tree Mistresses, or came here over the years."

"What does your mother have to say about it, Mistress?"

"She's perfectly fine with it. After all, she's a trained sex slave herself."

"Really, Mistress?"

"Yep. She and my father divorced shortly after she made a trip up here to see me. One thing led to another and she found herself collared. Master Joey upheld the collaring despite my pleading and she went on to serve as a breeding slave to her new Master."

"Honestly, that's pretty cool. Though I have no idea how I'd feel about my mother visiting and being turned into a slave. I've fought tooth and nail for months to keep that from happening and as of this morning she still hasn't heard anything from the blackmailer about being enslaved at home."

"Probably biding their time hoping to strike when your parents least expect it."

"Maybe. I'll stop wasting your time now Mistress. Thank you for giving me the time and answering my questions."

"You are not wasting my time, Sluttycunt. I am your Mistress and it is my duty to make sure you are taken care of both physically and mentally. If there's ever anything on your mind do not hesitate in asking."

"Thank you Mistress."

49

Three more months later...

Kim and Lana pulled into the parking lot of the Domination Farm and slapped the silver cuff bracelet around their right wrist. After dressing in their submissive clothes – obtained from former trips, they went through line, placed five hundred dollars on their bracelets and then headed inside. Not wanting to waste time and risk getting caught, Lana went straight for the main office.

"I want to look around a little," Kim said to her mother.

"No way! If you get collared there's nothing I can do about it. Just stay by my side and we'll be out of here in no time."

"But I've been here three times already and I want to look around. Just go take care of business and we'll meet at the exit in an hour."

"I said no!"

"And I said I'm over the age of eighteen and don't have to listen to you, so stop trying to run my damn life." Storming off with a huff, Kim didn't dare look back as she fast walked down Domination Drive – turning out of her mother's sight on Anal Avenue.

Thinking about going after her daughter, Lana sighed and entered the main office instead. "Hello Mistress Gwen. Do you have time to talk?"

"Of course. You dropping by to add more time to their training?"

"Yes, Mistress," Lana almost scowled – the thought of taking a submissive role demeaning to her. "I'm adding enough to keep them here at least two years. But first, can you do something about my daughter? She's wondering the damn Farm alone and uncollared."

"You know the rules, Lana."

"I'm paying you all this money so the least you can do is this one small favor. Just send someone to get her and bring her back here, or better yet, take her out to the damn car before someone slaps a collar around her neck."

"No can do."

"Look you fucking cunt, you either do me this one small favor, or I'll take my business elsewhere."

"Threats will get you nowhere, Lana. And I advise against them here."

"Whatever. How are the slaves progressing? How soon can they go up for auction?"

"They are coming along nicely, but have a long way to go. You knew from day one that it could take years so why the sudden lack of patience now?"

"I'm getting impatient because this place is bleeding me dry dammit! You, slave, go fetch my daughter for me," Lana said to Cockharlot.

"Cockharlot answers only to me. And if you continue to bark orders you're not going to have a good time."

"Bitch, I'll knock your fucking tits in the dirt," Lana threatened.

"What did I tell you about issuing threats around here?" Mistress Gwen asked. "Cockharlot, kindly escort Lana here to the waiting room. Maybe after another guided tour she'll have enough sense to know her place."

"Yes Mistress."

"I'm not going anywhere. I'm here for one thing and one thing only. And if you're not going to take my money then you can go fuck yourself."

"You can either go to the waiting room, or you can go to the registration office. The choice is yours. And remember one thing. The longer you stand here and argue with me, the greater the chance your daughter will be collared."

"Fine! Let's go, slave."

∞ ∞ ∞

Lana was barely to the door leading to the waiting room when Natalie walked around the corner of Bondage Boulevard and into the main office to show off her new golden showers mark of completion.

"You've got impeccable timing, Sluttycunt. Another three minutes and you would have walked right into your benefactor."

"You mean they're here, Mistress?"

"That is correct. Would you like to see who it is?"

"I thought that was confidential information, Mistress?"

"It was until one of them decided to toss threats around. Come with me."

Taking Natalie to a small back room filled with wall to wall monitors, Mistress Gwen walked over and pointed to one particular screen near the bottom row. "Tell me, Sluttycunt, does anyone in that room look familiar?"

Moving in for a closer look, Natalie nearly shit herself when she saw Lana sitting along the back wall bouncing her left leg up and down a hundred miles an hour. "It can't be. What is she doing here Mistress? Please tell me this is some sort of sick joke."

"It's no joke, Sluttycunt. She's the one that negotiated all of this. She's the mastermind behind everything that has happened to you and your friends and family from the moment you were handed that first photo album."

"But that's...she's...why? Why would she do this to me?"

"For the fun of it? Revenge? Because she can?" replied Mistress Gwen. "Who knows why anyone does anything?"

"But she's my best friend's mother!"

"I know sweetie and that brings me to surprise number two," Mistress Gwen said pointing to another monitor near the center of the back wall showing a woman of about twenty pulling the door to the golden showers open and stepping inside.

"Oh my god! You mean Kim's here as well? Did she know about all of this, or did her mother bring her to be trained as well?"

"They are both here to be fully trained," Gwen replied "although they don't know that yet. I thought it only fitting considering what they did to you and your loved ones. Lana believes she's here to discuss you and your friends and I would have taken her money and added the time to your training had she not been a bitch and ignore my warnings. You might have noticed neither of them are wearing collars. They are bare-necks right now, but they have no idea how much their lives are about to change.

Sinking to the floor, Natalie began to cry – her best friend's betrayal cutting her like a knife. "I d-don't know what I e-ever did to her to deserve this, Mistress. She played me for a fool! Claimed she got a commandment just to throw me off! Why? W-Why would she do this to us?"

"I honestly don't know, Sluttycunt. But her days terrorizing you and your family are at an end. I've been waiting for her to fuck up here at the Farm so I could claim her and that's exactly what she did."

"I always thought it was a man named Glen behind it. Or whatever his real name was. Thank you for showing me this, Mistress."

"You're very welcome. And as far as Glen is concerned, Lana made the mistake of telling me all about her plan. And from the bottom of my heart I am truly sorry I could not tell you this earlier, but my hands were tied until she did something to break the rules of the Farm. Had I divulged this information before now, I would have lost ownership of the Farm and been registered a Farm submissive."

"I understand Mistress. And you know what? I think I've finally made up my mind, Mistress."

"Concerning?"

"I want to remain and be trained as a Dominant, Mistress. And if they are here when the time comes, I know exactly which two slaves I'll be claiming as my own."

"That can be arranged, but know that training is not free. You'll be expected to participate in farm activities and do other work around here while you are trained."

"I understand, Mistress."

"I know this is a lot to take in and your first inclination is to hunt them down and beat the shit out of them, but please, please do as I say and leave them be. Any violence on another will not be tolerated and if you are reduced to Farm submissive you can kiss any chance of owning them goodbye."

"You're right, Mistress. I want to rip their heads off and use them ad soccer balls, but I'll do as you command and I'll make sure the others do the same."

"Go one then, I'll locate them and have them brought back to your room."

"Thank you Mistress."

∞ ∞ ∞

"Are you fucking serious!" Susan yelled. "Kim? Your best friend since the second fucking grade Kim? Where are they?"

"You cannot go after them," Natalie said holding her hand up to prevent her friend from making a huge mistake. I know we all want answers, and I promise we'll get them, but we have to keep playing the game for now. Mistress Gwen is planning on taking the money meant to keep us here longer and using it to pay for their time here at the Farm. Even now, Kim is in the golden showers being pissed on."

"Can we go back to the main office and see?" Mike asked.

"Mistress Gwen didn't say anything about going back so I suppose it'll be alright to see it for yourselves. And just so everyone is aware, I've decided to remain for Dominant training. I think it goes without saying who I want. What about the rest of you? Are you still planning on staying, or are you leaving now that your paid time is up?"

"I'm not leaving my fiancé," Mike answered. "I've decided to remain Mistress Gwen's slave for as long as she'll have me."

"Nice."

"And I'm here for you no matter what," Beth said. And since we're all here." Dropping to one knee, she removed a ring she was hiding in the top of her right boot, and held it out to her girlfriend. "Natalie, we've only been together a short time, but I can't imagine living my life with anyone else. Will you marry me?"

The tears falling before she could drop to her knees, Natalie hugged Beth tight and sobbed into her shoulder for several minutes before composing herself. "YES!" she exclaimed loud enough for the entire Farm to hear it. Holding out a trembling hand, she watched as her now fiancé placed the golden band on her finger.

"Well, congratulations!" said Susan.

"Thank you."

"Maybe we can plan a double wedding," Mike suggested.

"That would be wonderful," Beth agreed.

"Not to put a damper on the celebration, but how are you going to claim Kim and her mother as your slaves? Won't they be collared long before you complete your training?"

"Good point. I never really thought that far ahead. Anyways, let's go to the main office so you can see it for yourself.

50

"It's about damn time," Lana said angrily when Mistress Gwen finally walked into the room she had been moved to in another part of the Domination Farm. "Where the hell have you been? I've been waiting here for over an hour."

"I'm sorry," Gwen apologized almost sincerely. "I couldn't take you to my office as normal."

"And why the hell not? Maybe you don't appreciate my business as much as I thought you did."

"Oh I appreciate it just fine. I didn't think it was a good idea considering your slaves –in-training are currently in there. Now, have you cooled down enough to talk like a rational human being or do you need more time?"

"I'm sorry for my earlier outburst, Mistress Gwen. My daughter walking off has gotten me rattled. By the way, you haven't seen Kim wondering around have you?"

"As a matter of fact I have. Last I saw she was headed into the Golden Showers building."

"You mean where all those men pissed on Natalie?"

"Yep, the very same. Boy did she ever pick the wrong time to go wondering in there."

"Why?" Lana asked, suspicions raised.

"It just so happens that there are two submissives in there right now preparing for their golden shower with about fifty men. The men will see her as just another woman to piss in and on. She's sure to get a bellyful."

"What the fuck are you doing here then? Go get her the hell out of there!"

"You know I won't do that even if I could. You and Kim both know the rules better than any bare-neck and yet you let her run around here willy-nilly. Let's just hope no one puts a collar around her neck before I have a chance to."

"What in the hell do you mean by that? You're not making my baby into one of your filthy fucking slaves."

Gwen looked down at the watch on her left wrist. "Oh lord, look at the time. I didn't realize it was getting so late. "You'll want to come with me now."

"Why? Where are we going now?"

"This room will be filling up in about five minutes for the gang bang of three submissives so unless you want to participate you had better do as you're told and follow me. But before we go out put this on." Mistress Gwen said holding out a pink collar.

"I'm not putting that on. I'm not that damn stupid. I know what happens when a collar goes around the neck at this place."

"Would you rather one of the other masters or mistresses put theirs around your neck? That is a guest collar. It symbolizes you are a personal guest of mine and cannot be collared by another for any reason. It's all in the rules if you bothered taking the time to fully read them." That was a complete lie of course. There were only a handful of pink collars made and they weren't mentioned in any rules. Right now, she was relying on their length, complexity and unwillingness of most people to thoroughly read them to aid her now.

"Yeah, I think I remember reading that." Taking the collar, Lana placed it around her neck. As the ends got closer, she was unable to keep them apart and they snapped together almost of their own accord "What the hell?"

"It's magnetic," Gwen smiled. "Super strong at that. To put it simply, it takes either a special tool or about 3,000 pounds of force to remove it."

"Well I hope you have the tool to remove it."

"I do. It's in my office. Now come on unless you want to be gang banged."

"Where are we going now?"

"We're going to the Golden Showers to get your daughter before someone else slaps a collar around her neck. If they do I can't put this one on her," she said dangling another red leather collar between finger and thumb.

"I thought a submissive had until they got to the registration office to remove the collar before they were no longer permitted to take it off?"

"That's true," Gwen replied "but given Kim's youth and beauty how long do you think that would take? Now stop complaining and come on. They should be about done with the golden shower by the time we get there."

"I don't even want to think about my poor baby going through that. Uhhhggghhh," she shuddered in fake, yet convincing disgust.

"I didn't tell you the other part of it."

"What other part?"

"Well, the golden shower doesn't start until all of the men are inside the building. Until then those that are there will use the submissives as their personal fucktoys. It's more than likely she'll be gang banged long before being used as a urinal."

"Stop," Lana sighed "just please stop. I don't want to hear about it. I swear, if they hurt my baby I'm going to come down on you like hellfire!"

"As long as she complies with them she'll be fine," Gwen smirked "but knowing Kim, she'll struggle and they might have to put her in her place."

"Meaning?" Lana stopped and turned towards Gwen, her eyes burning with hatred.

"Meaning, they'll spank her ass, or anything else it takes to get her to fall in line. Now, if you want to get her out of there before she's collared then I suggest shutting up and following me."

∞ ∞ ∞

Natalie and friends watched as Kim entered the Golden Showers building and they all recalled with perfect clarity the day they did the same – Natalie going insane and doing all three required golden showers in one day to set a Domination Farm record.

"I hope she fucking chokes to death on it," Susan growled.

"Not me," said Mike to everyone's surprise. "What? If she chokes to death then we won't get the satisfaction of seeing her broken and trained."

"Fair enough," Susan huffed.

"Hey, there's another one," one of the men shouted over the sounds of moaning and groaning – a finger pointing to Kim.

"Come on over sweetheart," yelled another. "There's plenty of cock to go around."

"You just stay the hell away from me," Kim demanded. Turning to leave, she found the way shut – the door not budging no matter how hard she pushed or pulled on it.

"Sorry doll face," said a voice nearly in her ear "the door is magnetically locked until the shower is over."

"Shower? What shower? What in the hell is going on here?"

"Don't act all innocent now sweetie," he said reaching out to grab a handful of Kim's large breasts – laughing when she instinctively slapped his hand away.

"Don't you dare fucking touch me," she screamed. "Do you know who I am? I'll have your god damn balls cut off and fed to you if you lay another finger on me."

"We've got a firecracker here guys," the man laughed. "Look you stupid bitch, I can see you're a bare-neck, but that won't help you here. Read the rules written on the wall. You're not getting out of here until you've been pissed on and in my every man here. And then you're going to the body modification building where you'll receive your mark of completion."

"LIKE HELL!" Thought she had no problem pissing on another, she was not into being on the receiving end.

"You can get your sexy ass over here and participate as you're obligated to do under the rules you agreed to and signed before entering the Domination Farm, or we can go about this the hard way. Either way, you'll be drinking our piss."

You can do this Kim, she thought to herself. *Just do it and get it over with and they'll leave you alone afterwards.* Taking a deep breath, she walked over to the group and let them drag her to the ground. But instead of feeling warm urine splashing down on her nearly naked body, she felt three cocks penetrating her pussy, ass and mouth at the same time.

"W-What are you doing!" Kim demanded to know, pulling back long enough to complain.

"The golden shower doesn't start until the last participant arrives," a woman answered. "Until then, you're ours to play with as we see fit. Now shut up and start sucking."

"What's your name?" The man fucking her ass asked.

"K-Kim. My name is Kim."

"Well, Kim, from now on I think I'll call you Sluttymelons. With big tits like these I think it suits you," he added, reached under her and tweaking her nipples. Shame I don't have a collar with me. Oh well, enjoy your gang bang until the rest of the party gets here."

"How many are there going to be?"

"About fifty so I hope you're thirsty."

51

"Hey, look at this," Susan screeched. "Hurry up!"

Rushing over to the monitor their friend was pointing at, they caught sight of Mistress Gwen and Lana walking into the body modification building. It was a full house today with nearly every seat taken up by male and female bare-necks, submissives and slaves as their Masters and Mistresses stood nearby preventing them from running off.

"Is Master Jeromy free?"

"Yes Mistress," Milkymelons answered. "He's just having lunch. Shall I tell him you're here?"

"That's alright, he's expecting us. Come on Lana, let's go in back."

"Why? What's back there?"

"Why all the damn questions? Follow me to the back room, or go out onto the farm and be used as a slave."

"You said no one could use me!"

"No, I said no one else could collar you. Now get your ass in the back room so we can finish our business, or I'll remove the collar and let one of them replace it."

Looking around the large open room from bare-neck, submissive and slave to Master and Mistress, Lana quickly weighed her options, decided they were not good and proceeded to walk into the back room where she sat a tattoo-covered man eating a sandwich. She was spun around and pushed into a chair – her wrists secured to the arms before she even had time to realize she had fallen for the trap.

"What in the fuck are you doing?" she demanded to know even as Mistress Gwen attempted to restrain her right leg.

"Master Jeromy meet Lana. Lana meet Master Jeromy."

"Pleasure to meet you Lana," said Master Jeromy extending his hand. "Oh, where are my manners?" Standing up, he walked over to the half bound and struggling woman and shook her hand. "Here, let me get that other leg for you, Mistress."

"Let me go. You have no fucking right to do this!" Lana screamed. "God damn it I demand you let me go!"

"You're really not in any position to make demands you stupid cunt," said Master Jeromy as he strapped her other ankle and then thigh in place.

"I'm not one of your submissives, asshole, so let me go!"

"The collar around your neck says otherwise," Mistress Gwen laughed.

"You fucking bitch. You said it was a guest collar so no one else would collar me."

"Not my fault you're so naïve. No, you stupid woman that is a very special collar and soon your daughter will have one around her neck as well."

"You can't do this to us. Let me go right god damn now!"

"I can do this to you as you can plainly see. If you thought you could waltz in here and demand things of me you were sorely mistaken. The money you were going to pay to keep Natalie, Susan, Beth and Mike here another two years will instead go to training you and your spoiled brat of a daughter. Let's see, if my calculation are correct that means about four years of training for each of you."

"What would you like me to mark her with?" asked Master Jeromy.

"Her slave name will be Milfycunt. Go ahead and pierce her nipples, clit hood, and labia as well to get that out of the way. And her daughter will be here after her golden shower is complete. I believe her name is going to be Sluttymelons. When you're done with them could you please have them brought back to my office for registration?"

"Of course, Mistress Gwen," he smiled. "I'll make sure they're escorted right to your desk."

"Thanks a bunch."

∞ ∞ ∞

"Did you just see the same thing I did?" Natalie asked.

"If you mean Mistress Gwen enslaving Kim's mother, then yeah, I saw it as well," Mike answered. "And it looks as if she's headed back to the golden showers."

"Speaking of which, how's Kim coming along with that?" Susan asked.

Moving back to the other monitor, they watched as five men stood around Kim, pissing on her as another pissed down her throat. They had no idea how many loads she had eaten, but she was absolutely drenched – her hair matted to her head and face while more poured from her pussy and ass. The four friends continued watching Kim's debasement, laughing every time she choked and gagged.

The door eventually opened and Mistress Gwen stepped inside. "EXCUSE ME EVERYONE," Mistress Gwen shouted. "I NEED YOUR ATTENTION PLEASE!"

The action stopped and Kim fell to the floor spitting up urine by the mouthful. Looking up, she saw Mistress Gwen standing there looking over the group. "Get me out of here!" she demanded. "Do you know what they're doing to me? My mother will hear about this and she won't be happy!"

"Your mother knows all about it."

"What can we do for you Mistress Gwen," one of the men asked. "Are you here to join the party?"

"Not today boys," she replied to everyone's dismay. "I need a second of Kim's time if you don't mind."

"By all means, Mistress. She's all yours."

Mistress Gwen walked up to Kim and stared down into the young woman's pleading eyes. Smiling, she placed the pink collar around the piss-soaked woman's neck and stepped back. "She's all yours gentlemen. Make sure to fill her up until she's ready to burst. And in case you don't know what that collar means," she said to Kim "it means she now belongs to another. Don't bother trying to remove it for your own or you know the consequences."

"Yes Mistress. Are you sure you don't want a few loads for the road?"

"Oh, what the hell," Gwen shrugged. "You, you, you, you and you," she said pointing to five men. You may piss down my throat. If anyone else attempts to piss on me, or the five of you go anywhere other than down my throat, you'll be collared before you leave this building." Dropping to her knees on the piss-soaked floor, she opened her mouth and accepted the first cock. Relaxing her gag reflex, she let is easily slide down to her belly – softly moaning as it warmed her insides.

When the last of the five men were done, Mistress Gwen found herself incredibly horny. "Alright, you five may piss up my ass, while you ten cover my body," she said pointing to another fifteen men. When they were done, she crawled to the shower and cleaned herself before punching in a code to release the lock. Kim attempted to make her escape, but was dragged back on top of a big black cock. "Oh, and when you're done using her, make sure she makes it to the body modification building. Master Jeromy is expecting her."

∞ ∞ ∞

The door opened and the four friends watched as Mistress Gwen entered the monitoring room. "Hello Mistress," Natalie was the first to say.

"Hello Sluttycunt. And hello Sugarpussy, Jizznympho and Cummonkey."

"Hello Mistress," the three said as one.

"Did you enjoy the show?"

"Very much so. You drank all that piss like it was nothing."

"I meant with Kim and her mother."

"Loved it, Mistress. I can't believe they are collared. Do you think they'll try to escape?"

"Probably, but with the shock feature enabled it'll be fun to watch them try. And I wasn't kidding when I said those were special collars. I assume you were listening in as well as watching?"

"Yes Mistress."

"Well, those are your collars, Sluttycunt."

"Mistress?"

"They belong to you. You are to be their Mistress once you've completed your training. It will be your job to make sure they are fully trained while you are here. Do you understand?"

"Yes Mistress. I mean, no. I don't fully understand. Are you planning on keeping them here for another two years without training them while I finish my slave and Dominant training?"

"Oh, they'll be here every bit that long, but you will begin training them immediately."

"I don't understand, Mistress."

"Being my slave has its advantages. You will go through slave and Dominant training at the same time starting tomorrow. It won't be easy by any means, but I believe you have what it takes."

"Congratulations!" Beth exclaimed. "May I ask how many of those collars you have, Mistress?"

"I have eight more."

"I know I am here to be trained by you, but do you think it would be possible to be registered as Sluttycunt's slave?"

"Only when her training is complete."

"Do I have to wait until then to wear her collar, Mistress?"

"That's a very good question," Susan added.

"What do you think, Sluttycunt? Do you want two more volunteer slaves in training?"

"Three, Mistress," Mike said with a smile."

"Are you guys being serious?" Natalie asked on the verge of tears.

"You know I am," Beth answered.

"I don't deserve this," Natalie cried.

"Don't sell yourself short, Sluttycunt. I've been watching the four of you very closely and I've seen how the other three look up to you even if they don't realize it themselves. And did you notice how quickly they all asked to serve you? That should tell you something."

"But I don't know the first thing about being dominant, or training sex slaves, Mistress."

"No? Even after nearly a year of training, you don't know even the first thing?"

"We've only been here five months, Mistress."

"True, but you were being slowly trained for months before being sent to us. If I did not think you had what it takes to be an excellent

Dominant I never would have offered it to you in the first place."

"Are you sure you want me as a Mistress?" Natalie asked her friends.

"God yes," Beth answered.

"No offense Mistress Gwen, but I've known Gwen nearly my entire life," Susan said. "And as a fellow pain slut she'll know exactly how to punish me."

"No offense taken, Sugarpussy."

"I know I said I want to serve you Sluttycunt, but I don't want to be separated from my fiancé."

"I understand."

"I know how much my Cockharlot means to you and how much you mean to her," said Mistress Gwen. "And that is why, if it is your desire to serve your friend I will release Cockharlot to her as well."

"But she is your best friend," Mike gasped in shock at the offer. "I could never take her away from you, Mistress. No, I've made up my mind to serve you for as long as you'll have me. Besides, Sluttycunt has her hands full with four slaves already."

"Can I see them Mistress? Milfycunt and Sluttymelons, I mean."

"Master Jeromy should be done with them in an hour or so. I've got plans for Milfycunt, but you can talk to Kim in her room in a couple of hours."

"Thank you Mistress."

"Before I forget I have another present for you. Let's go out to the office."

"You've given me so much already Mistress. I don't deserve such treatment."

"You're right, Natalie," Gwen said using Sluttycunt's real name for the first time in nearly six months. "You deserve so much more."

It was all Natalie could do to keep from total breakdown as she followed her Mistress out of the small room, friends in tow. Going to her desk, Mistress Gwen grabbed a long, narrow box and handed it to Natalie. Opening it, Natalie saw a pink collar and armband. "What is this, Mistress?"

"Congratulations, Mistress Natalie. Those are your new collar and armband. I've already informed the rest of the Dominants that you are in training and they will not ask you to do anything as a submissive unless you want them to. Jizznympho, Sugarpussy, please step forward." When the two slaves did as commanded, she continued. "You may remain my slaves in training, or you may wear the collar of Mistress Natalie, but before you make a decision, know that there is no going back. If you chose her, you will be registered as her slaves and should you remove her collar after that, you will be registered as Farm submissives."

"I want to wear my fiancé's collar," said Beth.

"Me too Mistress."

"Very well. Kneel and I'll remove your collars so that your new Mistress can replace it with hers."

Beth and Susan did not hesitate in kneeling, causing Natalie to sob even harder. "Are you sure you want to wear my collar?" she asked Beth."

"I'm yours, body, mind and soul, Mistress."

"And me," said Susan.

"Thank you both so much. This means more to me than I can ever put into words," Natalie said, snapping the pink collar around her fiancé's neck. Next, she collared Susan and smiled down at them both before turning her attention back to Mistress Gwen. "So, does this mean I give them commands now? Mistress?"

"That is correct. They are yours to command just as you are still mine to command."

"Why did you do it Mistress Gwen?"

"Why did I do what?"

"Why did you show me who was blackmailing me and my friends? You could've kept quiet and kept us here for however long they paid, but you didn't. Why, Mistress?"

"Because I don't like arrogant bitches like Lana and Kim walking into my home and barking orders at me as if I were nothing more than a dog for them to kick around," Gwen replied. "They've had this attitude adjustment coming for a long time."

"Thank you again, Mistress."

"Anytime. Now, if you don't mind I have a lot of work to do and little time to do it and you have a couple of slaves to train."

"Of course, Mistress," Gwen said on her way out of the office. "What are you kneeling there for?" she said to Sugarpussy and Jizznympho.

"Sorry Mistress," Beth replied. "Dropping onto her hands and knees, she crawled to her new Mistress's right side while Susan took up position on the left.

"Before I go Mistress, Do I have the authority to remove the lacing from Sugarpussy's pussy?"

"As her Mistress, it is your right."

"Thank you Mistress." Looking down at Susan, she grinned. "Don't worry, Sugarpussy, I have no intentions of ever unlacing you."

"Thank you Mistress."

52

Kim sat alone in her room unable to move from the chair she was securely tied to. She hadn't seen her mother all day and thanks to the ropes binding her, had to piss herself because she couldn't go to the bathroom like a normal human being. She reeked of piss and it was still dripping out of her ass when Natalie entered the room. "What in the hell are you doing her you worthless fucking slave?" she yelled at her once best friend. "Untie me right fucking now and I won't kick your god damn ass."

"Shut the fuck up," Natalie said in reply. "I have some questions and you're going to answer them."

"I don't have to do anything you say. You don't own me. I'm not some stupid fucking idiot like you and your friends to be duped into becoming sex slaves."

"What do you think you are right now? That collar around your neck says you are exactly a slave and this armband means I am a Dominant. Why did you do it?"

"Why did I do what?"

"You know damn well what. Why did you want to ruin me and my family? What did we ever do to you to deserve such malice? I thought we were friends."

"Friends? Hardly. It was all a big fucking game. I've hated you for so long I can't remember ever liking you."

"What in the hell are you talking about? We were best friends. If you hated me so much why did you remain my friend all these years?"

"To get back at you," Kim said angrily.

"For what? What did I ever do to you? I've been nothing but nice to you ever since we met. My parents always invited you along on vacations and we spent entire summers at each other's houses."

"You've done nothing but humiliate me from the day we met."

"What on earth are you talking about? I saved your life! If it wasn't for me you'd be dead!"

"There it is again. Rub it in my god damn face every chance you get!" Kim growled, trying in vain to pull free of the ropes, but only managed to twist them tighter. "It's the first thing you tell anyone who asks how we met. You have to be the hero. You have to be better at everything!"

"It's the truth," Natalie replied. "So what that I saved your life. Would you rather I left you out there to drown? And I only ever told those that asked how we met. It's not like I went around telling every person I saw on the street. If it bothered you so much why didn't you tell me? I would've stopped saying it."

"So you'd rather lie about our friendship than tell the truth?"

"You're bat-shit looney you know that! You're pissed I told the truth all these years and now your pissed I said I should have lied. What is wrong with you? When did you lose your fucking mind?"

"YOU! You're what's wrong with me you stupid bitch. No matter what I did you always had to one-up me. I got A's in school and you had to get A+'s. We join cross-country and you win every race. I join the cheerleading squad and you make captain."

"They made me captain because I knew the routines better than anyone else and also came up with several new ones. It had nothing to do with besting you."

"It just goes on and on with you. It never fucking stops. I get a 3.99gpa and you have to get a 4.0 and beat me out for valedictorian. Hell I had to go to a different college just so I didn't have to compete with you anymore."

"It was a one-sided competition," Natalie said sadly. "I was never competing against you Sluttymelons. I was never anything but your friend and I'm sorry you never truly felt the same. I'll give you this though. You did succeed in your latest goals. I mean, your goal was to turn me into a slut and I have to say that worked out perfectly. I've done so many kinky things I couldn't be called anything else. And I do believe it was also your goal to humiliate me and rip my family apart and it almost worked. You should have stopped while you were ahead, however. Sending me and my friends here was your biggest mistake."

"It wasn't a mistake," Kim yelled. "You're all a bunch of low-life sex slaves at the beck and call of whomever will use you and that was my plan all along!"

"Pot calling the kettle black, Sluttymelons."

"Go to hell you worthless cunt!" Kim spit, practically foaming at the mouth with rage.

"That's Sluttycunt, but to you and your mother it's Mistress."

"I'll never call you Mistress! I'll be damned if I let you win over me again! You're nothing!"

"We are very well trained slaves, that's for sure. But instead of ripping us apart it did just the opposite. We're stronger and happier than we've ever been and nothing could ever tear us apart now. Mike found a woman he loves and Beth proposed to me. We're planning a double wedding in the spring."

"You're a fucking liar. I bet your girlfriend is getting gang banged by a hundred men right now and Mike is taking it up the ass by the men he loves so much."

"Actually they're waiting outside your room as we speak." Walking over to the door, Natalie opened it. "You may come in now." Stepping to the side, she waited for Sugarpussy and Jizznympho to enter before closing it again. Notice anything about them, Sluttymelons?"

"They're worthless slaves just like you!"

"Go on," Natalie said "take a good hard look and it'll come to you eventually. While you're trying to figure it out, I should inform you that the money you and your mother attempted to pay to keep us all here another two years is instead paying for the two of you. And guess what? I'm your new Mistress."

"Wait, why are they wearing…oh, you've got to be kidding me!"

"Ding, she's got it! Jizznympho and Sugarpussy have asked to be my slaves in training and I accepted."

"The second you let me free of this chair I'll leave the Farm!" Kim scowled.

"Have fun with that."

"I'll never serve you! Never! Never! NEVER! I'd rather die than be humiliated by you again," Kim screamed, rocking the chair so hard it tipped over.

"You don't really have much say in the matter, Sluttymelons. You're a marked slave now and you belong to me. By the way, I thoroughly enjoyed your gang bang golden shower. I hope you liked it because you'll be doing a whole lot more in the near future."

"Fuck you!"

"That's fuck you, Mistress," Natalie smirked. "I'll let that one slide, but if you disrespect me again you will be punished."

"Go to hell you fucking bitch!"

"You were warned." Leaving the room, Natalie went in search of something to use to teach her new submissive a lesson in respect. In the living room she found a small box of paper clamps – those black ones with the silver handles and really tight grip. From the kitchen she grabbed several wooden spoons and a bowl of ice cubes. Finding nothing else of use, she returned to the bedroom and sat everything on the bed. Starting with the ice so it did not melt before going into use, Mistress Natalie knelt between Sluttymelons' legs and spread her pussy open.

"Get away from me!" Sluttymelons shouted. "Keep your hands off of me you filthy whore!"

Natalie ignored her new slave and pushed one...two...three...four cubes into Sluttymelons' pussy. To keep her from pushing them out, she took out three of the paper clamps and clamped her slave's pussy shut. Next, she took the longest wooden spoon and brought it down across Sluttymelons' right breast as hard as she could.

"Ahgh! You fucking bitch! I swear to god I'll kill you for this! Stop hitting me!"

Not paying Sluttymelons and attention, Mistress Natalie took out two more clamps. Pinching some skin on Kim's left breast, she placed the clamp and grinned as her slave cringed. Another clamp went to the right breasts. Left. Right. Left nipple. Right nipple. Kim pulled against the ropes keeping her bound to the chair, but it was no use.

"PLEASE!" Kim begged. "Just let me go."

"Are you ready to calm down and call me Mistress yet, Sluttymelons?"

"Go...to...hell," Kim grunted through clenched teeth.

"Well, I'll just leave you like this for a while. I'll be back in the morning to see you again."

"What? You can't be serious! You can't leave me like this!"

"Come Jizznympho, Sugarpussy. Let's give Sluttymelons time to consider her position."

∞ ∞ ∞

Mistress Gwen sat in the surveillance room watching every second of Natalie's visit with Sluttymelons and she couldn't be happier with what she saw. "What do you think Milfycunt?" she asked the woman tied to the chair sitting next to her. "I think your precious daughter will make a fine submissive for Natalie. Personally, I can't wait to see her broken down day by day until she finally submits to the woman she hates so much."

"Kim will never serve that fucking bitch and neither will I."

"That's another fifty swats."

"Fuck you! I'll sue you for this! I'll have this place shut down and see you begging on the fucking streets!"

"Better people than you have tried. And that's another fifty swats. You're here for the next few years so you can fall in line, or face continual punishment day after day. What are we at now, five hundred swats?"

"I'm out of this fucking place the second you untie me."

"Good luck with that." Look, Mistress Natalie is coming back. I bet she'll be so happy to see you." Watching the newly minted Mistress and her new slaves walking down the streets, head held high, she opened the door and waited for them to enter. "Welcome back, Mistress Natalie."

"Thank you Mistress."

"Nice work with your new slave. We watched the whole thing and I gotta say, the ice was a nice touch."

"Thank you, Mistress. It just came to me in the moment."

"That's the kind of quick thinking that makes a good Mistress. I was worried you'd be afraid to try anything with her, but I'm glad you proved me wrong."

"Thank you, Mistress. I must say it felt pretty damn good, but I think she's lost her damn mind. She blames me for all her problems. Apparently our entire friendship was a competition to her."

"I heard it all. She's going to be a tough one to crack, but I think you're up to the task. Milfycunt is in the monitoring room. Want to say hi?"

"Sure." Stepping past her Mistress, Natalie entered the room and stared hard at her ex best friend's mother. The collar you wear around your neck marks you as my slave. You saw what I did to her and I will not hesitate to do worse to you. You can accept me as your Mistress and follow my every command to the letter, or I'll show you what it means to suffer."

"Neither of us will ever serve you."

"We'll see. Jizznympho, Sugarpussy, please escort Milfycunt here to the School of Discipline.

Leave her tied to the chair in case she thinks about escaping."

"Yes Mistress."

Picking up the chair, the two slaves-in-training carried Milfycunt out of the main office and down the streets to the School of Discipline – the one place on the Domination Farm guaranteed to teach an unruly slave a lesson in obedience.

"I hope I didn't just step over the line, Mistress."

"Of course not. It is your right as her Mistress to send her in for a much needed lesson. And I've been thinking and I've decided to see to your Dominant training personally."

"Thank you Mistress. With you in charge I'm sure to be the best Dominant possible."

"You'll be joined by Cockharlot."

"Mistress?"

"Cockharlot will be going through Dominant training with you, Natalie. And Cummonkey has agreed to be her slave."

"Sweet. I really think I'm going to love it here."

"I really hope so. It's been a very long time since I've had the opportunity to train a slave and Dominant in the same person."

Printed in Great Britain
by Amazon

17178345R00230